W9-DCH-297

ALSO AVAILABLE

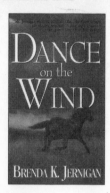

UNTIL
SEPTEMBER

"Spellbinding."
—Joan Johnston

BRENDA K.
JERNIGAN

PRELUDE TO LOVE

The campfire burned with an orange glow. The roasted rabbit smelled good as it sizzled over the fire.

"Are you hungry?" Claire asked Billy.

"Starved. I only have one plate, knife, and fork, but we can make do. Here is a canteen."

Billy removed the rabbit from the spit and placed it on the plate Claire held. "Ain't no delicate way to do this," he said, cutting the meat. It was so tender that it fell apart. "Give it a minute to cool, then dig in."

She took a bite, and chewed for a moment before murmuring her approval, "This is so good."

Claire chuckled and Billy glanced at her, puzzled.

"What?"

"I was just thinking about what my mother would say if she could see me eating with my fingers." Claire rolled her eyes. "I can hear the lecture now. But you know, it's fun doing things you're not supposed to."

"I take it you've always done everything the right way."

Claire smiled. "Pretty much."

He reached for another piece of meat and shrugged. "Sometimes you learn from doing things the wrong way."

"But I've never been given the chance," Claire said. She licked the grease off her fingers. "Are you going to teach me the things I need to know?"

Her voice was so soft that Billy found himself looking at her mouth and saying his thoughts out loud. "I'll teach you anything you want to learn."

Her eyes glistened. "Anything?"

"Anything," Billy replied.

Good, Claire thought. She just didn't know how to ask him to teach her how to love. . . .

BOOK YOUR PLACE ON OUR WEBSITE AND MAKE THE READING CONNECTION!

We've created a customized website just for our very special readers, where you can get the inside scoop on everything that's going on with Zebra, Pinnacle and Kensington books.

When you come online, you'll have the exciting opportunity to:

- View covers of upcoming books
- Read sample chapters
- Learn about our future publishing schedule (listed by publication month *and author*)
- Find out when your favorite authors will be visiting a city near you
- Search for and order backlist books from our online catalog
- Check out author bios and background information
- Send e-mail to your favorite authors
- Meet the Kensington staff online
- Join us in weekly chats with authors, readers and other guests
- Get writing guidelines
- AND MUCH MORE!

Visit our website at
http://www.kensingtonbooks.com

UNTIL SEPTEMBER

Brenda K. Jernigan

ZEBRA BOOKS
KENSINGTON PUBLISHING CORP.
http://www.kensingtonbooks.com

ZEBRA BOOKS are published by

Kensington Publishing Corp.
850 Third Avenue
New York, NY 10022

All Kensington titles, imprints and distributed lines are
available at special quantity discounts for bulk pur-
chases for sales promotion, premiums, fund-raising, ed-
ucational or institutional use.

Special book excerpts or customized printings can also
be created to fit specific needs. For details, write or phone
the office of the Kensington Special Sales Manager:
Kensington Publishing Corp., 850 Third Avenue, New
York, NY 10022. Attn. Special Sales Department. Phone:
1-800-221-2647.

Zebra and the Z logo Reg. U.S. Pat. & TM Off.

First Printing: November 2003
10 9 8 7 6 5 4 3 2 1

Printed in the United States of America

Until September is dedicated to
Star Helmer who saw the glimmer of a storyteller.
With her encouragement and training,
I saw the dream come true.
Thank you, Star.

A special thanks to Ute Hickman
for letting me use her name and
providing the German for this book.

In Memory of

My mother, Bonnie Dittman, who died much too
young of breast cancer. A portion of the
proceeds from this book will be donated to
HOSPICE, so they can help those who
can't help themselves.

Prologue

He'd been drunk for three damn days.

Billy West lay on a small cot, staring at the cracks in the white ceiling, willing himself to remain perfectly still for fear his head would explode at any small movement. He wondered what he'd gotten himself into this time.

He'd done some stupid things in his life, and he had a real bad feeling that this one ranked right at the top. Problem was he was none too sure what he'd done or where in hell he was.

The sound of someone in the distance, swearing, followed by the jingle of keys gave Billy a clue. He bet if he turned his head slightly he would see bars and, more than likely, he'd be on the wrong side of them, but the effort was just too much, so he went back to counting the cracks above his head . . . anything to stay conscious.

Billy felt lower than a snake's belly in a wagon rut after the wagon had run over him a couple of times. He managed a slight smile at that thought.

There had been happier days. Billy remembered

when he thought he'd known it all as he left the safety of his sister's and brother-in-law's ranch. Now he was forced to admit he hadn't known nearly as much as he'd thought.

Unfortunately, he had to learn everything the hard way. The next time he chose a friend, he would damn well be careful. No more trusting. If he ever bumped into Bad Joe Green again, he'd skin the man alive and enjoy every minute of it.

"You look like shit, kid!"

Billy winced at the loud voice intruding on his misery. He recognized that voice. And he knew it wasn't a voice that would go away.

"Are you going to lie on that cot and feel sorry for yourself all day?" Brandy asked.

Shit, Billy thought. Bad enough Thunder was going to see him like this but now his sister was here, too! And she didn't sound too happy. With a great deal of effort, Billy sat up, grabbing his head to stop the throbbing as the sheriff unlocked the cell and ushered Thunder and Brandy into the cell.

"Call me when you're done," the sheriff said on his way out of the room, his keys chiming like church bells to Billy's ears.

"I thought you were old enough to take care of yourself," Brandy started, "but I'm beginning to have second thoughts. Don't you remember what it's like to live with a bunch of drunks?"

Billy peered at his sister through eyes that felt like sand. It appeared Brandy was getting worked up because she'd started to pace the room, while Thunder casually crossed his arms and leaned against the window bars. He knew his wife would try to get her anger out of her system. Billy had learned that about her a long time ago.

"Now look at you—" Brandy stopped and glared at Billy for a moment. "You're no better than they were."

Billy knew she referred to the gunslingers he'd lived with before Father Brown had taken him in. When they got all liquored up, they would beat him, and he'd been too young to defend himself. Thank goodness, they had all been killed, and he had been sent to the orphanage. Finally, Billy said, "You're getting mighty worked up, Sis."

"You're darn right I am! I didn't bring you halfway across the country for you to end up like this." She threw her hands up and sighed. "And smelling of rotgut."

"Well, Joe Green swindled me and ran off with all the money I'd saved for the past year!" Billy's voice grew louder as his temper returned. He staggered to his feet and then reached for the wall so he wouldn't fall. "And you know what that leaves me? Absolutely nothing."

"We've had nothing before, Billy." Brandy's soft voice took some of the anger out of him.

"This is different. 'Sides, all I did was start drinking. Come to think of it, why am I in this stinking place?"

Thunder straightened and said, "You're in trouble, kid."

Billy frowned as he looked at his brother-in-law. "For getting drunk? When did that become a crime?"

"Since you busted up the saloon and took a horse that didn't belong to you," Thunder answered.

"Do you think I'd still be here if I'd stolen a horse? I'd be in another county by now."

Thunder shrugged. "Probably not, which is what

I pointed out to the sheriff. If he is going to accuse you of being a thief, he needs the evidence. So I got him to drop the charges," Thunder said.

Billy grinned. "It pays to have a lawyer in the family."

"And I paid the saloon for the damages," Brandy added.

If it were possible to feel worse, Billy did. He'd let down the two people he loved most. And he had nobody to blame but himself. When he left the ranch, his parting words had been . . . *"I am going where the wind blows me."* Well, this time it had blown him in the wrong direction. But he vowed that things would change.

"I'm obliged. I promise you'll not have to bail me out of jail again," Billy said, meaning it, and watching as his sister smiled her approval.

They had been through a lot together back in Independence, Missouri. He and Brandy had been orphans and Father Brown, the priest who'd been keeping them, had died. Billy had felt pretty low then, too, especially when they found out they were losing their home, and would have absolutely nothing. That he and Brandy had survived at all was a miracle.

He realized now that he'd been acting as if life didn't mean anything to him when he knew damn well it did. He was a fighter, not a quitter.

"I got a proposition for you, kid," Thunder said, breaking into Billy's thoughts. "I have been doing some legal work for a gentleman named Ben Holladay. He's known as the Stagecoach King, and he's thinking about extending his line into Denver. I mentioned you, and Ben said that if you were good with a gun, he could use a good man."

Billy straightened slowly so he wouldn't jar his throbbing head. "What do I have to do?"

"First, let's get you out of here and cleaned up. Then I'll take you over to meet Ben."

Maybe this would be a new beginning, Billy thought.

He needed something . . . and it damn sure wasn't a drink.

Chapter One

Claire Holladay's heart beat fast.

"Calm down, Claire," she whispered to herself. "Everything will be all right. You're just letting your imagination run away with you."

It was a cold winter's day and she sat rigid in the cane back chair, waiting for Doc Worden to return to his office. It was the waiting that had made her nervous—not that odd look on Doc's face during the examination.

It was just nerves. That's all.

This had been an unusually cold New York winter, or so it seemed to Claire. The wood in the old potbelly stove crackled and popped as warmth spread throughout the room. But today she couldn't seem to get comfortable. Her hands were like ice, and she rubbed them together.

She rose and moved over to the inviting warmth and held her hands out a few inches from the stove to warm them. She glanced around the room. How many times had she been in this familiar office?

Too many to count.

However, some things never changed. This office was one of them. She liked the familiar feeling she got every time she entered the room. The medicine smell, the old brown desk. . . . She stepped over and looked at the desk. A small "CH" had been carved in the corner of the wood by a brave child of ten. She could remember it as if it were yesterday. She had wanted to give Doc Worden something to remember her by.

Claire had figured that she'd be walloped for that little stunt, but punishment wasn't forthcoming. Instead, her family had just carefully scolded her the way they always did when she did something wrong. Because of "her condition" they always treated her with kid gloves. It was almost as if she didn't exist.

She was different.

Claire frowned.

She didn't' want to be different. She wanted to be normal.

A tickle started deep in her throat. She coughed and coughed and finally eased down upon the chair to catch her breath. She held her chest as she took a deep breath and reached for the glass of water that was on the edge of the desk. She carefully took small sips of water until the spasms were under control. At least, this time she didn't have to take any medicine. Once again, she was the prim and proper Claire Holladay.

A child crying in the next examining room caught Claire's attention. She smelled the ether just before the child's cries faded into a whimper, followed by silence. Claire hoped it was nothing serious because she knew firsthand what it was like to be sick.

Looking back at the old brown desk, she noticed how messy it was. As a matter of fact, she couldn't ever remember all the papers being in order. And the groups of brown bottles which sat in one corner must have been there for the last ten years.

It was a shame when a doctor's office felt like home. She sighed. The waiting was making her nervous.

The doorknob jiggled before the door swung open, and Doc Worden came into the room. He'd shed the brown tweed coat that he wore in the winter. His white shirtsleeves were rolled up to his elbows, and a stethoscope hung around his neck.

Instead of taking his chair as he normally did, Doc Worden ambled over to the desk and leaned back against it. He folded his arms across his chest, then looked at her over wire-rimmed glasses perched on the tip of his nose. "Sorry I took so long. It seems Mary Ann tripped and cut her knee."

"Oh, that sounds painful."

"She'll be fine," he said in an offhand manner, as if his mind were elsewhere. He drew in a deep breath as he rubbed his chin. Claire noticed that he seemed to be fascinated by his shoes, for he had yet to look at her.

And he was frowning.

A knot started to form in Claire's stomach. Doc Worden was taking much too long to talk about the pains she'd been having in her chest. What was he having such a hard time saying? And why wasn't he looking at her?

"I thought I could do this," he said finally in an odd voice.

Claire swallowed hard. "D-do what?"

Slowly, Doc Worden brought his head up and his gaze settled on her. He had the kindest eyes, the eyes she'd learned to trust. He ran his right hand through his hair and finally said, "There isn't anything else I can do for you, Claire." He sighed.

"I—I don't understand. You have always taken care of me."

Reaching over, he took her hands in his soft, warm hands. "I know. But the truth is, I cannot make you well. I've tried for a very long time. But Claire, you're going to die!"

Claire gasped. She jerked her hands from his and gripped the chair for support. She felt as if all the blood had left her head, leaving her light-headed. "I-I I'm going to die?" she asked in a hoarse whisper.

This is not fair! she wanted to scream.

"I am afraid so, child. Consumption is a strange disease that we don't understand. You know how much you cough at times, and you have told me you have night sweats. I expect violent pains over your left chest will be next. When you start coughing up blood. . . ." He paused, and she could see that he was choked up. He looked as helpless as she felt. "The only thing I can do is to give you opium in the form of an atomizer spray to relieve your coughing. And maybe if you stay in bed. . . ."

He didn't bother to finish his sentence. He didn't have to. Claire knew. . . .

He kept talking, but she had tuned him out. Who wanted to stay in bed all the time? She felt like her body and mind were separating. None of this should be happening.

She should be hysterical.

She should be weeping.

But all she could feel was this cold empty feeling inside her as if somebody had sucked all the air from her lungs. "How long do I have?" she finally managed to ask as she pushed herself to her feet.

"I-I'm not sure. Perhaps until September," Doc Worden said and handed her a new bottle of medicine.

Claire nodded. Then she stood and hugged the doctor. His arms wrapped around her in a strong hold. Somehow his hug said it all. He was saying goodbye to her.

"Thank you for all you've done."

When Doc Worden released her, he nodded, with tears in his eyes.

Claire gave him a small smile before heading for the door. She had just touched the doorknob when he said, "You take care of yourself, and remember when the pain gets too bad, I'll give you more opium."

She turned back, tears brimming in her eyes as she said, "I will take care . . . until September."

Five days later, Claire sat by the window looking at the large icicles that hung from the eaves of her upstairs bedroom. There was a very large one in the center of her window.

The numbness she'd felt for the last few days had started to lift and a weird feeling she couldn't put her finger on remained.

Her family had wept when she'd told them. Then they'd looked at her with such sympathy and pity that she had finally broken down and wept, too.

After two days of crying, her tears finally dried. She had wept for all the things she would miss.

She'd never get married . . . never have that little house and children. She cried for the injustice of it all. She was too young to die. But finally she stopped feeling sorry for herself and dried her tears, swearing that from this day forward she'd never cry again.

Claire summoned the courage to tell her fiancé, David Ader. They had been engaged for two years. He had wanted to wait until he had his mercantile store running properly before they married. She shut her eyes and remembered two nights ago when David had come to the house.

"Claire," David had said as she'd entered the parlor. "I haven't heard from you in over a week, so I've come to see if everything is well." He placed his hat on a chair then stepped closer to her. He took her hands in his when she finally stopped in front of him, placing a kiss on the back of her hand. He was dressed in his usual no-nonsense plain brown suit.

"No, everything isn't all right," Claire said.

"Well, you do look a bit peaked, my dear. It isn't that dreadful cough of yours, is it?"

Claire looked at him for a long moment. "Yes, David, it is my cough."

"I hope you have asked Doctor Worden for more of your medicine. It always makes you feel better." David loosened his bow tie, frowning. He finally said, "You wouldn't believe what a day I had." He reached for her hand. "You should come down to my store more often, Claire, and not stay in the house."

As usual, he had only listened to her for a moment before he started talking about his business.

"I'm going to die!"

David let go of her hand, taking several steps backward to put some distance between them.

Evidently, he was afraid he'd catch whatever she had.

"I—I don't understand," he stammered in bewilderment. "Look at you—other than your color, you look fine."

"I have consumption, David. Doc Worden told me a few days ago. He hadn't been sure until now." Claire waited for David to tell her that he'd love her no matter what. But the look on his face told her everything. She could see the loathing in his eyes. There was no love, only pity. He wanted to get out of the house as soon as he could. And it was now apparent that he wanted nothing more to do with her.

"What are you going to do?" David finally asked.

She made sure her expression became a mask of stone. "I'm not sure," Claire said honestly, and then with the courage she didn't know that she possessed, she said, "David, I think that it's better that we end our engagement." She saw the relief that washed over his face as a knife stabbed through her heart. The fact that she could be rejected by someone who was supposed to love her hurt her more than she'd ever been hurt.

"I think that is the wise thing to do, my dear," David said. Then he turned and took his hat from the chair. "I do hope that you'll get better." And with those parting words David left her house and her heart. He hadn't even bothered to kiss her goodbye. No kiss on the cheek. No handshake. Nothing.

Claire sighed, weary of the thought as she traced a "C" in the condensation on the windowpane. She had hoped that he would take her into his arms and assure her that everything would be all right.

But he hadn't.

Claire could still picture David's face. After the look of relief, she saw pity in his eyes. She never wanted anyone to look at her like that again.

She wiped the moisture off her finger and again focused on the large icicle. A drop of water clung to its very tip, waiting to fall. It looked as if it were hanging on for dear life.

Just waiting.

Something inside Claire snapped. She sat a little straighter in her chair as a strange kind of warmth spread through her. A light . . . a spark from deep within her had ignited, and realization washed over her. It was the light that she'd been missing.

The spark of hope. It had been taken away from her.

She was much like that tiny drop of water . . . hanging on with her bare fingertips, waiting to die.

Well, no more.

She would not sit around and wait. Everybody needed a spark, and she would hang on to that spark as long as she could.

Abruptly, she got to her feet, tossing the quilt aside. A plan began to form, and if it worked she'd be changing her life forever.

Fetching her cloak from the peg on the door, she slipped it on and went downstairs.

Margaret Holladay was strolling through the foyer when her daughter came down the stairs, her soft hair framing her heart-shaped face. Margaret smiled. What a beautiful young woman Claire had become. Her hair was as black as soot and her porcelain skin made her look like a fragile doll.

And in many ways Claire was fragile, waiting to be broken by the disease that had plagued her over the last few years.

Margaret sighed. She wanted to reach out and pull her daughter into her arms and assure her that she'd stand by her no matter what. But Margaret held back, not wanting to upset her daughter. How could anyone so beautiful be so sick?

Margaret's heart ached for her daughter, and she felt utterly helpless as to how to help Claire.

"Why are you not in bed resting?" Margaret asked.

"I'm sick of resting and being told to do this or that. I'll not rot in bed anymore," Claire said.

"But you know what the doctor's instructions were."

"Yes, but I don't care."

Margaret saw a glow in Claire's expressive aquamarine eyes. "I see you have on your cloak. Where are you going?" Margaret asked as she handed her daughter a gray wool scarf and a fur muff.

"I'm headed down to Harper's," Claire told her as she wrapped the warm scarf around her neck and reached for the doorknob.

"I thought you'd given up that reporting job," Margaret said. She'd never liked the idea of her daughter working at a magazine when there were more dignified jobs for young ladies.

"No, I didn't quit. I am not a quitter, Mother," Claire's chin rose. "As a matter of fact, I have just had a brilliant idea that I want to tell my editor about."

Margaret knew how headstrong her daughter could be. "Well, at least let me summon the coach. You'll catch your death."

Claire swung around and gave her mother a

half-smile. "Mother, I'm going to die anyway."
Claire's laughter could be heard all the way down
the icy steps.

Margaret almost smiled at Claire's jest. She didn't
want to lose her daughter but she had to admit that
she liked the spark she'd just seen in her daughter's eyes. Anything was better than the blank stare
Claire had worn upon returning from the doctor's
office.

A few snowflakes began to fall as Claire walked
toward the stable. A path had been cleared, so it
was easy to walk though the snow. She felt so alive
as the snow crunched under her boots. The air was
crisp and felt good in her lungs. This was so much
better than sitting in her room thinking and wondering and—worse—waiting. She had done way
too much of that. And she wasn't going to let her
condition stop her from living anymore. She'd
been careful and done everything that Doc Worden
had wanted and what good had it done her?

The carriage ride down to the ferry town took
about a half hour. They boarded the ferry, then
Claire stepped out of the carriage as the driver
placed wooden blocks behind the wheels. She
stood at the side rail and looked out over the river
as the steamboat made its way across the river.

Once they were off the ferry, the carriage was
on its way through the streets of New York City.
Soon they were passing between the tall rows of
business buildings. Finally, they reached the five-
story home of her publisher, Harper's. Once she
was there, she instructed the driver to return for
her in about an hour.

She straightened her cloak and entered the red

brick building, and climbed the stairs to the second floor. Pausing at the top to catch her breath,
she realized how weak she'd become by staying in
bed so much.

When she regained her composure, she hurried
down the hall to the familiar glass door that said
Harper's Weekly. She strode into the office.

"Good morning," Claire said to Alice, the recep-
tionist. "Is Ann in her office?" Claire asked.

"She sure is," Alice said with a bright smile.
"How are you feeling this morning?"

Claire smiled as she removed her wool cloak and
hung it on the coat rack. "Much better, thank you."

"We've been worried about you," Alice told her.

"Thank you," Claire replied and then went to
Ann's office. She rapped lightly on the door but
didn't bother to wait for an invitation.

Ann glanced up as Claire burst into the small office. "What are you doing out of bed? I thought
you were going to stay home."

Claire sat in the straight-backed chair across
from Ann's desk. "I have had the most wonderful
idea, and I couldn't wait to run it past you."

Ann's eyebrows arched. "Oh, really?"

"Really. I've decided that I want to write articles
about the West."

Ann looked over the small reading glasses
perched on the end of her nose. "How are you
going to do that from here?"

Claire gave her editor a slow smile. "This is the
best part . . . I'm going to do it from out there, not
from here."

Ann leaned back in her chair, completely startled. And it was hard to startle Ann. "But—"

"I can wire you the articles. It will be something
fresh. Exciting. What do you think?"

"Well—"

"I know . . . my health. But look at it this way. I can die out there just as easily as I can die right here in New York. I have nothing to lose."

Ann frowned, then she said, "I don't like to hear you talk about—about—well—you know. However, you do have a point and it would be something different for the magazine."

"What do you think Henry will say?"

A thoughtful smile curved Ann's lips. "He'll probably moan and groan and then rephrase the whole thing as if it was his idea. And once it is his idea—he'll love it. I'll ask him after you leave, but what about your parents? Have you brought up the subject with them?"

Claire frowned. "Not yet. I wanted to talk to you, then wire my Uncle Ben before I tell my family."

"Uncle Ben?"

"He is my father's brother. He owns the Overland Stage, so I should be able to get quite a few ideas from him."

Ann leaned forward and rested her arms on the desk. "It sounds so very exciting. I almost wish I were going instead of staying behind this desk all the time."

Claire stood. "You can always come with me."

Ann gave her a wistful look from under her brown bangs. "Oh, how I'd like to, but who would make sure that the magazine got printed so our customers could read your fine articles? No." Ann sighed. "I suppose I'm doomed to sit behind this ugly brown desk. However, I do hope that you'll have the time of your life." And then Ann must have realized what she'd said, for she blushed a tomato red. "That was a figure of speech."

Claire gave Ann a slow smile. "I intend to. No

more being careful. I'm going to have fun. Now I had better go send that telegram. Give Henry my best."

A week later, Claire received the telegram from her uncle that she'd been waiting for. He said he couldn't wait to see her and that she could stay as long as she wanted. Claire shouted for joy.

Tonight she would break the news to her family over dinner. She took a deep breath for courage then smiled as she thought this would be one dinner where there wouldn't be a lull in the conversation. She could hear their protests now.

When she reached the dining room, her family had already sat down. "Hello, Father," Claire said as she took her seat at the long mahogany table. One of the maids had made a centerpiece of evergreens with holly and red berries.

Donald Holladay was a large man and still nice-looking for his age. He had a beard that ran along his jaw line, and his hair was as black as Claire's except for a few gray hairs.

He ran a prosperous shipping business with his three sons: Heath, Albert, and Bobby. They also raised thoroughbreds so there was never much idle time around Green Hills.

Heath and Albert barely glanced her way as she sat down across from them. Bobby, the youngest of the boys, sat beside her. He had already snatched a roll before taking his seat, and was tearing off small bites as his brother spoke.

They were discussing one of their ships that had gone down in a bad storm three days ago. Claire pulled out her small pad of paper and a pencil and began jotting down notes as their plates were served. What a good article this would be, she thought as she scribbled bits and pieces down. She could see the headlines: "Ship Lost at Sea." A tingle started racing through her body as it always did when she began writing a good article. Maybe she would, one day, give Samuel Clemens a run for his money. She had seen him several times at the magazine but had yet to meet him.

"You shouldn't be writing at the table, dear," Margaret scolded. "It's considered bad manners."

Claire put down her pencil, then unfolded her napkin and placed it on her lap, feeling much like a twelve-year-old reprimanded by her mother. Somehow, her family refused to let her grow up. They had been overprotective because of her illness. "Writing stories is what I do, Mother. The ship sinking will make a good story."

"You should be writing about women's things, like fashions or the latest hair styles," Bobby piped up from next to her and received a swift kick from Claire under the table.

"Women do have other interests, brother dear."

"It isn't ladylike, Claire," Margaret pointed out, "And boys," she shifted her attention to the other three, "that will be enough business discussed at the table." Margaret looked to her husband for help. "Say something, Donald."

"Your mother is right. Business shouldn't be discussed at the dinner table," Donald said in an offhand manner before taking his first sip of tomato soup.

"All right, Mother," Albert said, reaching for a roll. "What else do we talk about?"

Claire couldn't believe that the perfect opening had been handed to her. "I have something."

Heath, the oldest at thirty and set in his ways, looked at her. "We're all ears, puss."

"I'm going out West," Claire said.

Her father choked on his soup. A spoon clattered on the fine china as he snatched up his napkin. Suddenly, everyone was talking at once.

Bobby jerked his head sideways to look at her. "You're what?"

"But you're sick," her mother cried.

Heath shook his fork at her. "That is the craziest idea you've ever had."

"Well, I might be crazy, but I'm still going, and for the very reason that you just said, Mother. If I'm going to die, I'm going to do it my way. I intend to live life to the fullest over these next few months."

Margaret dropped her soup spoon. "Donald, speak to your daughter."

"When you bring up a topic at dinner, puss," Heath said as he buttered his biscuit, "you choose well."

Claire wanted to stick her tongue out at her brother, but didn't get the chance as her father spoke.

"Have you thought about how hard this trip will be on you?"

Claire nodded. "Yes, father, I have. I wired Uncle Ben, and he is sending one of his men to escort me West."

"No daughter of mine is traveling across the country with a perfect stranger. I'll not have people talking about you," Margaret said.

Claire glanced at her mother. "I am a grown woman."

"An *unmarried* grown woman."

"I'm sure Uncle Ben wouldn't send somebody he didn't trust," Claire argued.

"We'll have a talk with him once he gets here," Heath said.

"I have the perfect solution," her father said. "Why not send Aunt Ute with you? She is an experienced world traveler and can help Claire get settled. Ute will be the perfect chaperone." He smiled at his idea and added, "She'd box the ears of any man who made advances to Claire."

"She is also a nurse," Margaret added. "Excellent idea, Donald."

Claire watched as her family talked amongst themselves as if she weren't there. Would they ever let her do anything on her own?

Probably not.

The whole group was too protective, so it was probably for the best that she was getting away. Claire smiled. She knew they loved her, but she had to go. And she really didn't mind Aunt Ute. She was a large German woman who came from the old country. She had a wonderful sense of humor, and she didn't take any guff from anyone.

"I think Aunt Ute is a wonderful idea," Claire said.

"Good. Then it's all settled. You'll be leaving next month," her mother said, as if the whole idea had been hers.

Chapter Two

"You're a dead man, Billy West!" Ralph Kincade swore, glaring up at Billy as he clutched his wounded son.

Billy re-holstered his Colt. "I'm sorry you feel that way, Kincade, but Jake drew on me first." Hell, Billy thought, he could have killed the snot-nosed kid who was looking for a reputation. At least the kid wouldn't be drawing a gun on anyone else anytime soon, if ever. With Jake's hot temper it was just a matter of time before someone killed him. Just maybe, Billy had saved his life.

Billy rode on the Overland stagecoach, which hit a deep rut and jarred him out of his thoughts about the Kincades. He grabbed at the side of the wooden seat, his gaze moving over the trail ahead. Why the hell the Kincades were on his mind today was a mystery to him. Unless it had something to do with that bullet which had barely missed him last night—a bullet that seemed to have come out of nowhere. Or maybe it was the fact that Billy heard that Jake was dead, having taken his own life. Again the coach hit another deep hole.

"Shit, Rattlesnake," Billy swore at the stage driver, sitting next to him. "Are you going to hit every damned hole in the road?"

"Yer so danged boring today," Rattlesnake Pete said as he spit tobacco juice out of the side of his mouth. "I keep nodding off."

"All right. All right," Billy said as he replaced the rifle across his arm. He'd ridden shotgun for so long that every once in a while he'd get complacent, which wasn't good if robbers or Indians attacked the stage. "You miss the holes, and I'll keep you awake. I reckon I haven't been much company today."

"Dang it, boy, what's ailin' you?"

"Damned if I know. Feel kind of restless . . . like I have an itch I can't scratch. I seem to be doing the same damned thing over and over, day after day. I'm ready to do something different, but I'm not sure what."

"Yer complaining about my gol-danged company?"

"Why would I complain about that?" Billy twirled a piece of wheat straw in his mouth. "I've seen your ugly hide forever."

"It is right handsome," Rattlesnake said, stroking his scraggly whiskers with his gloved hand. "Maybe that little filly at the way station has gone and got you all stirred up! I seen how she bats them pretty eyelashes every time we stop there to eat."

"Nelly's a good cook," Billy admitted and then cut his eyes to Rattlesnake Pete, who was one of the best damned drivers Billy had ever ridden with. Pete had white hair and his whiskers were pepper-colored, which made him appear a lot older than he really was. Pete had been around for a long time, and he knew these roads like the back of his hand.

Ben Holladay, owner of the stage line, was careful to employ only experienced and trustworthy men. At last count, he employed seventy-five drivers on the stage line, and Billy had ridden with most of them. However, Rattlesnake was his favorite by far.

The stage drivers were the kings of the line, like the captains of ships, and Holladay dressed them for the part. All the Holladay drivers dressed alike. They wore broad-brimmed sombreros, corduroys trimmed with velvet, and high-heeled boots, and they all carried a nine-foot rawhide whip with a big leather handle. All the drivers were well respected around town because Holladay didn't put up with drunks or derelicts. Nor did he allow swearing around the passengers.

Billy chuckled. Once, when Rattlesnake had gotten the stagecoach stuck in a deep rut, he had to ask the passengers to get out so he could have a word with his team of horses. After one more good cussing to those nags, he got the wagon moving, put the passengers back on the coach, and made it to his next stop on time. Rattlesnake had told the tale one night over supper, and Billy still laughed when he thought about it. He felt privileged to be a part of the Holladay organization and one day he hoped to be part owner of the stage line.

"Then I'm right?" Rattlesnake persisted.

Billy blinked a couple of times. "Right about what?"

"Nelly?"

"I just said I like her cooking."

"Shucks boy, there's a few other things about her to like," Rattlesnake said. " 'Sides, I'm kind of partial to that other filly you been seein'."

"Mandy. I think she's getting much too serious,

so you need to find another favorite. She's all yours." Billy said.

"Wonder how she'd feel about me?"

"Won't know till you try," Billy said.

Rattlesnake threw back his head and laughed as if what Billy had said was the funniest thing in the world. Finally, he stopped and cleared his throat. "I could use a danged drink of something cool."

Billy reached for a canteen, but before he could grab it, a shot rang out of nowhere. "Damn!" Billy grabbed his shoulder. "I've been hit!"

"Yer all right, son," Rattlesnake shouted as he gripped the reins and urged the horses to go faster. Another shot whizzed over their heads.

"Yep, I'm hit, all right. But I'll live," Billy yelled. He turned and crawled out on the top of the stage, dragging his rifle behind him. "Get those nags going. I'm tired of being somebody's target."

"Ah-wooh-wah!" Rattlesnake bellowed, in what could be called a warpath yell, then cracked his nine-foot rawhide whip above the horses' heads. Instantly, the team responded. Billy stretched out flat on his stomach, his elbows propped up on a trunk as he took aim at the group of riders galloping behind them. He fired twice, taking one rider down and then another. Whoever these men were, they couldn't possibly have shot him. They had been too far away. It must have been somebody on the cliffs, waiting for them to pass by.

Somebody wanted him dead, and Billy needed to find out just who it was before he was successful and finished him off. Thankfully, by the time he picked off the fourth man the group of outlaws gave up the chase.

The stage barreled along into the edge of town,

dust flying from beneath the wheels. "Whoa!" Rattle-snake yelled and yanked back on the reins until the horses obeyed. Then, at a slower pace, they made their way to the hotel where the passengers were to disembark.

"Come on, boy," Rattlesnake said, pulling off his heavy buckskin gloves and tossing them under the seat. "I'll get you to the doc."

"I'm all right, Pete. Let's get the passengers off first. You remember Holladay's rules—the passengers are always our first priority."

"Not when you have a gaping hole in yer shoulder. But who am I to argue? Iffen you drop dead, I'll just have the passengers step over you as I welcome them into town."

Billy couldn't help but smile. The gruff old buzzard really did care.

As the passengers filed off the stage, most asked if Billy and Pete were all right and then thanked each of them for bringing them safely into town. However, the last passenger complained about the wild ride. He said his hat would never be the same again, and he was going to make sure Mr. Holladay knew about how the passengers had been tossed around like sacks of potatoes.

Billy bit his tongue, causing him to wonder if he was truly mellowing with age. When he was younger he would have had a pistol under the fellow's nose, asking if he had any further comments he'd like to make.

"Consarned fool looks like a sack of potatoes," Rattlesnake grumbled. "Let's get that bullet out and then get a drink," Rattlesnake said, giving Billy a shove.

* * *

Ben Holladay stared at the young man sitting in front of his desk. He was staring out the window as he waited for his instructions.

Ben could barely recognize the kid who had come to him looking for a job three years ago. Now a man sat before him. His black Stetson was pulled down so low that you couldn't see his eyes, nor read his thoughts.

Billy looked dangerous—like any hired gun, but Ben knew there was so much more to Billy West than his outside appearance. He was a survivor. Billy would be successful one way or the other, and he was no man's fool.

That's what Ben liked about him most. He smiled as he shuffled the papers on his desk to gain Billy's attention. Ben wanted Billy to be successful, and he was about to put him to a test to see how well he could do.

"Can you realize it has been three years since I started the stage route?"

Billy shook his head and smiled like he was casually amused. "Time has gone by fast. I'd almost forgotten that headache I had the first day I met you."

"It's a good thing you gave up drinking." Ben chuckled. "I don't think you could have handled another hangover like that one."

"What's that saying? Older and wiser?"

Ben threw back his head and laughed. "For some . . . and some only get older and never wiser." He leaned forward on the desk. "How's the shoulder?"

"Stiff. Actually, the bullet hit the fleshy part of my arm."

Ben let out a slow, disgruntled sigh. "I don't think Kincade is going to let up. When Jake took his life, Kincade had to blame somebody. He wants blood. Your blood."

Billy's mouth spread into a thin-lipped smile. "I'm beginning to think the same thing, and I'm not too sure what to do about him."

"I think I have a solution," Ben said and watched as he now had Billy's full attention. Ben just hoped the young man would agree. "I need you to do something for me. It will get you out of town for a while."

Billy's jaw tightened. "I'm not running."

Ben noted the kid's set face, his clamped mouth and fixed eyes. "Whoa." He held up his hand, having forgotten the temper the boy had. "That's not what I meant. I have something back East that I want you to bring out here for me."

"It must be one hell of a cargo if you want me to travel that far to get it."

Ben chuckled. "You could say that. It's my niece. She wants to come and spend some time out here."

"And she doesn't have any family that can bring her?"

"Yes, she has a large family, but they have never been farther West than Kentucky. I want to know that Claire is safe and in your company, and I have no doubts that she will be. How much trouble could it be to bring one girl to Denver?"

Exactly what Billy was thinking. To bring one child across the country had to be easier than what he and Brandy had gone through when they had brought the orphans out West.

"I'll have my nephew, Fredrick, go with you. His family lives near Oak Hill. My sister's place is just past Oak Hill, so he can show you the way and introduce you to the family."

"What's Oak Hill? A city?"

"No. It's my brother's estate. He has a large horse farm, among other property."

Horse farm got Billy's attention. He'd always thought about raising horses. This little trip could provide some valuable information. "Why don't you send Fredrick?"

"Because the kid is still wet behind the ears. Hell, he'd get sidetracked halfway across the country and forget what I'd sent him for. He's so green that somebody would take one look at him and try something. On the other hand, they'd take one look at you and think twice before crossing you."

Billy's smile turned into a chuckle. "Thank you. I think. But I don't know—."

"Well, I heard about your sudden engagement to Mandy, so I understand if you don't want to leave her."

"What?"

"She's told everybody in town that you were going to marry her. I figured that you'd finally gotten serious about someone. She is pretty enough."

"She's pretty, all right, but that engagement business is news to me," Billy muttered, his voice full of sarcasm. "You know, I'm damned sick and tired of women. You pay them a little attention, and they try and put a rope 'round your neck."

"All the more reason for you to accept my offer," Ben said. "I'll pay you five thousand dollars for your trouble."

Billy's brow shot up. Something sounded fishy, and he had the feeling he wasn't getting the entire story. "That's a hell of a lot of money. What's wrong with the kid?"

Ben shrugged. "Nothing. Absolutely nothing. But Claire means the world to me. With your gun,

I know I'll not have to worry. It's a simple job. All you have to do is bring her back here. What could be easier?"

That was the problem. It sounded much too easy. But on the bright side, it would get him away from scheming females. And it was only a child he would be getting.

"Why do I have the feeling that you're not telling me something?" Billy pressed. He knew Ben paid good money for whatever he wanted. Price was never an object, so his niece must be very special to him.

"I don't think I've missed anything. Besides, it will get you out of town," Ben said, while thinking at the same time, I merely omitted the fact that my niece isn't a child, as Billy assumed but he would find that out on his own. Ben smiled. "Then you'll do it?"

"Add two more grand, and you've got yourself a deal."

Ben gave a slow, satisfying nod. "Good. You leave first thing in the morning."

Billy left Ben's office with the strange feeling that he'd been hoodwinked. But on the bright side of things, it would give him a chance to see a part of the country he'd never seen before. He'd read in the books that Brandy had made him study that everything was different back East.

Billy removed his jacket, rolled it up, and tied it behind his saddle. The days were starting to warm up, and the sun felt good on his shoulders. Speaking of his sister . . . if he didn't tell her he was leaving town, he'd have hell to pay when he got back.

It was midafternoon when Billy reached his sister's place. They had named the ranch The Wagon

Wheel. His family figured they had spent so much time living in a wagon that it was an appropriate name. He glanced up at the wheel they had hung over the archway as he now passed under it. There had been a time when he thought the wagon would be their only home forever.

Billy nudged his horse into a trot to cover the short road to the house. He dismounted and tied his horse to one of the white aspen trees.

The front door flew open, and Scott, his brother, came running out, slamming it loudly behind him as he scurried down the steps. Billy noticed that Scott's britches had a tear in the knee. He was still as energetic as he was at seven, and he still talked just as much, too. But that's what was so lovable about Scott. His black hair was cut in a bob and his brownish-green eyes bubbled with personality.

"Billy! You're just in time for dinner," Scott called as he ran over and jumped into his brother's arms. "You hungry?"

Billy swung Scott around, then said, "Depends. Who's cooking?"

Scott giggled. "Not Brandy. They don't let her near the cook stove. Ellen and Mary are cooking."

"In that case—" Billy chuckled, rubbing his sore shoulder, "I'll stay." Billy held Scott at arm's length to get a good look at him. "Look at you, I bet you've grown two inches. Pretty soon I won't be able to pick you up at all."

"Yep. And one day I'll be taller than you. Then you'll have to look up at me."

"I doubt that." Billy ruffled Scott's straight black hair. "Let's get some grub and catch up. Were you out helping Thunder?"

Billy and Scott started up the steps to the front porch. "Nope. I was milking that blamed cow."

Billy couldn't help chuckling. "You just can't seem to get rid of that cow, can you?"

"When I grow up, I ain't having no milk cows," Scott grumbled as he reached for the door.

They moved through the large living room and headed back to the kitchen. The minute Billy walked through the door, Mary and Ellen rushed over to hug him. Everyone was talking and laughing at once. It was good to come home to his family, Billy thought.

The girls were turning into real beauties. Mary's long, blonde hair hung halfway down her back and her eyes were just as blue as he remembered, and just as rebellious. Ellen, who had once been a mousy little thing, had filled out very nicely, Billy couldn't help noticing. Her long, brown hair complemented her hazel eyes—eyes that had lost the sadness that had been there for such a long time.

He hadn't realized that it had been four months since he'd been back to the ranch. "What's for dinner?"

"Chicken and biscuits," Ellen said, placing a pan of buttermilk biscuits on top of the counter.

Mary took a plate from the cupboard. "I'll set another place. It's about time you brought your sorry hide home!"

Billy's brow raised a fraction. "I see you're as charming as ever," he teased and gave Mary a swat.

A half-smile crossed her face. "What's this I hear about you being engaged?"

"That's what I'd like to know, too," Brandy said as she entered through the back door, carrying a bucket of water. Quickly, she set the bucket down so she could give Billy a hug. "You look thin. Are you eating? And tell me about the engagement." Her violet eyes glistened with questions.

"There is no engagement. Ain't nothing to it," Billy said, moving away from her. "Don't you think I'd tell you first? Mandy must be spreading rumors."

"I see," Brandy said. She wiped her hands, slung the towel over her shoulder and crossed over to sit down at the table. Pushing her brandy-colored hair over her shoulders, she said, "I thought it was Nelly, not Mandy."

"It's kind of been both." Billy smiled as he took his seat at the table on the long bench next to Scott.

"A real ladies' man," Mary added.

"Once upon a time I had you charmed." Billy smiled at Mary.

Mary placed a napkin in her lap, then looked at him. Raising her eyebrows she said, "That's before I came to my senses."

"There was a time when we didn't think you had any senses," he teased her affectionately.

"Did I say that I missed you?" Mary shot back. "I take it back—every word."

"Where's Thunder?" Scott asked. "I'm starved."

Brandy smiled at Scott. "When haven't you been hungry?"

"Did I hear my name?" Thunder said as he finished wiping his face and arms with a towel. He tossed the towel aside and took his seat at the head of the table. "It's good to see you kid. About damn' time you showed yourself."

Billy eyed the man he admired most. Thunder had been dragged into their life when he really didn't want any part of them, by his sister, Brandy, but the man seemed happy enough about it now. Maybe it just took the right woman . . . or blackmail. Billy smiled.

He thought back to when he'd first met Thunder. He hadn't changed much except that the hard look that had always lurked in Thunder's dark eyes had been replaced with something . . . Billy wasn't sure what. . . . Maybe it was contentment. For a long time Thunder had been torn between the Cheyenne and the white man's world.

Thunder had once told Billy that he felt as if he were dancing on the wind, not knowing where he belonged, or who he was.

Well, Thunder had a family now. Billy smiled. It was ready-made when Thunder made the mistake of bumping into Brandy, and she blackmailed him to take them out West.

Thunder still wore his slate-black hair a little long and his coal gray eyes could still make people freeze in their tracks. It had always worked on Billy, he remembered with a chuckle. As fast as Billy was with a gun, he still couldn't outdraw Thunder.

Even though Billy still thought of Thunder as half Cheyenne, he now knew that Thunder was white and used the white name of Thomas Bradley. But they all called him by his Indian name. Thunder's mother, Helen, had been captured from a wagon train when she'd barely conceived him. She'd been smart enough to pass Thunder off as her Cheyenne husband's child.

"Have you forgotten how to speak?" Thunder asked.

Billy shook his head. "Sorry. I was just remembering when we first met you. You really didn't want any part of us. Did you?"

"Like a toothache. Even when I was forced to take care of you, which I might add didn't sit well with me, I still didn't want this rag-tag-lot," Thunder admitted, waving his hand at the group. "Pass the biscuits."

Billy received the plate of hot biscuits from Mary and handed them to Thunder. "So what made you change your mind?"

"I'm not sure," Thunder admitted as he put a biscuit on his plate. "I've never told any of you this, but the second night I stayed at the parsonage, it was the night of the big storm. Maybe you remember. I saddled Lightning and rode away from the compound with the intention of never returning. I rode through town and headed for the open prairie. It seemed like I rode all night, the rain pelting down on me. After I'd ridden all my anger out, I finally noticed my surroundings, and I realized that I was back at the parsonage. Why? I don't know."

"Well, I'm glad that you came back," Brandy said softly. "None of us would be here now if you had kept on riding. Of course, I could have had you arrested."

"And, no doubt, you would have."

"I'm glad I came back, too." Thunder looked at his wife affectionately. "I wouldn't have missed our adventure for anything, although I wouldn't have admitted it at the time. One thing you can definitely say is that we didn't have a smooth road, it was full of bumps along the way."

"I agree with that," Billy chuckled. "Some of us were very hard to get along with." He glanced sideways at Mary.

"Oh, shut up," Mary grumbled and gave Billy an elbow in the side. "I couldn't have been that bad."

Brandy choked, and Thunder had to pat her on the back.

"I just had to go though an adjustment period," Mary said with a smile.

"And thank God you adjusted," Billy teased. They were quiet for a moment as they ate and then Billy thought about Thunder's mother. "Have you heard from Helen?"

"We received a letter this week," Thunder said, then took a sip of water. "She is enjoying her stay with my grandparents. However, my grandmother has become sick, so Mother is taking care of her at the moment. I'm glad that she finally made it back to Boston. I'm sure she'll come back West once my grandmother is well."

Brandy put her fork down and looked at Billy. "Why do I have a hunch that your sudden appearance is more than just a visit?"

Billy stared at his sister for a moment then burst out laughing. "Well, I did miss all of you."

Brandy rested her head on her chin. "And?"

"And, I'm going back East," Billy announced.

"For good?" Scott asked.

"Nope." Billy shook his head. "Ben Holladay wants me to go to New York and bring his niece back to Denver."

"What do you think about making this trip?" Brandy asked.

"It'll be a good chance for me to see a horse farm and I must admit it will be a change," Billy admitted.

"Our covered wagon is broken," Scott said.

"I won't need one." Billy reached over and ruffled Scott's hair. "I'll travel by train and stage."

"I guess you'll be gone a couple of months?" Thunder asked.

"That's what I figure," Billy said.

"Well, the only thing I can tell you, kid, is that life is very different back there, so be prepared."

"I can remember your stories about Boston. I think I'm going to take my horse. At least then I'll have something familiar with me." Billy chuckled. "I'll see you before you know it."

Mary reached over and placed her hand on Billy's arm. "Promise me you'll be careful."

Billy smiled and kissed Mary on the nose. "I will. After all, I seem to be the only one who can keep you straight."

Chapter Three

The sun had barely risen when Billy put on his white duster to ward off the crisp morning air. Even though the days promised the warmth of the spring, the chilliness of winter still clung to the mornings.

He rode to the stage station to wait for Fredrick, but when he arrived, he saw Fredrick leaning against a post, drinking a cup of coffee. Billy wondered if he'd ever looked as young as the kid did to him now. Sometimes he felt as if he'd been an old man all his life, having had a lot of responsibility at a very young age.

Fredrick was tall, lanky, and scatterbrained, which his uncle complained about constantly, along with the fact that the boy lacked any ambition at all. Billy figured that Fredrick just hadn't found his calling yet—but he would. You didn't live in this part of the country long without becoming a man. However, the sooner the better.

Billy had to admit that Fredrick had an easy-going charm that made the tow-headed kid likable.

He reminded Billy of an overgrown puppy who hadn't filled out yet.

"Are you ready to go?" Billy asked, not bothering to dismount.

Fredrick tossed out the remains of his coffee. "As ready as I'll ever be," he said as he pushed his rangy body away from the post. "Just as long as I don't have to stay." He must have seen Billy's puzzled look because Fredrick added, "I'm sure when I see my folks, they'll try and talk me into staying at home and learning the shipping business."

"It sounds profitable."

"It is. It's just not for me."

Billy nodded. He understood quite well. It was one of the reasons he'd struck out on his own. "We'll tell your folks that I need you," he said.

Fredrick nodded with a boyish smile. "Sounds good to me."

"I thought we'd ride instead of taking the stage, so that we can take our horses on the train. Don't like to be without my horse. Are you up to it?"

"You betcha." Fredrick mounted his horse. "Can you call me something besides Fredrick?"

"How about if I call you Fred?"

"I think I'd like that better, but I really prefer F. D. Out here Fredrick sounds sissy, and it has gotten me into plenty of fights. Been lucky they haven't involved shooting, but I'm learning not to use my name. However, my uncle will not call me anything but by my given name—unless it's 'hey you'." Fredrick laughed.

"Your uncle is one hell of a man."

"Yeah, but set in his ways," Fredrick said.

When they reached the edge of town, Billy felt a little strange leaving Denver for a reason other than work. Of course, this was work, only a different kind. But he'd be back, he thought as he turned in his saddle to glance back at the tall buildings as he rode away. He hadn't realized until this moment that he thought of Denver as home. He wasn't sure where he was from originally, but it didn't matter anymore. All that mattered was his adopted family. Whoever his real parents had been, it was evident that they had never wanted him. Billy had learned the hard way that your family is the people around you, who were there from day to day and cared if you got in trouble.

"What does F. D. stand for?" Billy asked.

"Fredrick David. It sounds more like a man's name than Fredrick."

"All right. It will be F. D. from now on. I figured that you'd be glad to be heading home."

"I'm looking forward to seeing my aunt and uncle and going to visit my folks, but Denver is home now. You'll see what I mean when we go back East. Give me the wide open range any day," Fredrick said, then he glanced over at Billy. "Where are you from?"

"It's funny that you should ask. I was just thinking that Denver is also my home. Can't say I know where I started, but I don't relish the idea of going back to Independence where Father Brown found me. I ended up in his orphanage."

"I bet it was tough being an orphan."

Billy nodded. "Yeah. You could say so. The first thing you learn is that the only person you can count on is yourself."

Fredrick looked at Billy for a long moment. "Looks like you turned out all right."

Billy chuckled as he glanced at the kid. "Glad you approve." He watched Fredrick turn red.

"Well, you know what I mean."

"Yeah, I know," Billy said. "I've never been East before, so I guess I'll be the greenhorn once we board the train and leave Missouri."

"Hey, I like the way it sounds. You can depend on me."

Billy frowned. He didn't like depending on anyone, but the kid was right. "Just remember, F. D., don't steer me wrong," he warned. "Looking foolish isn't something I care for."

"Yes, sir," Fredrick said with a smile.

They rode a long way in silence before Billy finally said, "Tell me something about Claire."

"She's my cousin," Fredrick said simply and shrugged. Then he chuckled at Billy's scowl.

"No shit. Quit horsing around."

"All right, all right. She looks ordinary. Kind of small with long back hair and blue eyes. I guess she's okay, for a girl."

"Do you like her?"

"Who doesn't like Claire? Everybody loves her. I don't know if she still has it, but she did have a terrible cough."

"Well, the young lady is going to be in for a big change," Billy said. "I just hope she's up to the trip. It's going to be a long journey," he said, wondering just what the youngster would be like. His one consoling thought was that he'd probably enjoy dealing with a child instead of a fickle woman. He just hoped the kid wasn't scared of him. It had been a while since he'd been around children, so he'd have to remember to be gentle.

Instead of the snarling bear that he could be.

Claire had everything packed except for a couple of items lying on the blue and white quilt on her bed and the few gowns she'd wear and the ball gown she chosen for the farewell party her mother had planned.

Normally, she didn't give a fig about parties, but she was looking forward to this one. It would probably be her last ball, so she wanted to enjoy every minute of it.

Glancing at her aquamarine gown, she smiled at the elegance of the cut. She wanted to make sure she looked her best to show David that she was doing just fine without him. Maybe he would regret letting her go.

She had to admit that she did miss him. Having grown up together, he'd always been a part of her life. She'd planned to marry David. Now she realized that she'd been viewing him through rose-colored glasses. David had many flaws, the worst being that he thought only of himself. She'd never want anyone like that. Too bad she'd not seen his true colors earlier.

Claire wasn't sure what kind of man she wanted, not that it mattered anymore, since she wouldn't likely live to see him. Perhaps she'd just have a few flings with several men. Her reputation would not matter, and she'd be very careful not to fall in love with anyone in the short time that she had left. Tears threatened to fill her eyes so she took a deep breath.

The intake of air tickled her throat and she began to cough. Quickly, she grabbed her handkerchief from the dressing table and pressed it to her lips. She coughed and coughed until she finally had to sit down. Grabbing for the brown medicine bottle, she held it to her lips and took a sip, frowning at the bitter taste, but desperately needing its relief. She coughed again.

"Here, let me get you some water," Aunt Ute said, entering Claire's bedroom.

Claire nodded then took another sip of medicine.

"Drink this, Claire." Ute said in her thick German accent. She held a cool glass of water out for Claire.

After Claire drank several sips, her spasms eased, and she set the glass back down and whispered, *"Danke schön."* It was the only German words she knew.

Ute patted her back. "That's my girl. Take a deep breath and wipe the tears from your eyes. Much better, *ja?"*

"Uh-huh," Claire said as she nodded, feeling that if Aunt Ute slapped her back any harder she wouldn't have any breath left!

"Have you had many spells today?"

"No." Claire took another soothing sip of water. "I've been lucky. That was the first."

"Good." Ute nodded then moved over to the high four-poster bed. She finished putting the folded garments into the trunk. "I see you are already packed. This is good, *ja?* We don't want any last minute frazzles."

Claire looked at her aunt and smiled. "I knew you'd be pleased." She really liked her aunt. Being extremely tall for a woman, she could intimidate most men. Although large, she was pretty, with shoulder-length brown hair and green eyes that had specks of gold in them. Having never been married, she was considered an old maid, but Claire liked to think that Ute just hadn't met the right man. There had to be that special someone out there waiting for the right woman.

Thoughts of David sneaked back into Claire's

mind. She had thought she'd met the right person but she knew now that she'd been terribly wrong.

Oh, well, Claire sighed. She was glad to have Aunt Ute as a nurse. She was a great deal of comfort.

Aunt Ute nodded. "Margaret said to tell you that your escort should be arriving this afternoon."

"Really? That's wonderful! He will arrive in time for my party this Friday. Then the next day, we're off on our great adventure."

"You're a little sad about leaving home, *ja?*"

"No." Claire shook her head emphatically. "Oh, I'll miss my family, but I want to see other things beside Oak Hill. I want to see the world. Or at least, the Wild West."

"There's nothing like traveling. It enriches the soul, and I'm really glad that you're getting the chance. But I've heard that the frontier can be a wild place. They have uncivilized creatures out there: some who would scalp you. Can you believe it?"

"Indians," Claire supplied. "I'm sure we won't run into any. I think they are mostly in books and uncivilized places. We'll be riding the train to Missouri and from there the stagecoach, I think we're safe."

"Well, I will tell you one thing." Ute put her hands on her hips. "If they want this head of hair, they will be in the biggest fight they have ever seen," Ute proclaimed. "Because I'm not a frail little thing."

Somehow, Claire couldn't picture anyone tangling with Aunt Ute. She grinned. They wouldn't stand a chance.

"I'm going to Doc Worden's office to get a few bottles of your medicine," Ute said as she moved toward the door. "We don't want to run out. Would you like to come?"

"I don't believe so. I've seen enough of his office to last a lifetime."

"I guess so."

"I think I'm going to lie down for few minutes. I really feel tired after that coughing spell. Besides I don't want to miss my escort when he arrives. I wonder what he'll look like," Claire said, voicing her thoughts out loud.

"Does it matter?"

"No, not really. I guess I've been trying to picture him because I know he's going to be different from the men I know. I'll bet he'll look like a real cowboy."

"As long as he leaves his horse outside, he will suit me," Ute said as she shut the door.

After Ute left, the soft bed called to Claire so she lay down and pulled the fluffy comforter over her. She'd never tell Ute how very tired she felt. The coughing spell had taken more energy than she wanted to admit, but nothing was going to stop her from making this trip, and that included her awful cough. She would just shut her eyes for a few minutes and rest, and then she'd be fine.

She could make this trip. She could.

But what kind of man had her uncle sent for an escort? Perhaps, an older gentleman like Doc Worden? Someone to advise her and protect her? She could picture him in an old brown suit with spectacles perched on his bony, sunburned nose. She just hoped he was pleasant, or it would be a long trip. At least, her cousin Fredrick would be with them, so she'd have someone to talk to besides Aunt Ute.

Claire sighed. She'd much rather have some real excitement. She'd been living peacefully for so long that she was bored.

Well, no matter. She yawned and her eyes watered. She'd soon find out who the stranger was and then they would get a few things straight.

She wanted to do things her way instead of being told what to do by some man who thought he knew it all. So, whoever this stranger might be, he needed to learn that she was the boss.

With a soft smile, Claire drifted off into a deep sleep . . . a place where there was no pain nor sickness.

By the time he reached New York, Billy was so tired of sitting that he felt like a caged animal waiting to pounce and stretch his legs. It wouldn't take much to set off his temper. He wasn't accustomed to such idleness. He looked out the window toward the long platform just coming into view. It was full of people and children dressed in their Sunday-go-to-meeting best.

The train hissed to a halt as it pulled into the station, steam pouring from the big engine. A sign nailed to the side of the long wooden building proclaimed them to be in Kenton, a small town outside of New York where the Holladays lived. Billy couldn't help wondering if Spot, his horse, was as restless as he was.

"We're here," Fredrick said as he rose to his feet and stretched. "I'd forgotten how long the trip is. Now I remember why I haven't returned home before now."

"You should try covering the distance by wagon train." Billy chuckled. "Believe me, this is faster, though just as boring." He glanced out the window again before he scrambled to his feet.

"Let's go get the horses," Fredrick suggested.

Once they left the passenger car, Billy began to realize that he and Fredrick were dressed differently from everyone he walked past. He noticed how they took second glances at him, even if they tried not to stare. He hated their stares because there wasn't any way in hell he was going to dress like those fancy dudes.

At the cattle car, they led Billy's pinto and Fredrick's big red roan down the ramp, where they saddled the horses. Then they mounted and started off, Fredrick leading the way.

Soon the many buildings disappeared behind them, and they were in the countryside where the trees were just beginning to show their spring foliage and the roadways were sprinkled with wildflowers.

Kenton was a lot greener than the prairie, Billy thought as they rode. He was beginning to relax now that they were in wide open country. "How far?"

"Go left here," Fredrick said and pointed. "My aunt and uncle live down this road about a quarter mile. That way," Fredrick said, pointing to the right, "is where my folks live."

"At least their property is away from town. Thunder told me what it was like when he went back to Boston to see his grandparents. Said it was nothing but one house after another, all jammed side by side. He said he sometimes had to look to find the sun. Don't think I'd much care for that."

Fredrick chuckled. "If you go into the city, you'll see what Thunder was talking about. Nothing to see but tall buildings. I don't like it either."

Suddenly, Oak Hill came into view. Billy pulled back on Spot's reins, bringing him to a halt. "Jesus, F. D! Is that a house?"

"Yep. Something, isn't it?"

A mansion, sitting on a small hill between two large oak trees, came into view as they came to the end of the drive. A veranda surrounded the house—but not a normal veranda—this one reached around all four façades and extended from the ground to the main roof cornice. The veranda floor was elevated about three feet above ground level so that when they rode closer to the house, the porch was still above their heads. Billy counted the pillars. There were twenty-eight. "You might say that it is very impressive. How high are those pillars?"

"Thirty feet," Fredrick said as he dismounted.

They climbed the wooden steps up to the porch. When Fredrick lifted the brass knocker on the front door and rapped, it was only a moment before the door swung open, and a man dressed in a black coat came out and said, "Might I help you, sir?"

Fredrick glanced at Billy. "He must be new." Then Fredrick looked at the sharp-looking doorman. "I'm Fredrick Holladay and this is Billy West. I believe we're expected."

"You could have tried F. D.," Billy said with a grin.

"I will announce you," the man said stiffly, bowed sharply at the waist and rang a bell. In a flash, a small boy came flying around the veranda. "Willie, take the gentlemen's horses to the stable."

The little boy scampered down the steps and took the reins of both horses to lead them around the massive house. "I like this one," Willie said, patting the pinto and glancing back at Billy. "What's her name?"

Billy stared at the little guy who looked much too young to be working. "Spot."

"Looks like somebody dropped paint on her."

Spot was all white except for a brown mane and a brown left shoulder and leg. It did look as if someone had spilled paint on her. Billy smiled at the little boy and then followed Fredrick into the house. A monumental staircase faced them as they entered the front door, and rooms to the left and right.

They were led into the parlor at the left to wait. The room had white walls and woodwork. The rosewood furniture with gilt copper mounts was upholstered in a most handsome Aubusson tapestry with a pale green background and a medallion in the center. It looked very uncomfortable. Billy had seen a settee like this one in Miss Ruby's fancy sitting parlor, which was, after all, the fanciest whorehouse in Denver. Billy actually smiled at that thought, which he discreetly kept to himself. Best not to start out on the wrong foot.

A woman swept into the foyer. She was a beautiful older woman, her dark hair swept up on top of her head and away from her face. She was smiling and looking at Fredrick as her arms spread wide.

"Fredrick, it has been much too long since you have visited us. Look at you. Your skin is so tan, but other than that, you look none the worse for living out there."

"Aunt Margaret, it's called the West. How did you think I'd look?"

"Well, you know how wild it is in that part of the country."

"You've read too many books, Aunt Margaret," Fredrick said with a chuckle. "I want you to meet someone. May I introduce Billy West? He's going to make sure we have a safe journey back out to *that place.*"

Margaret, wearing a stricken expression, stared at Billy for the first time. "Is that why you're wearing a gun, Mr. West?"

"Exactly, ma'am."

"Well, let us hope that you do not need it around here. We are most certainly civilized in this part of the country."

Before Billy could respond and assure Mrs. Holladay that he wasn't going to shoot her, a young woman came into the room and whatever he was about to say flew completely out of his head. My God, she was a beauty, Billy thought as all his breath left his body. It was as if a gust of fresh air had swept through the room.

This young woman looked nothing like the women where he came from. She had an elegant quality about her instead of the worn-out look that the women out West had. Her skin was pale, and her hair was black as coal. Her eyes resembled two pools of ice blue water. Yet, there was something about her—some unreal quality—that seemed if you reached out and touched her she would vanish, like the many beautiful butterflies he'd tried to catch when he was younger.

As she moved toward him, Billy noted the graceful way she carried herself. He lifted his hand to his jaw to make sure his mouth hadn't dropped open. This wasn't the way he usually felt when he met attractive women. He had always felt in control, but at this moment, he felt as if he'd been slugged in the gut.

He'd sworn off women. Was he loco?

She gazed at him with vivid blue eyes that reminded him of fresh mountain streams when the sun reflected off the silver-blue rushing water. Her gaze roamed over every inch of his body, and Billy wondered what she was thinking.

"We have company, dear," Margaret said.

Claire didn't say anything, she just stared which, of course, was very rude, but what she saw before her was a far cry from what she'd expected.

"Did you hear me, dear?" Margaret said.

"Yes, Mother, I see," Claire answered in an almost breathless voice. She blushed. Her escort wasn't some elderly advisor she'd thought her uncle would send. He was a cowboy . . . in *every* sense of the word. His shoulders were broad and he was dressed in black from the Stetson on his head to the toes of his worn leather boots. He was ruggedly handsome, his face was bronzed, and his dark brown hair hung just below his ears, giving him an untamed look.

He stared at her with eyes that were so brown they appeared black: as black as the handkerchief tied around his neck.

Evidently, he didn't know that it was rude to stare . . . or perhaps he just didn't care. More than likely the latter, Claire thought. For just a moment, she was aware of nothing but the man before her as he held her gaze with his warm chocolate eyes. Her stomach quivered. Odd feeling, she thought.

"My dear, this is Billy West," her mother said, trying to gain Claire's attention.

Get hold of yourself, Claire thought. *You've seen plenty of men before.*

But nothing like this cowboy, a tiny voice inside her said.

"Mr. West," she nodded politely, and then looked immediately at her cousin. "I am surprised that you came, too, Fredrick."

Fredrick stepped over and hugged Claire. "You have changed, cousin, since the last time I saw you."

Billy got a queer feeling, watching Fredrick embrace the young woman, but he chalked it up to being tired. He smiled slightly. This woman was a real looker. She hadn't bothered to hug him. All he got was a polite nod. Good thing she wasn't the one going on the trip. It was the other cousin that Billy wanted to meet. The one he would be responsible for. "Where is the child that we are escorting back to Denver?"

The three other people in the room turned and gaped at him. And then the woman and Fredrick said together, "Child?"

Billy wondered if these people had a hard time understanding plain English. "Claire. The child that we're taking back with us."

"There is no child," the beautiful young woman answered him. "I'm Claire."

Billy had to grit his teeth to keep from slinging a few choice cuss words. Ben knew how sick Billy was of women, and now he'd saddled him with a female for several thousand miles. And a beautiful female at that. He thought back to their conversation. Ben hadn't really said anything about a child, but he also hadn't corrected Billy either. The sly devil. Ben had known exactly what he was doing.

Well, what was done was done. Maybe it would work out better than Billy thought. At least, he wouldn't have to worry so much about a grown woman getting lost or in trouble. The biggest problem that he could see would be some cowboy making an improper advance to Claire, and then Billy would have to beat the daylights out of him. That would be more an aggravation than anything else.

"Is there anything the matter?" Claire asked.

Billy realized he was still staring holes through the young woman. "Just a slight misunderstanding. I understood that I would be taking a child back to Holladay."

"Well, I'm sorry to disappoint you, but I promise I'll not be as much trouble as a child would be," Claire said.

You had better not be, Billy thought. He could tan a child's backside if she didn't mind him, but turning Miss Holladay over his knee brought a whole different thought to mind.

"Let me show you to your rooms," Claire said. "I'm sure both of you would like to freshen up after such a long trip."

Billy nodded, then followed Claire up the stairs, taking note of the sway of her hips. Lord help him. What had he gotten himself into? He cursed himself for allowing his thoughts to wander down the wrong path. What the hell was the matter with him? He was acting like he'd eaten locoweed.

Just castrate me and get it over with 'cause that's what Ben would do if Billy touched one little hair on the lady's head. He grunted.

"Is something wrong, Mr. West?" Claire asked.

"Yes, sweetheart, but I'll get over it."

Billy liked looking at the pretty young thing. He'd admit that much. But he'd just have to remember to look and not touch and the trip would be easy.

Claire pointed to a door. "This is your room, Mr. West."

"The name's Billy."

"Is there anything else I can do for you?"

"I'd like to check on my horse after I stow my gear," Billy said, looking past her to Fredrick.

"That won't be a problem," Fredrick answered. "You might like to have Claire show you around. Oak Hill is one of the best horse farms in the East. Uncle Ben said you've always been interested in starting your own farm."

Claire's eyes lit up with interest. "Is that right? I'll be glad to show you around the stables. Would you like to meet me in the foyer in about an hour?"

Billy opened the door and stepped in. "I'll see you then."

Once the door was shut, Claire looked at her cousin. "He doesn't talk much, does he?"

"Not a lot." Fredrick laughed. "But he'll warm up to you, as soon as he gets over the shock. Uncle Ben led Billy to believe that he'd be picking up a child to bring back to Denver."

Claire opened up the next bedroom door for her cousin. "Why would he do that?"

"Well, back home there have been several young women who have been trying to get Billy to the altar. One even went so far as setting a wedding date, and told the whole town while Billy was out on a stage run. It took him by surprise and embarrassed him. One thing you don't want to do is embarrass Billy West. He doesn't hold kindly with anyone who does. And for that reason, he's more or less sworn off women. If he'd known it was you he was picking up, he never would have agreed."

Claire leaned against the door frame. "Such a shame," she said, then she laughed at her cousin's dumbfounded look. "Well, he *is* good looking. I'm sure there will be some disappointed women."

"I guess you could say that," Fredrick said. "But I wouldn't go getting any ideas if I were you. You'd just get hurt."

"Oh, Fredrick, I don't mean me. I was just teasing. Mr. West can rest assured that I don't want any entanglements." She straightened. "And before I forget, I don't want anything said about my condition."

"So Uncle Ben told me." Fredrick frowned. "I'm real sorry Claire."

"Thank you." She gave him a little smile. "Now don't you go getting sad on me. I'm so excited about this trip that I don't think about my sickness anymore, and I want to leave it that way." She decided to change the subject. "Are you going to see your parents?"

"Sure. Then I'll come back here at the end of the week."

"Remember, there is nothing wrong with me but a slight cough. We haven't told anybody outside the family except my editor."

"Your secret is safe with me," he answered her, then asked, "Are you sure you'll be able to make the trip?"

"Yes. I have plenty of medicine, and Aunt Ute is to accompany us."

Fredrick laughed.

"What's so funny?"

"I would save that bit of information until the day we leave. Billy isn't going to be happy with another person to look after."

Chapter Four

The smell of beeswax surrounded Claire as she waited in the foyer. The maids had been busy all morning waxing the floors and woodwork, and it showed. Everything gleamed. Of course, her mother would never stand for anything but perfection in her home. And with the ball coming up, her mother had the entire staff cleaning everything not once, but twice.

Claire glanced in the hallway mirror, smoothed her hair, then quickly yanked her hand away. She wasn't trying to look pretty for *him*. It was just that when she'd changed into her dark blue riding habit, she had disordered her hair. And, she had planned on going riding even before she'd met Mr. West—Billy, she corrected herself. It seemed odd to call him by his given name when she hardly knew him, but she had to admit he didn't look much like a Mister.

But stranger or not, she was going riding today. It had been several months since she had last ridden Run for Glory, her prize thoroughbred, and she wanted to take him on the train, so at least she'd have something familiar with her out West.

She hadn't been able to judge Billy, but she was sure he would be reasonable. She was sure he wouldn't mind her taking her horse. After all, he had brought his mount.

He certainly was different from any man she'd ever known. Billy was bigger than life . . . rugged looking, and so masculine that she found she really liked watching him.

One thing was certain, she wouldn't be afraid of traveling with his protection. There was something about the way he stood, his square jaw jutting outward that said, "Don't mess with me!" A stranger would think twice before antagonizing him or anyone traveling with him.

"Are you going out riding, dear?" Margaret said as she strolled through the foyer with her arms full of freshly cut flowers for the dining room. "Do you think you should?"

"Yes, mother. I agreed to show Billy around the stables, and then I'm going to ride. I intend to take Run for Glory with me on my trip."

"I see it's 'Billy' already." Her mother shifted her basket to her hip. "What do you think of your young man?"

Claire could feel her cheeks heating. How had her mother known whom she'd been thinking about? She couldn't have known. She was just guessing. "For heaven sakes, Mother, he isn't 'my young man'," Claire said. "I have just met him."

A noise on the staircase caused Claire to swing around to find Billy coming down the stairs. She sure hoped he hadn't heard what they had just said. She would die on the spot.

"I hope I haven't kept you waiting," came the rough masculine voice.

"No, not at all," Claire said, noticing that at least he wasn't smirking. Maybe he hadn't realized that they had been talking about him.

She watched him approach, noting he had changed clothes. He wore a dark brown homespun shirt. The handkerchief was missing, revealing tanned skin with a sprinkling of dark hair peeking out of his shirt. His hair was still damp on the sides where he'd washed, and as he neared her, she could smell the fresh scent of soap. She realized that she was gawking at him in the most unladylike manner. She quickly averted her gaze.

Billy nodded toward Margaret. "Ma'am."

"Shall we go?" Claire asked.

Billy didn't answer, he simply put on his Stetson indicating he was ready.

He was a man of few words, Claire thought as she placed her gloved hand on his arm. Even through two layers of fabric, she could feel his heat.

Margaret cleared her throat. "Take care of my little girl. She's fragile."

"Mother, I'm just going for a ride," Claire protested, but didn't stop.

Billy was a little surprised by the comment, but he didn't know what to say, so he just reached for the door. Before he could grasp the knob, the gentleman they had seen yesterday appeared.

"Allow me," he said stiffly.

Billy wondered why in the hell he couldn't open the door by himself, but the fool man seemed hellbent on doing it. He waited for Claire to precede him, then he followed her out. They walked down the steps in silence and started toward the right side of the house.

"I could have opened the door," Billy said off-handedly.

"That's Webster's job," Claire said.

"You mean you have a professional door-opener?"

Claire giggled, and Billy found he liked the sound. "He's called a butler."

"Oh, yeah. I've heard of them. In fact, my kid brother said he wished he had a butler, so he could milk the cow."

"I've never heard of a butler milking cows. I certainly couldn't imagine Webster doing so. They direct the household staff. However, I guess there could always be a first time."

"In my household, lots of things would be different from here," Billy said, glancing at Claire and wondering how in the world Margaret saw a child in her. Claire was definitely a woman in every sense of the word. She was a mite thin—hell, he could probably encircle her waist with his hands—but with a little food, she would fill out just right. Come to think of it, it might be better to keep her a mite thin.

"Is something wrong?" Claire asked.

"Just thinking. You don't look fragile to me," he said with a smile.

"You'll have to excuse my mother," Claire told him, her blue eyes dancing with a smile. "She's a little overprotective."

"And do you need protecting?"

Her eyes widened, as if she were surprised by his remark. "Most certainly not. I am a grown woman."

"I'll say," Billy shot back before he thought.

"I beg your pardon?"

He made sure to keep a blank expression before he answered, "Nothing." Better not have her getting any ideas that he thought her attractive. He didn't want another female latching onto him. He pointed. "Is that the barn up ahead?"

"No. It's the stable where we keep our horses. We have a separate barn where hay and feed is stored."

"It's a big one."

"We stable twenty-four horses, twelve on each side. We have another building where we keep the pregnant mares. I'm sure they put your horse in the main stable. I'll take you to him."

"Her," Billy corrected. Spot was the only female he trusted.

They entered the double doors and immediately smelled fresh hay and horses, a scent Billy was familiar with. Some things didn't change whether in the country or the city.

Spot had poked her head way over the half-door of the second stall, looking around with curiosity. Billy smiled as he neared the stall. Hell, Spot probably figured she'd died and gone to heaven. Neither of them had ever been in a place this fancy.

Claire rubbed the horse's muzzle. "She's pretty. We don't see many pintos this far East." She noted that the filly was all white except for the one brown shoulder and forefoot and one large brown spot across her rump. "What's her name?"

"Spot."

Claire chuckled. "Surely you must be teasing me."

"Nope. Don't you think it's a good name?"

Claire thought about it then nodded in agreement. "Yes, it definitely fits. And it is a simple name. My horse's name is Run for Glory."

"That's one hell of a name. What do you call her . . . Run?"

"No." Claire smiled. "I call her Glory. Would you like to see the mating barn?"

Mating barn? Whoa! Billy's thoughts were headed down the wrong path fast. "You have a special barn for that?" Hell, back home they put horses out in the pasture and let nature take its course.

"Yes, we do." Claire pointed. "Right over there. Come on, I'll show you."

He followed her to the next building where several men were standing around and looking into a rather large stall.

"Come on, Black Boy, get up there," the man in the stall was saying as he held a lead rope, hoping to get the stallion to mount the mare.

Billy watched for a few minutes before saying to Claire, "Let's go back to the stable."

Once they were outside, Claire asked. "Is something wrong?"

He stopped and looked at her as if weighing his answer. "Where I come from, you don't have to encourage animals to mate. It comes naturally."

She looked at him with those pretty blue eyes, and Billy thought, *Speaking of mating* . . . Damn, he was doing it again.

Finally she said, "We breed horses. People from all over bring their mares out here to breed with our stallions, and they want to see that they are getting their money's worth. So it's something that happens all the time. We can't leave such things up to nature. There's far too much at stake."

Billy stared at Claire. She talked about breeding so matter-of-factly. Where most women would be blushing, she looked as if it was an everyday conversation. He sensed a passion in her. And she was much too tempting. Her color was high, which made her just that much more attractive when she met his gaze.

"I'm going riding," she finally said. "Would you care to join me? You can take one of our horses since you rode yours in and she probably needs to rest."

"Sure. Why not?"

Once they were in the stable, Claire spoke to a short gentleman who nodded his capped head and then left.

"Who was that?"

"Harvey. He's our stableman."

The stableman and the young kid, Willie, who Billy had seen earlier, brought out two of the most magnificent horses Billy had ever seen. They were a chestnut color with black manes and tails. Their coats glistened.

Harvey began to saddle the horses.

"I can do that," Billy said, feeling useless and in the way. He wasn't used to having people do for him when he was perfectly capable of doing for himself.

"Yes, sir," the man said while he continued his task.

Billy whispered to Claire, "Don't you people do anything for yourselves?"

Claire smiled and whispered back, "It's his job."

"Whoa. What's this thing?" Billy pointed at the rinky-dink saddle the man was putting on the horse.

"It's an English saddle," Claire supplied.

"I can't ride on something so dinky. I'll use my own saddle, if you don't mind." Billy grabbed his Hamley saddle off a sawhorse and tossed it to Harvey. "Now *there's* a saddle," he said to Harvey.

"I agree, sir."

"I sure do like your horse, Mister," Willie said. "She's real pretty."

"Your name is Willie?" Billy asked.

The child nodded his head, his green eyes dancing.

"I tell you what, Willie. If you'd like, and your folks don't mind, I'll let you ride him before I leave."

"Really, mister?"

"Sure thing. And the name is Billy."

"Just tell me when."

"You need to ask your folks first."

He looked down at his feet and sighed. "Don't have any."

"Willie, don't you have some chores to do?" Harvey called sharply.

The child took off, running. "Don't forget," he called over his shoulder.

Billy felt a strange connection with the child as he watched him run down the walkway and disappear into a stall.

Soon he and Claire were cantering over green rolling hills, the likes of which Billy had never seen. This is paradise, Billy thought.

The horse Billy rode was magnificent, overflowing with energy and spirit. His black silky mane bounced along his neck. How Billy would love to own a horse like this one.

He glanced at Claire and admired how well she

rode. Who would have thought such a frail thing could handle a horse so well, especially from that lop-sided sidesaddle she used. Maybe there was more to the little lady than he'd thought.

Watching her, he gave a nod of approval. "I'm impressed. You don't look big enough to handle such a large horse."

Claire gave him a sassy smile. "Looks can be deceiving. It's not so much strength as it is control."

"You're right. You know your horses." And then he thought about the question that had bothered him since they left the stable. "Who does the kid belong to?"

"Willie?"

Billy nodded.

"He doesn't belong to anyone. Willie is an orphan. One of the many orphans who roam the streets of New York. I found him sitting on the steps of my office building one afternoon."

"Your office building. You own an office?"

"No. No. I write articles for *Harper's Weekly*. It was their office building where I found him."

"I see."

"Anyway, I was leaving work and there was Willie, sitting on the steps, all bent over, his head resting on his knees. I touched his forehead, and he was burning up with fever. Like you, I asked him where his parents were, and he said he didn't have any," she said.

They reached a split-wood fence, Claire didn't hesitate. She nudged her horse and they sailed over the fence.

Billy was amazed, but he couldn't let her outdo him, even if he'd never jumped before. He leaned down and whispered in the horse's ear, "It's up to you, boy." Billy kicked the horse with his heels.

They dashed toward the fence, clearing it with ease. Damn good horse, he thought as they galloped at full speed to catch up with Claire.

"I just couldn't leave him," she continued with her story when Billy had caught up with her.

"Most folks would."

"Well, I'm not most folks. I don't turn my back on people, so I brought Willie home and nursed him back to health. We gave him a job in the stables so he'd at least have a roof over his head."

Billy nodded. He understood exactly where the boy stood. He'd been dependent on the kindness of strangers when he was a child. And Billy hadn't been nearly as lucky as Willie. He'd make sure he took the boy riding before he left.

"I'll race you to the top of the hill," Claire challenged. She didn't bother to wait for Billy's answer as she and Glory took off.

The wind whipped at Claire's hair, loosening half the pins, but she didn't care. It felt good to feel the breeze all around her. She'd been cooped up in the house much too long, she thought while heading for the elm tree that stood on a small rise.

She glanced back at Billy, who seemed to be gaining ground, but she knew with her lead that he'd never catch her. Run for Glory was one of the fastest horses in the stable. She reached the hill first. "I won," she proudly proclaimed, her cheeks burning with excitement as Billy came in second.

"You cheated."

Claire laughed. "Well, perhaps a little. Let's give the horses a chance to rest before we start back. We can enjoy some of this lovely weather. We've had a long cold winter, so I've missed the chance to get out and breathe in the fresh air."

Billy dismounted and tied his horse to a small tree.

"I'll need some help getting down," she said.

Billy turned and lifted his hands to her. "Ready?"

Claire nodded.

He slipped his hands around her waist and lifted her off the small saddle as though she weighed nothing, Claire thought. She grabbed his shoulders, feeling the hard muscles beneath his cotton shirt and wondering at their strength.

Billy set her on her feet and, just for a brief second, she was very much aware of every inch of Billy's body. She forgot that she'd just met him and that she was much too close.

"Th-thank you," she stammered, stepping away from him. For a moment she felt his power. It made her feel giddy. Billy was much too attractive. The line of his jaw was almost startling, and there seemed to be a tic in his cheek. She wanted to reach up and touch his face, but knew it would be forward to do so.

"Let me tie my horse." She needed a moment to collect herself.

"These are some fine horses. You should be proud," Billy said.

"I am." Claire smiled. "Let me show you something." Taking his hand, she pulled him to the very top of the rise. She shouldn't be holding his hand, but she didn't want to be rude, so she kept it clasped. "Look as far as you can see in all directions."

She watched him, noting his strong profile as he carefully surveyed the countryside.

"It's beautiful," Billy said approvingly. "Lush green pastures and plenty of trees."

"And it's all mine," Claire said with a smile.

"Why do you want to leave when you have all this?" Billy swept his hand to encompass the wide vista before them.

"I have many reasons," Claire admitted but, of course, she couldn't tell him any of them. It probably would be best not to answer any of his questions directly. "Would you believe that I've never been anywhere? Except an occasional trip to New York, but that doesn't count because it's right here."

"That is hard to believe," Billy agreed. "I was just the opposite. There was a time when I never thought I'd quit traveling." He studied Claire's face before he asked, "Are you sure you want to go and leave all this? It will not be easy."

"Wouldn't you want to go?"

She had a good point, Billy thought. Would he want to stay on all this beautiful land and never get to see any of the country? He'd probably stay, since he'd traveled so much, but if he were like Claire, he could see what she meant. "Since you've put it that way, I guess I'd want to go, but you see, my traveling was a little different from yours."

"Let's sit under the big shade tree and you can tell me about it." She pointed to a nearby tree. "How was it different?"

They sat down and leaned against the thick tree trunk. "I had to travel," Billy said, shrugging. "I never had a home to leave."

"I don't understand," Claire said, and Billy noticed the softness in her eyes. "Everybody has someplace they come from."

"I was an orphan, pretty much like Willie," Billy said, picking up a blade of grass.

She sat up and looked at him. "That's awful. And very sad."

"It would be hard for someone like you to understand."

Claire shifted and looked at him. "I resent that remark. I can imagine what it would be like."

"The key word there is *imagine*. Here you sit in the middle of paradise with the finest horseflesh money can buy, with your fine clothes and a staff that does everything for you, and you're going to tell me you know what it's like to have absolutely no one? And you're going to tell me, you know what it's like to be so hungry that there is a constant gnawing pain in your stomach?" He wrapped the blade of grass around his finger.

Claire opened her mouth but no words came forth. Billy was right. She couldn't possibly know, but neither was she the uncaring creature Billy seemed to think. Before she could come up with the words to defend herself, Billy jumped to his feet.

"Jesus Christ!" Billy swore and drew his gun from the holster strapped down to his leg, so fast that Claire didn't have time to scream.

He was going to shoot her!

Chapter Five

Everything happened so fast Claire didn't have time to scream.

She started to jump out of the way, but before she could, Billy reached down and jerked her up toward him. Then he fired his gun.

Scared to death, she wrapped her arms around his neck and clung to him.

But why was she hanging on to the person with the gun?

It took a moment before Claire realized that the gun had gone off, and she hadn't been hit. If he wasn't shooting at her . . . then what?

Slowly, she leaned back. Was Billy trying to frighten her? If so, he'd done a good job.

"You can let go anytime, sweetheart. You're safe," Billy said with a half grin.

Claire frowned. Evidently, he thought the whole thing was funny. Well, she didn't. Her heart was still pounding like a drum. "I thought you were going to shoot me," she snapped, then realized that his arm was still around her waist, and she was pressed intimately to him.

"I'll probably want to shoot you several times before the trip is over," he said slowly. Then he took her face gently and turned her head around. "Look behind you."

A rather large snake—or what was left of it—lay on the ground right where she'd been sitting. Apparently, the thing had been behind her, and she hadn't seen it.

Billy had just saved her life!

"Thank you," she reached up and placed a soft kiss on his cheek.

Finally, he let her go and lazily drawled, "And that's why I wear a gun."

"And I'm so glad that you do." The snake twitched and Claire gasped. A tingle started in the back of her throat, and she began to cough and cough. She tried to stop, but she couldn't. This time the coughs were deep and close together; she could feel the air supply leaving her lungs. Gasping, she fumbled for the bottle in her pocket, but before she could successfully reach it, she fell over in a dead faint.

Billy jumped and managed to grab her as she keeled over. Damn, he hadn't meant to cause all this. Now what was he going to do? The gunfire had scared the horses and they had managed to break the branches they'd been tethered to. Now, they were nowhere to be seen. He should have brought his own damned horse instead of these skittish creatures.

He checked Claire's pulse and breathed a sigh of relief when it felt strong. Billy lifted her up into his arms.

Now what?

He sure as hell couldn't carry her back to the barn, so he propped her up against the tree. Then he disposed of the snake.

Billy sat down beside Claire and tried to figure out what he was going to do. He couldn't just sit here and stare at her, lying there with her chin resting on her chest, so he pulled her into his arms and patted her face. "Are you all right?"

She didn't respond.

Billy blew out a disgusted sigh. He knew how to take care of cuts and wounds, but swooning females were beyond him. If she fainted often, this journey could prove to be very long. He remembered her terrible cough and wondered if that could be the cause for her fainting.

He patted her cheeks again. Still no response. Summoning patience, he leaned back and waited.

Looking down at the woman he held, Billy noticed what a fascinating creature she was. She had long sooty black lashes and her cheeks were creamy and soft. He raised his hand to her cheek and brushed a stray strand of black hair off her face. It felt silky slipping through his fingers.

She seemed to have everything in the world, yet he sensed Claire wasn't completely happy, and he wondered why. He had a feeling she probably wouldn't tell him if he asked, so he wouldn't bother just now. But it didn't keep him from wondering what deep, dark secrets she was hiding from him.

Her beauty was one of those things she tried to hide with her pale skin and hair twisted up into a spinsterish knot. He much preferred her hair down as it was now, hanging softly around her shoulders. As she slept, the worry lines had disappeared from her forehead. He liked that.

Claire was much too young to worry about anything. Hell, she had her whole life before her. All right, Billy thought. He'd admit that he was attracted to this woman. Running a finger down the side of her face, he noted her flushed cheeks, and reached down and unbuttoned the first two buttons of her blouse to give her a little more air.

This was a first, Billy thought. Stopping after only two buttons.

He glanced out at the rolling hills. What would he have been like if he'd grown up in Claire's family? Would he be a better person? Would he be happier to have what he now worked his ass off for?

He sighed. That would be something he'd never know. One thing for sure, if he'd had that life he would dress differently and be wealthy beyond his imagination. *But,* if given the choice to switch lives, Billy figured he'd stick with the life he had.

True it wasn't much fun at times when he was growing up. Some of it had been downright awful, but he realized that all the orphans had become stronger having survived their personal ordeals. When you started at the bottom the only way to go was up. Rattlesnake had always given Billy his words of wisdom, "Son, it ain't worth having if you don't have to work for it."

Claire moaned, and Billy looked back down at her, seeing the dark circles under her eyes that shouldn't be there. "Are you all right?"

She batted her eyelids a couple of times before they finally snapped open. Her eyes held confusion in their depths.

Claire tried to focus as she found herself gazing up into warm brown eyes that looked very concerned for her. She felt as though she'd been transported on a soft and wispy cloud. Then she remembered what had happened.

Billy simply took her breath away. Everything about him was electric and untamed. She found herself extremely conscious of his virile appeal when he was so close to her. Her body ached for his touch, but Claire quickly realized that such an attraction would be perilous. She felt embarrassed that she'd fainted. He probably believed she was a weak female. Before she could say anything in her own defense, she heard horses somewhere in the background, and somebody shouting her name. She mustn't be caught in Billy's arms.

"I—I'm so sorry, will you help me sit up?" she said softly.

Once she was in an upright position with her back to the tree and not sprawled all over Billy, she could see Heath approaching with their horses behind him. "How did our horses get away?" she asked Billy.

"Evidently, they don't like gunfire," Billy said and then nodded toward the rider, "Who's that?"

Slowly, Claire got to her feet. "My oldest brother, Heath."

"What happened?" Heath demanded, his tone sharp as he dismounted. He didn't bother to tie the horses; instead he held the reins. "Your horses came back to the stables. Were you thrown?" And then Heath focused on Billy. "Who is this?" But Heath didn't give his sister a chance to say anything. "If one of the hired hands has taken advantage of you—" Heath was so angry he choked on his words.

Billy looked Heath over from head to toe. This hot-headed city slicker needed to be brought down a notch or two. He gave the man a daring look, hoping he'd take the bait and then Billy could beat the shit out of him. Maybe a good fist-fight would get rid of some of this pent up energy. When that didn't work, Billy said, "Why don't you ask me who I am? Since I'm standing right in front of you."

"Why you—" Heath gritted out and took a step toward Billy.

Billy grinned. *Come on, I'm more than ready.*

But the first punch never came because Claire jumped between them.

Heath's eyes narrowed. "What's going on here? I want an answer. Now!"

"Nothing is going on," Claire snapped.

"Don't tell me that." Heath cut her off with a wave of his hand. "Look at you. I ride up and find you in this stranger's arms with your hair down, and your clothes half off."

"They are not!" Claire's hand flew to her throat, and she felt the open buttons, which surprised her. "Oh," she squeaked. Then she glanced at Billy.

Heath glared at Billy. "I've got a good mind to punch you in the mouth."

"I wouldn't if I were you," Billy drawled, not scared in the least, as he added, "If you think you can, do it."

"Who the hell are you?" Heath tried to take a step toward him, but Claire shoved him in the chest as Billy's hand hovered above his gun, poised and ready.

"You bull-headed moose!" Claire yelled. "If you'll shut up for a few minutes, I'll explain what happened."

"I'm listening," Heath said, easing his stance only slightly.

"This is Billy West. The man Uncle Ben sent to escort me West. Didn't Mother tell you?"

"I've not been by the house," Heath answered curtly, "but if you think that we're going to let you go across the country with the likes of him, then you had better think again."

"So, why didn't you volunteer to take your sister?" Billy shot back.

"I've had enough," Claire said flatly as she put her hands on each man's chest and shoved them apart. "Both of you be quiet." She looked at her older brother. "My blouse is unbuttoned because I got choked and fainted, so Billy loosened the buttons. And the reason I choked was because Billy saved my life from a snake that was coiled and ready to strike. I didn't see it." She watched as her brother's face reddened. "I am going out West and there isn't much that any of you can do about it. Billy is right. You could have gone with me, but not knowing the country you probably wouldn't be much protection." She planted her fists firmly on her hips. "Now, I expect you to apologize to Mr. West right this minute."

Heath frowned. Billy could see that Claire's reprimand didn't sit well with Heath, but this time he had little choice but to eat crow. Billy liked that. He tried to suppress a triumphant grin.

"It seems I jumped to the wrong conclusion, Mr. West. I apologize," Heath said. "We have always been protective of Claire."

"I can see that," Billy said with a nod. He looked at Claire. "Tell me. Am I going to run into any more like him?"

Claire laughed. "I'm afraid I have two more brothers. However they are not as hot-headed as Heath."

"I resent that," Heath said as he handed the reins to Billy.

Sometimes the truth hurts, Billy thought but decided he'd had enough excitement for today. He was damned tired from traveling, and Claire appeared tired, as well.

As they rode back to the stable, Billy asked. "Tell me, Claire, do you have these fainting spells often?"

"No," she quickly replied. "You can rest easy. I guess, with the excitement of the snake and then the cough, it surprised me. I feel perfectly all right to travel," Claire assured him.

Heath glanced at her, and she gave him the keep-your-mouth shut look. She would be fine on this trip. She was sure of it.

After Billy had returned to the house, Claire went to find Heath who was in the tack room with Albert.

Heath glanced up at her when she walked through the door. "You should probably go to the house and rest."

"Do please be quiet," Claire stormed, immediately liking the shocked look on Heath's face. She'd been babied until she was sick of it.

"What's got her in a twist?" Albert asked.

"I'll tell you," Claire volunteered. "Your brother was rude and very unpleasant to Billy West."

"He's your brother, too," Albert pointed out.

"Not if he keeps acting like a jackass."

Albert chuckled, gaining a glare from Heath.

"I was not out of line," Heath told her. "I was

worried sick that you'd broken that pretty little neck of yours when your horse returned without you."

"I was just fine."

"I could see how fine you were lying in that man's arms."

"What man?" Albert asked.

Claire glanced at Albert. "He is my escort. You'll meet him tonight at dinner."

Albert cocked a brow at her. "He just arrived today and you are already in his arms?"

"See." She raised her arms in exasperation and let them fall to her side. "You are just as bad as Heath, jumping to false conclusions."

"Were you not in his arms?" Heath asked.

"Yes."

Albert started toward the door. "Where is the son-of-a-bitch?"

Claire reached out and grabbed his arm. "Wait a minute." Then she told Albert about the snake and her fainting.

"I think you're being a little hard on Heath," Albert finally said. "I'd probably have done the same thing. Now, why don't you two kiss and make up?"

"I guess he's right, puss," Heath said pulling her to him and squeezing her in a great hug.

"I want both of you to promise me that neither of you will tell Billy about my condition."

"He's bound to notice," Heath pointed out.

Claire shook her head. "Uncle Ben told Billy that I had been sick. He didn't tell him that I still was, and I don't want him to know. I want to be treated as normally as possible."

"I think he should know," Heath protested.

Why her brother had to be so set in his ways, Claire didn't know. "Please."

"All right," her brothers agreed reluctantly. "We'll keep your secret."

Claire started to walk off. "And do try to be nice to Billy."

Heath frowned. "That's asking a lot."

"Well, I'm looking forward to meeting him," Albert said. "Anyone who can get under Heath's skin so quickly must be one hell of a fellow."

Billy had been told that Fredrick had gone to his parents' home and would be back in two days. So Billy decided that they would leave on Thursday. The sooner they were out of here, the better. If the other two brothers were anything like Heath, Billy wanted to spend as little time as possible in this household.

Once he was downstairs, the maid showed him to the dining room. Billy saw that everyone had already been seated at a large oblong table. There were three candelabrums: one on each end of the table and another in the middle. Two maids, dressed in black with little white aprons, stood on one side of the room.

"Come, sit beside me," Claire said, gesturing toward the empty seat.

Billy nodded and made his way over to her. "Evening, folks." Why did he feel like he was walking into a courtroom and he was the defendant?

Immediately, a servant appeared and pulled the chair back as he approached. Didn't these damned people do anything for themselves? He wasn't sure he could ever get used to having a handful of strangers living in his house. Evidently this was the way rich people lived, and hadn't he always wanted to be rich?

"Gail, you may serve," Margaret instructed the maid, placing her napkin in her lap.

Upon that instruction, two maids came through a swinging door with bowls of soup on trays and served everyone. As soon as Mrs. Holladay reached for her spoon, everyone else followed her lead.

Billy tried his soup and found that the odd-looking brown stuff tasted like onions. It was very good. At least they ate well in these parts, he thought.

"It's a pleasure to have you in our home, Mr. West," Margaret said. "Let me introduce you to my family." She gestured toward the end of the table. "My husband, Donald."

Mr. Holliday nodded, then said, "My brother speaks highly of you, Mr. West. We appreciate you taking our Claire out to visit her uncle."

Evidently, Donald Holladay didn't know that Billy was being paid handsomely to do a job, so he'd just keep that information to himself. Donald went on talking, and Billy realized that Claire's three brothers were staring holes through him.

"And we have complete trust in you," Donald Holladay finished.

Billy almost choked on his water. *You might, but your sons look like they could string me up to the nearest tree.* Finally, Billy nodded at Mr. Holladay.

"My sons," Margaret said. "Heath, Albert, and Robert."

"Mr. West," they all said on command.

At least they were better mannered than the family he came from, where nobody did anything together unless they had to.

"Do you work for our uncle, Mr. West?" Albert asked.

"Please call me Billy. I'm not used to formality. And yes, I do work for your uncle. I ride shotgun on the stage."

"Sounds exciting," Robert said. "I'd like to do something like that."

"Forget it, young man," Mr. Holladay said. "We have a horse farm and a shipyard to run."

Robert frowned. "I know, Father. But Claire is getting to go. I thought . . . just maybe."

As the Yankee pot roast was being served, Billy said, "It does sound exciting, Robert, but when you're being shot at you might have a different opinion."

Robert's eyes widened. "They actually shoot at you?"

"There is a reason they call it the Wild West." Billy chuckled as he cut into the juicy roast meat. "It isn't anything like what I've seen, so far, in the East. Out there, they would sooner shoot you as look at you."

"And this is where you want to go, Claire?" Albert asked.

"The very place. I intend to write articles on the stage and my travels for the magazine," Claire said as she picked up her goblet of water.

Billy glanced at her. "You work for a magazine?"

"Yes." She nodded. "For *Harper's.*"

"I've seen copies of *Harper's Weekly* once or twice," Billy commented.

"You can read?" Heath asked.

Billy knew Heath had been quiet for too long. Too bad, Heath had finally found his voice. Slowly, Billy placed his fork down beside his plate. He could tell that he and Heath were like two bulls in a pen and there just wasn't room for both, even if Billy was the visiting bull. Trying very hard not to lose his temper, he took a deep breath before answering, "And write, as well."

"Heath!" Margaret's voice held a sharp reprimand.

"It was just a simple question, Mother. I've read that most people out West can't read."

Billy wondered for a moment if this was how Thunder had felt when people called him a half-breed. "Heath does have a point, Mrs. Holladay. I was just lucky to have had a good teacher who was determined I would be educated."

"Well put," Donald Holladay said, "My brother said you were sharp. I see he wasn't wrong. Ben also said you were thinking about buying into a stage route and starting your own horse farm."

"That's correct."

A maid entered the dining room with dessert. She placed a huge piece of yellow cake with chocolate icing down in front of Billy. His mouth watered.

"Tell cook she outdid herself on this cake," Albert said. He wiped his mouth and looked at his sister. "I saw David today. He said to tell you hello."

"That was nice of him," Claire said, but Billy heard an icy tone in her voice.

"I still can't believe that you broke off your engagement. You two have been promised forever," Robert added.

"He broke it off with me," Claire corrected her brother, although she'd never told them it was because she was sick. She knew it would make them furious. She glanced at Billy. "They are talking about my ex-fiancé."

Must have been a damned fool, Billy thought.

So far, he liked Claire and that, in itself, was un-usual. Of course, this was the first day, and he was sure in a day or two she'd become just as boring as the other females he'd encountered. But she had a fiancé? Interesting. Did she still love him? Billy frowned. And why should he care? A stab of jeal-ousy stirred inside him. The knowledge that the woman beside him could stir such emotions didn't sit well with him at all. As a matter of fact, it irri-tated the hell out of him. It was as if he had been turned upside down since setting foot in this house, and he had only been here a day. He'd be plumb loco by week's end.

He was used to calling all the shots. Therefore, his next words were sharper than he meant. "We leave Thursday. I assume that you're already packed."

"I'm afraid that will not be possible," Margaret spoke firmly, drawing Billy's attention to the other end of the table. "We are giving Claire a going away party. We don't know how long she'll be out West, or if we'll ever see her again."

Billy thought he heard a catch in Mrs. Holladay's voice before she continued.

"So we want to give her a large party, to which you are invited, of course. I'm sure it isn't neces-sary that you leave on Thursday, since I had a wire, just yesterday, from Ben who said that you could take all the time you need. He also wanted to wish Claire well with her party."

Damn. Billy felt his jaw clench, knowing there was no way out of the situation. Worse, he had to attend a party. Finally, he nodded. "Then we will leave Saturday morning. We should get the tickets for the train."

"Good." Margaret smiled. "I'll take care of the tickets. Claire has to go into the city tomorrow. You can accompany her and be fitted for your formal wear. The tailor has already been notified, so there will be no problems. I'm sure you want to look your best when we introduce you to all our friends."

Billy leaned back in his chair and shrugged. He could not care less what their friends thought of him. But attempting to be cordial, he didn't say his thoughts. He wasn't used to this. He felt as though they were squeezing the air from his lungs. And there wasn't a damn thing he could do about it. But it was only for three days, he quickly reminded himself . . . he could survive anything for three days . . . he hoped.

"I bet you've never been around big ships and harbors," Claire said softly.

Surprisingly, the sound of her voice took the fire out of him. "No, I haven't."

"Good. We can go by the docks tomorrow."

Billy got to his feet and stood, then said to Claire, "Until tomorrow." Then he turned and addressed Mrs. Holladay. "Supper was wonderful, thank you. I'm going to call it a day."

Claire watched Billy leave the room. He stood tall and carried himself in a way that simply took her breath away. If only things were different . . . Billy West wouldn't stand a chance.

Chapter Six

The next morning, Billy found he was looking forward to seeing New York City as he left his room and started down the hallway of the sprawling house the Holladays called Oak Hill. He'd heard many tales about how high the buildings were in New York and how crowded the city was. After living in the wide-open plains dotted with the occasional small towns, he thought Denver was a large town. He couldn't imagine larger. However, if this house was any indication of how they built things in the East, nothing should surprise him.

When he reached the bottom of the staircase, Mrs. Holladay was passing through the foyer. She turned and called to him, "Good morning, Mr. West. Excuse me, I mean Billy. You're looking much better this morning."

"Are you trying to tell me that I looked pretty rough yesterday?"

"No—no, not at all," she rushed to assure him.

"I was just teasing you, ma'am," Billy said with a smile. "Have you seen Claire this morning?"

"Certainly. She is waiting outside on the veranda. She wanted to enjoy the fresh air this morning. I do believe that you'll have a lovely day for a trip into the city."

"I hope so, ma'am," Billy said and started out the front door, but not before the butler opened it for him. "Thanks." It still bothered him that he couldn't just open the door himself.

The first thing Billy noticed when he stepped outside was that it was a bright sunny day, and he smelled something sweet in the air, possibly honeysuckle. He looked around and found Claire on the far end of the veranda, her face turned away from him. Her head was bent and the morning sun bathed her with soft light. For a moment, she didn't look real. She looked more like an angel.

A chill ran up Billy's arms. It kind of scared him, and he hadn't been scared in a long time. He felt as though he was looking at a very special person who puzzled him more than he cared to admit.

Claire seemed engrossed in something in her lap and had yet to see him, so it gave him a good chance to observe her.

The first thing he noticed was that her long black hair was down and pulled up on the side and fastened with combs. She wore a rose-colored gown that complemented her skin. A delicate white shawl was pulled around her shoulders and had slipped slightly down on her right side.

Perfection, he thought.

As he drew closer, he could see a brown journal in her lap. She was jotting down notes in the book. He wondered if she had bothered to write anything about him.

Claire finally must have heard him because her

head came up and she looked his way. She gave him a dazzling smile.

"Good morning, Mr. West. I hope you slept well," she said in that soft voice that made Billy's stomach turn to mush. A voice that he was growing accustomed to much too quickly.

Billy leaned against the porch rail in front of her. "As a matter of fact, I did. I didn't sleep well on the train."

Claire shut her book and looked up at him. "I've never been on a train. This will be my first trip."

My first everything, she thought.

"I would imagine that you might be tired after your journey," she said as she stood. "But today will be fun. I want to show you around New York. After we go by the tailors, that is."

Billy's pleasant expression turned grim as he shoved away from the railing. "Great."

"I can see that you're not happy with that idea," Claire said as she moved past him. "But I assure you it's better than getting shot at all the time."

"I wouldn't count on that," Billy mumbled.

When Claire reached the steps, she looked back at Billy, who was still frowning, and noticed he was wearing his gun. She would have to persuade him to remove it . . . later, she thought. "Are you coming?"

"Do I have a choice?" he grumbled, but Claire was glad to see that at least Billy was moving toward her. And he did look very handsome this morning. He wore denim trousers and a chambray blue shirt that made his brown hair and eyes appear very dark and dangerous in his tanned face.

"Not today. Today, you are mine to do with as I

please." She grinned at the shocked look on Billy's face. His eyes spoke to her with a warmly intimate look and she quickly glanced away.

Together, they started down the steps. Then Claire added, "I'll have to take your advice once we leave here, so today, you can humor me and let me show you New York. However, leave your gun in the carriage. Nobody wears guns in the city, and you do want to fit in."

The carriage was waiting for them at the bottom of the steps, and the driver held the door open, making Billy feel like everyone in New York thought he was incapable of doing anything for himself. "Who says I want to fit in?" he muttered, taking the seat across from Claire.

"You are ornery this morning, Mr. West." Claire looked up and gave him a sly smile. "But I do believe that I can handle you."

"You think so?" Billy flashed her a devilish smile. "We'll see about that." He leaned back and folded his arms across his chest in a defiant and confident gesture.

Claire didn't say another word, much to Billy's pleasure, and the lovely blush that stained her cheeks gave him a great deal of satisfaction.

The carriage ride was pleasant and the open carriage gave him a good view of the countryside. Of course, the view inside wasn't too bad either. He smiled as Claire pointed out different things of interest along the way.

Damn it! Billy thought. *He liked Claire's company way too much.*

A little later without warning, the carriage stopped. Billy reached for his gun and was almost out the door, but a giggle from Claire stopped him.

He twisted around to look at her.

"You can relax, Mr. West. We're not being robbed." Claire laughed again. "We have to get out and board the ferry." She noted his set face, his clamped mouth and fixed eyes.

"You're not going to think it's so funny when we're out West," Billy said tersely. "And the name is Billy."

"But we're not out West," Claire reminded him as she started out the carriage door "Don't forget to leave your gun under the seat. I'll protect you."

Glowering, Billy followed Claire out of the carriage.

He turned and gave her a long look, brows raised. Were they having their first standoff, she wondered?

Slowly, Billy untied the holster strap from his leg, then he unbuckled his gun belt. Carefully, he folded the leather straps and slipped the gunbelt under the seat. "I don't like this." He felt naked without his gun, although he didn't bother to tell her.

"I know," she said and grabbed his hand, tugging. Then she gave him a slight smile. "Thank you. Now let's go and wait for the steamboat." She stopped and pointed. "Look, she's coming now."

Billy glanced out over the East River. It was much larger than anything he'd ever seen, and he couldn't help being glad he'd never had to cross something like this while they were on the wagon train. The Missouri was bad enough.

"Why are you smiling?" Claire asked.

"Just remembering a time we had to cross the Missouri River when we were on the wagon train.

And believe me, we didn't have a boat like that."
Billy inclined his head toward the steamboat chugging toward them.

"What did you have?"

"Something like a raft. It was called a scow, which was basically a flat barge with no sides. We rolled the wagon up on the scow and it was guided across the river by ropes."

"I can't even imagine," Claire said with a shake of her head. "It would take a very large rope and raft."

"It was a long rope," Billy confirmed. "Crossing the Missouri and trying to keep the wagon from plunging into the river wasn't any small feat. When we crossed the river one of my sisters fell in and darn near drowned."

"How awful." Claire wondered what it had been like for Billy without a father and a mother. She knew he must have felt lost more than once, yet he had been brave enough to travel out to Denver.

"Sure was, but Mary survived."

"How many brothers and sisters do you have?"

"Too many," Billy shot back with a smile.

Claire nodded. "I know the feeling."

"I have four sisters, Brandy, Mary, Ellen, and Amy, who doesn't live with us anymore. She was adopted by a nice family we met on the wagon train," Billy explained. "And I have one brother, who will talk your ears off. Scott is the youngest."

"They sound fantastic. I hope I get to meet them one day," Claire said.

Billy looked at her in the oddest way as he softly said, "I do, too."

The steamboat whistle blew, drawing Billy's attention back to the scene at hand. Smoke belched from the large smokestack as the steamboat pulled up next to the dock. The *Sylvan Glen* was a wide-bodied boat painted a gleaming white with its name blazed in red on the side.

The gangplank lowered and horses and wagons started filing off, led by their masters, and then the passengers that had been on the upper deck began to disembark.

When it was time for them to board, Billy held Claire's elbow as she stepped up on the gang-plank. It was amazing how small and delicate she was. The woman needed to put some meat on her bones.

"Thank you," she said as they trudged up the stairs. She turned and waited for Billy to join her. "John Roebling will be at my party. Do you know that he is going to build a suspension bridge over the East River?"

"Impossible," Billy said, following her to the front of the boat.

"He is supposed to bring his drawings to show Father and a few other men. Perhaps, you can see the drawings for the bridge at that time."

"It's hard to believe a bridge could ever be that long."

"Oh, it isn't the first bridge that Mr. Roebling has built. He calls them suspension bridges. They have cables that make them strong." Claire motioned toward a chair. "Let's sit here so we can see the city as the boat approaches."

Billy sat in one of the big, wooden chairs next to Claire. She reminded him of a very delicate flower, something he needed to protect. He wasn't quite sure how she was going to do out West. Would she be too fragile to survive? Would she feel as out of place as he felt here? That was another good reason not to get attached to the woman. She might not be staying long. She belonged in a fancy house with servants.

As the city loomed before him, Billy felt as if he were in a completely different world. The buildings were much taller than out West, and it was definitely far more modern than the familiar places he knew.

Some white birds flew overhead. "What kind of birds are they?" Billy asked.

"Seagulls. Over that way on the other side of the city is the Atlantic Ocean. It stretches as far as the eye can see. You cannot see the end of it."

"I find that hard to believe. Every body of water that I've ever seen you can always see both banks. However, I do remember reading about the Atlantic and Pacific Oceans in school," Billy said, and then he grew quiet and enjoyed the ride. A ride, for once, where he didn't have to provide the power . . . this ferry was a definite plus for crossing rivers.

As the *Sylvan Glen* approached the dock, Billy observed that the buildings of the city were all made of brick. He had to admit that they appeared much sturdier than the wooden buildings back home and there were so many of them. He remembered Thunder complaining about that very thing when he'd returned to Boston.

"Look over there." Claire nudged him.

Great Eastern was written on the ship's hull. "It is hard to believe that anything that big can float," Billy said. "How is it powered?"

"Actually, two ways, by steam and by sail. The *Great Eastern* is a fifty-eight foot paddle wheeler. See those big round things on the side?"

Billy nodded.

"That is where the paddle wheels are, and there are big boilers below that produce the steam. The ship has six masts and carries 6,500 square yards of sails, making her the largest vessel afloat."

"Are you sure?" Billy chuckled. "It seems every time you show me something, we turn around and you show me something even larger than the first thing."

"Yes, I'm sure. She is the largest."

"How do you know so much about ships?"

"My father and brothers built the *Great Eastern*. So I got to see the ship first hand. I grew up hearing them talk facts and figures. If we have time, we'll go by the shipyard, and you can see a boat under construction."

"I'd like that."

"See, the trip isn't bad so far," Claire teased. "Now let's find the carriage. I believe that we should visit the tailor first."

"This trip just got worse," Billy said with a frown.

They arrived at a small brown building wedged between two taller buildings. A sign hanging out front with a needle and thread painted on it indicated that it was Anthony Wiggle's Tailor Shop, Billy noticed as they entered the front door.

A bell tinkled, announcing to the shopkeeper that someone had entered his place of business. Very promptly, a small bald man shuffled from the back room to greet them.

"Are you Mr. Wiggle?" Claire asked.

"That I am, Miss. What can I do for you?"

"I'm Claire Holladay. I believe my mother sent a

message that we will be needing to fit Mr. West."
She motioned toward Billy.

"Yes, she did. I'll have his suit ready by tomorrow and will have a messenger deliver it to Oak
Hill." Mr. Wiggle wrinkled his nose, and then said,
"But first things first. I must measure your young
man."

Claire's cheeks heated, but she didn't bother to
correct Mr. Wiggle, and neither did Billy, she
noted.

"Come stand over here, Mr. West. I must say that
you're a large one. Maybe just a tad larger than
Heath Holladay."

Billy thought the little man could have mentioned anyone but Heath. Billy had just gotten the
sorry cuss out of his mind. But it wasn't this man's
fault. "They grow 'em big where I come from."

"Where are you from, son? You most certainly
are not from around here with that accent," Mr.
Wiggle said as he stretched out Billy's arm and
started measuring.

Claire watched in fascination. She could observe Billy without getting caught gawking at him.
She wanted to get to know the man she'd be traveling with. So far she felt comfortable with him,
and she definitely liked looking at him. His shoulders were so broad that they made his light blue
shirt stretch across his back. And she really liked
the way he wore his brown hair longer than most
of the men in the East. It just covered his collar
and was streaked with gold on the tip ends where
the sun had bleached it.

Her gaze traveled over Billy's body as she noted
everything about him. Even his stance was different from that of the men she knew. He was so sure

of himself that he stood tall, not bent over like some men who worked slumped over a desk.

This man was meant to ride a horse and be surrounded by the wide-open range and green trees: all things she wanted him to show her. Claire wondered what kind of a man Billy was. She had a feeling he had a temper. Like now when he was doing something he considered a waste of time, she could see he was tense and trying to control himself. She glanced at him in the full-length mirror, and found he was staring just as intently at her.

Their eyes locked. The warm intimate look in his eyes was vibrant, making her heart beat faster. She was very much aware of something going on inside her.

She felt dreamy, and her legs weak as she remembered him holding her in his arms yesterday afternoon. She had enjoyed their closeness, as she did now. He almost looked at her possessively, she thought. There was also a smoldering flame in Billy's eyes that startled her, but she found she couldn't look away like any decent lady should.

Last night, she'd dreamt about Billy, of being crushed within his embrace and kissed. Remembering the kiss, she licked her lips. It had made her feel alarmingly alive. She drew in a shaky breath.

"Mr. West. Mr. West," Mr. Wiggle repeated, attempting to gain Billy's attention.

"Sorry," Billy finally said. "Did you say something?"

"Several times," Mr. Wiggle replied as he draped the measuring tape around his neck. "That must have been a good daydream you were having."

Billy smiled. "It was." His gaze slid back to

Claire's in the mirror. Knowing that she felt the same attraction to him as he felt for her, they were like a pot of water getting ready to boil.

And God help them if it boiled over.

Chapter Seven

Billy and Claire didn't say much to each other as they left the tailor shop and headed for the waiting carriage.

"Take us to South Street, James," Claire told the coachman as he opened the door for her.

Once she was settled and the carriage had started moving, Claire glanced to her right at the buildings as they rolled past them, but she quickly fell into thought.

She wasn't completely sure what had happened a few minutes ago, but she felt that she and Billy had made some kind of connection and she knew that he had felt it too. However, she wouldn't pursue it now. She wanted to be light-hearted today because it was her day to show Billy around the city.

Besides, she felt wonderful, almost giddy, in the bright sunshine. She really couldn't ever remember feeling quite this way before.

For once, she felt like a normal young lady instead of the one who was sick and fussed over.

She glanced at Billy. It seemed that he found the scenery interesting as well.

She looked forward to showing Billy things he'd never seen before. She also decided that she wasn't going to let them ride in silence any longer. She'd just pretend that nothing had happened. It was evident that neither of them was willing to take the next step, but she wanted to have a good mood. "Are you hungry?" she asked, breaking the silence.

Billy turned and looked at her. "I could use some grub. How about you?"

Good. At least, he didn't sound funny. Perhaps, he'd been waiting for her to break the silence. "Grub? What a strange word. I assume it means food."

Billy nodded.

"I'm famished," Claire said. "I've instructed the driver to take us to South Street so you can see the wharf, and then we'll have lunch. How about a few clams and oysters? I'll bet you've never eaten those before."

Billy laughed. "I'm not even sure what they are. But you're the boss," he said, then gave her a slow smile. "For now."

Claire returned his smile as the coach pulled to a stop. "We're here."

In a moment, the coachman had opened the door and helped Claire out, and then held his hand up to Billy who frowned at him. The coachman quickly dropped his hand and stepped back.

"Where do you want me to wait for you, Miss Holladay?" The driver asked.

"You can wait outside Harper's Publishing. We shouldn't be more than a couple of hours," she said. "Make sure you get yourself something to eat."

Billy stepped out of the carriage, took one look around, reached back into the carriage and grabbed his holster from under the seat. This place she called the wharf appeared a little unsavory to him.

"That's really not necessary," Claire said from beside him, "But, then again, sometimes the people around the docks can be rough. We will avoid those places today."

Billy finished strapping on his gun. "Just in case we bumped into one of 'those places,' I want to be prepared. You never know when somebody is going to take a notion that he doesn't like the way my face looks."

Claire laughed. "I don't see anything wrong with your face." *You're beautiful,* she almost added. "You look perfectly acceptable to me. Just not like a New Yorker."

"As long as I pass your inspection," Billy shot back, "then I don't care what anyone else thinks."

Claire's smile brightened as she swung her arm up and gestured toward the wharf. "I can see that you're not going to let me have the last word in this matter, so let's go."

They walked along the dock where a broad-beamed, three-masted schooner was docked. "That's a big one," Billy commented. He hadn't thought much about ships in the past because the opportunity had never presented itself to see one, but he'd bet it would be enjoyable to sail.

"If you were going to stay in New York longer, we could go sailing on my father's yacht. Perhaps, someday you'll get a chance to sail. There is nothing like skimming along the water with the wind blowing your hair," Claire said, her voice sounding wistful.

"I must say that you make it sound wonderful.

Maybe, when I bring you back home, you can show me this sailing."

Claire's smile faded. She wanted to curse her fate. She'd dearly love to show Billy how to sail, but she knew that she wouldn't be around to do so. The thought that she wouldn't return from her trip West saddened her. She sighed, and then that damned tickle started in her throat, and she began to cough.

"Here, sit down," Billy took her arm and guided her to a bench in front of one of the buildings that overlooked the water. "You're not going to pass out on me again, are you?"

Claire was still coughing as she shook her head while, at the same time, fumbling in her pocket for the bottle of cough medicine. She took several sips before her coughing eased.

Billy took the bottle from her hand and examined it. "This must be some good stuff. What is it?" He removed the cork, sniffed, and jerked his nose away. "This is some strong stuff, lady. Are you sure that you're well enough to travel?"

Claire snatched the bottle back from him. "I'll not have you asking me that question every time I start coughing. I'm fine. I just have a nagging cough that will not go away. The medicine helps." She could feel the drugs taking effect, and she began to relax. It always made her a little light-headed, and before she knew it, she let her guard down. Just a little. "Do you think that I would make the trip if I were not well?"

"I don't know you well enough to say," Billy replied. "I just know that I don't need a sick fe-male on my hands once we start traveling. The journey will be hard enough."

"You must think of me as a burden," she said

with a frown before taking another sip from the medicine bottle, liking the way it made her feel. She crooked her finger and motioned for Billy to come closer. "I assure you, Mr. West, that you'll not even know that I'm around." Her lips were so close to his, she wondered what he'd taste like. If she just moved a little. . . .

"What the dickens are you doing down here at the docks?" Heath's booming voice came from behind her, causing Claire to jerk straight. Must her brother always show up at the wrong time? And, of course, he appeared peevish.

"I'm showing Billy the docks and then we're going to get something to eat," Claire said. "What are you doing down here?"

"I needed a few things from the foundry. There is also a problem in a design I need to straighten out," Heath said as he shifted a package in his arm. "You know you shouldn't be down here by yourself."

"She isn't by herself," Billy pointed out.

Heath frowned. What was it about Billy West that made him want to challenge him? Then it dawned on Heath, Billy was a lot like himself. And *that* was who he was sending his sister off with.

It was like sending a lamb out with a wolf. And Heath could see the experience in Billy's eyes which made Heath all the more uncomfortable. Well, the fellow had better not hurt his sister, Heath thought. He had a good mind to inform Billy just how fragile his sister was, but knew he couldn't. He wanted this man to know, but Heath had promised his sister he'd tell no one outside the family of her condition.

"Do you have time to join us for lunch?" Claire asked.

"I believe so, puss. Thank you for the invitation." Heath gave Billy an evil smile. He could see that Billy wasn't happy for his company in the least. "It will take about an hour to get what I need from the foundry. What do you have in mind?"

"Let's go over to the barges and have oysters and clams," Claire said. "Are you ready, Billy?" She noticed that he was frowning again.

"If you're sure that you are all right," Billy said.

"Do you think I'd let her go if she wasn't feeling fine?" Heath demanded.

Billy glared at Heath. "I don't believe I was speaking to you."

Claire let out a disgusted sigh. What was the matter with these two? "I am perfectly fine. Or, at least, I was until you two started sniping at each other. Let's go."

They walked by the brass foundry, a big grayish building with big black doors that stood open to let some of the heat escape. "And here is the fire hose and sail makers. Anything that you need for a ship can be found down here in these two rows of buildings," Claire explained.

"Interesting. But what is that smell?" Billy asked, wrinkling his nose with disgust.

"It's a combination of many things. The sea and river mix together to make brackish water. That's water that is part salt and part fresh water. The wood from the vessels and the salt from the sea all mix together to give it this special smell of the sea. It is rather a rotten smell, but refreshing in an odd sort of way. Does that make any sense?"

Billy smiled. "Kinda."

"I can't imagine never seeing the ships and the

ocean," Heath said. "There is something about it that enters your soul."

"I kind of sense that myself," Billy commented. "But then, I bet you've never seen buffalo or mountains."

"I guess you got me there," Heath admitted as he walked beside his sister, "but I do mean to visit your country someday."

As they strolled past an empty alley, three men sprang out upon them and two of them grabbed Heath from behind. "He'll do," one of the thugs said. "Get the other one."

Billy swung around and shoved Claire behind him. Two men were holding Heath as he struggled, reminding Billy of a bucking bronco. "Get your hands off him," Billy demanded.

"And what you going do about it?" the bigger man challenged as he took a step toward Billy. A bowie knife was in his right hand as the thug moved toward him.

Claire had never been in this situation before. Alarmed, she watched over Billy's shoulder. The man coming their way held a huge knife, and he looked very menacing. Her stomach churned with anxiety. Could Billy handle him?

Before she could blink, Billy had drawn and fired his gun, taking the robber's finger along with the knife.

The man howled in pain. "My finger's gone!"

"If the rest of you want to keep your body parts, I suggest that you let my friend go," Billy said, his words cold as ice.

The two men dropped their hold on Heath and backed off. Billy shot at their feet, and all three hightailed it. After the sound of the gunshot, workmen appeared in the doorway to see what all the commotion was about. "Do people usually appear out of nowhere and grab you in what is supposed to be civilization?"

Heath laughed. "That was a first for me. Guess I let my guard down. Thank you." He offered his hand to Billy. It was the least he could do.

Billy smiled, slightly as he accepted. "I had to lie about the friends part."

Heath chuckled. "Perhaps that will change some day," he said.

Still trembling, Claire placed her hand on Billy's arm. "Are you all right?" she asked in a quavering voice.

"I'm fine."

"What about me?" Heath said, frowning.

"I know you're fine. You never get hurt. But I must say, I'm a little shocked. I've been down here many times, and I've never been attacked."

"You didn't have what they wanted, sister dear," Heath replied curtly.

"What were they going to do? Rob us?" Billy asked.

"No. Sometimes unscrupulous captains need people for crews on their ships, so they send out some of their men to knock them out and grab them up off the docks. When their victims wake up, they are at sea, and it's too late for them to do anything." Heath slapped Billy on the back and grinned. "That would be one way for you to learn about the sea really fast!"

"No thanks. I like to learn things on my own terms."

Claire touched both men's elbows. "I don't like it out here. Let's keep moving and get something to eat."

"You're probably right, puss." Heath crooked his elbow toward Claire. "Shall we?"

"Amen to that," Billy said, offering his elbow as well.

They made their way to a small café that overlooked the water and was situated next to a barge with huge fishing nets draping from beams.

They were shown to a table in front of a big window that offered a view of the bustling waterfront. Claire took the seat pulled out by the waiter and spread her napkin in her lap. "Let me order for you," she said to Billy, and he nodded in agreement.

After the waiter left, Billy glanced out the window and saw a man sitting on a long pole thing that extended out from the ship. "What is he doing?"

Heath glanced out the window. "It's a sailor securing flying and outer jibs."

"He's securing the sail," Claire simplified.

"It's a wonder he doesn't fall off that thing and break his neck," Billy said.

"You should see them when they are out at sea," Claire said. "They have to climb the riggings like monkeys."

Heath leaned back in his chair. "I can take you out sailing if you'd stay another week."

"Thanks for the offer, but we need to be getting back to Denver. I'm already staying longer than I planned," Billy said.

The waiter walked toward them carrying a bucket of clams and oysters. Billy gave Claire the most befuddled look, causing her to giggle. She picked up on oyster. "Here. You take an oyster, insert your knife like this, and open the shell. Then you take your fork and eat the oyster." She demonstrated, then offered one to Billy. "Here, you try."

Billy didn't look very enthusiastic as he followed her instructions and placed the oyster in his mouth and chewed.

"What do you think?" Claire asked.

"Mmm," Billy said as he rolled his eyes toward the ceiling then back to her. "I like it." He shook his fork at the empty shell. "Don't believe that I ever had anything that tasted like this."

Heath reached for a clam. "Would you like a beer?"

"Nope. Gave up drinking a few years back. I'll stick with water," Billy said as he reached for several more oysters and concentrated on the task of opening each one. Then he took his time and enjoyed the seafood.

As they ate, Billy told them a little about Denver and then decided to ask the question that had been puzzling him since he met the brothers. "Why is it that none of you has married?"

Heath laughed, then wiped his mouth with the napkin. "Couldn't find anybody to have me."

"I don't doubt that," Billy joked. "But seriously, it seems strange that none of the Holladay children ever married."

"Well, Albert was married, but his wife died," Heath said. "However, the rest of us ..." He shrugged. "Don't know. Guess we just got wrapped up in business and never found the right woman. Claire here was engaged for a couple of years but—" He paused a moment as if he caught himself. "She broke off the engagement."

Interesting, Billy thought. He looked over at Claire. She was glaring at her brother, but when she glanced back to Billy she smiled . . . a smile that lit her eyes and warmed him. A breeze tousled her hair, and she appeared so carefree at the moment that he would have loved to have a picture painted of her just as she was now. And then he caught himself.

Come on Billy, she is the boss's niece. Get a grip on yourself. Claire isn't in your class. You come from two very different worlds. Haven't you noticed the way they live?

"How about you?" Heath asked, breaking into Billy's thoughts.

"I guess that's fair," Billy said. "Like you, I've had things to do." Billy chuckled, then added, "I heard I was engaged just before I left town. Hope she's changed her mind by the time I get back."

Happy that the two men were finally getting along, Claire had been listening as they talked. However, the moment she heard the word engaged, first from her brother, whom she could have killed for even mentioning the engagement, then she felt a little strange about what she'd heard about Billy. She'd never expected that Billy might have a sweetheart back home. Of course, it would only make sense that he did. She did note, however, that he didn't sound particularly happy about the fact.

The more time Claire spent with Billy, the more she liked him. That didn't mean that she had any claims on him, but she wanted . . . what? She wasn't sure. As for her new vow, she wouldn't worry about it and just let time take her where it would.

Claire placed her napkin upon the table. "We must go by my office. It will be the last time I'll get to see everyone before my trip," she told her brother, although she knew it would be the last time she saw them . . . ever. "Thanks for having lunch with us."

Heath shoved his chair back and got to his feet, and said, "I will see you tonight at dinner." He then looked at Billy. "You should be safe once you leave the wharf. However, after seeing the way you handle your gun, I'm not worried about my sister."

Billy stared at Heath. He was surprised by the compliment, especially from a man who'd made it plain that he didn't like Billy.

"But don't let it go to your head," Heath said over his shoulder just as he reached the door. "Because I'm still watching you."

That was better, Billy thought. He knew what to expect when Heath was acting like a jackass. It just wasn't in Heath to be civilized for long.

It didn't take Billy and Claire long to walk along the brick streets to the publishing house.

"So this is Harper's," Billy said as they entered the front door. "I've plunked down many a nickel to buy a *Harper's Weekly*. What exactly do you do for them?"

"I write articles and draw sketches of what I see around me."

"So those are the drawings that I see in the paper?"

"Not exactly. I send in my sketches to Harper's, and then they are reproduced through the medium of wood engraving."

"They actually carve the pictures in wood? That would take a skillful hand."

"They sure do. Otherwise, they couldn't ink

them and print so many papers," Claire explained as they climbed the stairs. "They did a wonderful job of covering the War between the States. We've grown to sixteen folio pages," she added proudly.

"Good. More for my money," Billy teased as he followed her. He noticed that Claire's footsteps were slowing as they reached the second floor.

"Well, they do have to pay me," she said with a smile, pausing to catch her breath. "So, I appreciate every nickel that you've spent."

Billy gave her a questioning look. "Are you all right?"

"Now don't you start," Claire warned, holding up her hand. "My family is always asking me that question just because I've had a cough. I am fine, and I'm making the trip."

Now it was Billy's turn to hold up both hands. "Whoa!"

Claire couldn't help but laugh at the surprised look on Billy's face. "Sorry. It's a touchy subject."

"I'll say."

"Come on, let's go into my office." She took Billy's hand. His fingers were warm and strong as he grabbed hers; his grasp gave her comfort. What a strange feeling, she thought as they entered.

"Hello, Alice," Claire said to a woman sitting at a desk just inside the door. "Is Ann in her office?"

"Isn't she always? Can't seem to pry her away from the desk." Alice chuckled. "Go on in." Then Alice must have noticed Billy. "You can leave the cowboy with me if you'd like."

Billy glanced at the lady and smiled.

"If you want to, sit over there," Claire pointed to a couple of wooden chairs. "I shouldn't be long."

"Take your time," Billy said. "Appears I'll be in

good company." He gave Alice a wink, and Claire could see that he could charm the pants off any woman.

"Alice, this is Billy West. He will be my escort to Denver," she told the woman. "Be sure to take care of him."

"No problem, honey," Alice replied, but she wasn't looking at Claire. "It'll be my pleasure," Alice added as she batted her eyelashes at Billy. "Anything you want, Mr. West, you just let me know."

Claire was shaking her head as she entered Ann's office. "I've come to say good-bye, and see if you have any last minute instructions for me."

"Instructions?" Ann looked over her spectacles and motioned to Claire to sit down. Then Ann looked up at the ceiling and repeated. "Instructions. Let me see . . . get some good stories, have fun, and be careful," she said, looking back at Claire. "Did your escort arrive?"

"He certainly did," Claire said, smiling as she thought about him.

"And—?"

"He is like no one I've ever met before."

Ann folded her arms and leaned on her desk. "Really? Now you have my curiosity up. Tell me about him."

"I can do better than that." Claire gave her a wicked smile. "I've brought him with me. Take some papers out to Alice so you can see for yourself."

"What a wonderful idea," Ann said. She picked up a few sheets of paper and headed for the door. "I'll be right back."

After several long minutes—many more than Claire thought necessary, Ann returned. She shut the door behind her and moved behind her desk, then slumped down in her chair. "My legs have gone weak. That is one handsome cowboy you've got yourself. Have you touched him to make certain he's real?"

"He most certainly is real," Claire told Ann. "I'm afraid I had a coughing spell and fainted in his arms."

"Convenient."

"It wasn't intended, I assure you." Claire sighed. "He is certainly nice to look at."

"Look at, hell," Ann, never one to mince words, snorted. "You need to be touching him and finding out how much muscle is under that shirt."

"Ann!" Claire felt her cheeks grow warm. "That isn't very ladylike."

"To hell with being a lady," Ann said, and took Claire's hand. "Didn't you tell me that you wanted to live? To do things you've never done before?"

Claire nodded as she released her hand and sat back in the chair. "Yes."

"Well, you've never had a cowboy before, nor any other man, for that matter, so now is your chance. Forget about the ladylike ideas you've had all your life."

"Ann, I can't believe you're talking like this!"

"Desperate times call for desperate measures." Ann smiled, moving around to the front of her desk to face Claire. Ann evidently was having a jolly time with this subject. "Listen, you've been a proper lady all your life, waiting for David; although I can't understand why. How many times did he put off marrying you because his business wasn't big enough, or that he didn't have the right house? It was always one excuse after another and, of course, *you* waited and waited, putting all your desires aside. And, I ask you, for what? What good did it do?"

"Not much. He broke the engagement," Claire said.

"Precisely. You got nothing but heartache. Of course, I would have hated to see you marry that dull-as-dirt simpleton anyway. But this one . . . I suspect you won't hear the word wait come out of his mouth."

"But I can't get sweet on him because—well, you know."

"So." Ann reached out her hands, palms up. "You enjoy your cowboy for as long as it lasts. Take a chance for a little happiness. Remember, you don't have to worry about getting married or saving yourself. *You* go after what you want and get it. You do like him, don't you?"

Claire nodded. "Yes, I do. Earlier today, I could feel something between us, but I don't know, I don't want to get serious about anyone."

"You don't have to be serious. Just have fun. Seduce him. Admit it, I bet you'd like to know what it's like to kiss him?"

"Yes. I would."

"Good. That's my girl." Ann patted Claire on the shoulder. "No more rules, but one. We go after what we want. Agreed?"

Claire stood, thought a moment, then said, "Absolutely."

"And when you send back your articles from out there, I expect a full report on your handsome cowboy."

"I'll do that," Claire said and then hesitantly asked. "But how do I start?"

"At your party." Ann thought for a moment. "You'll be all dressed up, and he won't be able to take his eyes off you. That's when you get him. You're just not very experienced at flirting, but it will come to you. Hell, I might even come to your party."

"Please do, just in case I need a shove," Claire said with a smile. "You know, I've followed the rules all my life. I hope I can change."

Ann took Claire by the arms. "Close your eyes."

Claire did as she was told.

"Now imagine your cowboy. Got it?"

Claire nodded.

"Picture yourself being kissed by your cowboy."

"All right," Claire said.

"Now, can you break a few rules to get what you want?"

Claire's eyelids flew open, and she gave Ann a triumphant smile, then said, "You're damned right I can!"

"That's my girl. Give me a hug and go out there and get him."

Claire gave Ann a final hug good-bye, knowing that Ann had just made it easier for her to leave. Ann had probably done so to avoid tearful good-byes, and Claire was grateful for that.

As Claire reached the door Ann said, "Don't forget to write to me. And I want details."

Claire gave Ann a sly smile. "I'll report back every intimate detail. Provided there are some."

"Oh, there will be." Ann sat back in her chair. "If I were a little younger, I'd break him in for you."

"I don't doubt that for a minute. 'Bye," Claire said as she shut the door and went to find Billy.

Once they were in the hall, Billy asked. "Do you always laugh so much with your editor? I could hear you as I waited."

Claire smiled at him. "Only when we have something wonderful to talk about."

"Well, today's subject must have been a good one."

"I guess you could say it is certainly one of the most important conversations we've ever had. She more or less gave me an assignment." Claire smiled a lopsided sort of smile.

"I hope it isn't too difficult."

Claire wanted to laugh as she looked into Billy's warm brown eyes. "Sometimes difficult tasks can be the most rewarding."

Chapter Eight

When Billy went down for breakfast, he noticed that the entire staff was scurrying around as if they had a thousand tasks to do. Armed with brooms, mops, and dust rags, they paid him little attention as he walked by.

He heard them talking about the party that would be held tonight, and knew the staff would be rushing all day to accomplish their tasks, so he decided to make himself scarce so he wouldn't get in anyone's way. And the idea of staying inside all day really didn't appeal to him. Since when had he spent this much time inside? He was used to being outside in the wide open spaces. Just the thought of being in this part of the country made him feel trapped.

Just one more day of the eastern life, he told himself as he strolled through the front door, beating the butler to the punch. Tomorrow they would be on a train heading back to Denver, and the big pay day. He looked forward to getting his money because he knew what he wanted to do with it.

First, he'd put it in the bank and then start looking
for his own land. And after he found his land, he
could start building his house, followed by a stable.

It still seemed like a dream to him, owning his
own land. But he also knew that dreams could be
shattered in an instant, so he cautiously kept his
dreams to himself.

But today, he was going to spend his time looking around the Holladay's stables. He might as
well learn from the best and pick up some useful
information that would be useful when he finally
bought his own ranch.

As Billy strode along the dirt road, he noticed
the split-rail fences that ran on both sides of the
roads and divided the land into pastures. The
grass had turned green and the horses seemed to
be enjoying themselves as they grazed on the tender blades of grass. In the distance, some men
were white-washing fences. Then he noticed his
pinto, Spot, in a smaller pasture by the stables. You
couldn't miss her as she was the only one who
looked like she didn't belong in such lush sur-
rounds. Billy laughed, he was sure he stood out
like a sore thumb himself. Spot was running
around, kicking up her heels. Evidently, his horse
was as restless as he was.

Billy entered the large white stable and found
four grooms talking to each other. One held a
pitchfork, the other three were frowning and shaking their heads. At the other end of the stable,
Albert came out of the tack room. "So why haven't
at least one of you mucked out Firebrand's stall?
Standing around talking won't get the job done."

Suddenly a horse's head came over the half-
door, mouth wide open, ears flat back.

"That's the reason," the taller boy said, taking a step backwards.

Albert noticed Billy and smiled. He pulled Billy to the side. "I see you had to get away from all the hustle going on at the house, too." Albert chuckled. "You would think that we were announcing my sister's engagement. Mother has always wanted Claire to have the grandest wedding, so I guess this is Mother's way of giving Claire what she'll never have."

Billy thought that was an odd statement. "Surely, Claire will marry one day," he said.

Albert was quiet for a moment and he looked a little sad before he said, "Sure, she will." And then Albert abruptly changed the subject. "Is there something I can show you?"

"If you don't mind, I thought it would be more to my liking down here at the stables."

"That's fine. You've arrived just in time to see our most difficult horse." Albert nodded toward the stall. "The boys here were deciding who was going to clean the stall and curry the horse."

"None of them look too eager," Billy commented as he walked over to the stall. A stallion paced. He was so brown his coat looked black and his mane and tail were black. His hind hoofs were white and a small white spot was in the center of his forehead. He spotted Billy and stared at him with cautious eyes. "He seems nervous and underweight."

"That's putting it mildly," Albert said. "He's underweight because he won't eat."

"Hi, Mr. Billy," Willie said, carrying a bridle that was almost as big as himself, the boy couldn't be over seven years old. He had dark curly hair and eyes as brown as Billy's. "I finished cleaning the bridle, Mr. Albert." Willie held it up so Albert could see.

"Good job. You can hang it up with the rest," Albert said, and then looked at the other grooms, dismissing the child. "Get to your other chores while I try and figure out what to do with this horse. If Father would agree, I'd get rid of him," Albert grumbled, then looked at Billy. "My sister said that you were interested in horses."

"I hope to raise them one day. Not these thoroughbreds but mustangs and quarter horses. That's the kind of horses we use out West. However, I must admit these animals are magnificent, especially that one."

Albert motioned toward the stall. "Firebrand is an Alter Real."

Billy frowned. "I hate to sound ignorant, but I didn't understand a word you just said."

Albert chuckled. "Not many people would recognize the breed name. I'll explain. This horse's ancestors date back to 1747 and were the results of the Braganza royal family wanting their own horses. They bred Andalusian mares imported from the Jérez region of Spain to get this special breed. And that probably sounds confusing: so, simply, this horse comes with an impeccable bloodline that makes him intelligent and a quick learner."

"If he's so intelligent, why don't you talk to him about his behavior?" Billy suggested with a smile.

Albert grunted. "Unfortunately he's a high priced, prickly thoroughbred. Do you have any suggestions?"

"What do you think is wrong with him?"

"Firebrand, a name he well deserves as you can see. Used to be a fine race horse, but he was in a stable fire a year back. After that, his owner couldn't do anything with him, so he sold him to us. Firebrand is a fine thoroughbred. We'd hoped to race him again, but as you can see we've not been successful calming him down. He paces his stall and lunges at anyone who gets near. I'm not sure we'll ever be able to do anything with him."

Willie had come back to stand between them. "I bet Firebrand's lonesome."

"Horses don't get lonesome. They're not people," Albert said.

Billy looked at Albert. "I disagree. I once knew an old Indian who taught me to talk to horses. He always said that horses needed friends just like people. Mind if I give your horse a try?"

"Talk to horses?" Albert looked at Billy like he'd been eating loco weed. Finally he shrugged. "Help yourself. I've got some other things to tend to but if Firebrand kicks you, just remember I warned you." He walked away shaking his head.

Billy touched Willie's shoulder. "Willie, do you have a few carrots?"

"Sure. Be right back."

Billy eased his way closer to the stall ignoring Firebrand's snapping jaws and ears pinned back. "Now you know that you don't really want to bite me. I'm here to help you."

Firebrand didn't look convinced.

Willie was out of breath by the time he returned. "Here are the carrots. Whatcha going to do?"

Billy took the carrots. "I'm going to have a talk with Firebrand. Stand back," Billy warned Willie. "I'm going into the stall."

"Are you nuts, mister? That there horse will kick the mud out of you."

"Maybe not," Billy said as he shut the half door of the stall behind him. "How about a carrot, big boy?" Billy said in a soft tone as the horse eyed him from the corner of the stall, his skin quivering with nervousness. Billy took a step forward. Firebrand reared up on his hind legs and pawed the air.

Patiently, Billy waited until the horse had all four feet down on the ground. Firebrand eyed him, unsure of what to do next as he pawed the ground.

An hour later, they were still in the same position.

"You might as well stop that fuss because I'm not going away," Billy told the prickly horse as he took another step closer to the animal. "I know you'd like this great big carrot." He held it out and Firebrand stretched his neck out to sniff.

Billy pulled the carrot back just out of reach so that Firebrand would have to move closer. "You'll have to come to me if you want this carrot."

The horse stepped side to side, his eyes never leaving the snack. Finally, he took the few steps toward Billy, reached out and bit off the carrot top.

Billy let him munch on the carrot as he slowly raised his other hand to rub Firebrand's thick, muscular neck. At first Firebrand jerked back but then he finally relaxed. Billy began to whisper to Firebrand. His heavy ears swept back and forth. Billy waited for the horse to calm down and the restlessness to leave him. He needed to gain the horse's trust. "Let's try some of these." Billy held up a bucket of oats and the horse began to eat.

"Golly, I can't believe you got him to eat," Willie said as he leaned on the half door. He'd pulled up a small wooden stool, so he could stand on it to look over the door. "What did you say to him?"

Billy chuckled at the boy's surprised expression.

"It was just a little horse talk," he said. "Let's take Firebrand outside for a little while." Billy reached for a lead rope that hung from a nail inside the stall and fastened it to Firebrand's halter, then Willie opened the door so Billy could lead the stallion out.

Willie ran along beside Billy. They had just passed his office when Albert walked out the door, papers in his right hand.

"I don't believe what I'm seeing," Albert said, lifting his cap and scratching his head. "You must be some miracle worker. Maybe we need to keep you around here for a while. Then you can teach me to talk to horses."

"Nope. Too civilized for me." Billy smiled. "I think you can have one of the boys muck out the stall now." He didn't wait for a reply as he led the horse over to the corral where Spot stood.

The pinto obediently came over to Billy who reached out and stroked her finely drawn muzzle. Then to Billy's surprise, Firebrand leaned over the fence and sniffed Spot. Spot seemed just as curious.

"I think they like each other," Willie said.

"I do, too. Why don't you get Spot and lead her over there where I can saddle her. Then I'll take you for that ride I promised."

Willie was already moving when he thought of a question. "What about Firebrand?"

"I'll put him on a long lead rope and let him come with us."

As Willie ran around to the fence gate, a female voice came from behind Billy. "So here you are! I was beginning to think that you'd left and started back home without me."

Billy turned and saw Claire, the sun making her

hair shine like a black raven's wing. She was dressed in yellow and white and reminded him of a sunflower today.

"It didn't look like you needed my help at the house," he said as his gaze traveled over her face, "so I came down here to give Willie that ride I promised."

Claire looked past Billy to Firebrand, so she wouldn't give away that each time she saw Billy, the pull was stronger. "And apparently tame our horse. Can I pet him?"

"Sure."

Claire moved slowly as she reached out to touch Firebrand's muzzle. "This is the first contact that anyone has had with him." She smiled slowly, regarding Billy curiously. "Are you good at everything you try, Billy West?" she finally asked.

He gave her a slow smile before answering. "Pretty much."

"Then I'll be in good hands," she said in a whispery voice. Suddenly, her heart was beating way too fast. She didn't usually flirt with men, but she was deliberately doing just that, and she could see a spark in the depths of his dark eyes. She should be ashamed . . . but she wasn't.

"I'm ready," Willie yelled as he ran over to them. "Are you going ridin' with us, Miss Claire?"

It was hard, but Claire managed to pull her gaze way from Billy and looked at the child. "I'm not dressed for riding, Willie. I guess you two will have to go and have all the fun, while I go back to the house." She turned toward Billy, his lithe body relaxed as he held Firebrand's lead rope. "Your clothes arrived a half hour ago, so you'll be all set for the party."

The corner of his mouth twisted with annoyance. "I'd rather stay out here."

Her lips twitched with the need to smile at Billy's apparent unhappiness. She knew she was asking him to do something that he preferred not to do. "I know, but please . . . come for me. You might even have a good time."

"I doubt it."

She touched his arm. It was so easy to get lost in his eyes, the way he looked at her. "It's the only party that has ever been held for me," she said softly. "And I probably won't have another."

"All right," Billy finally said. "But I might not stay long."

She studied his lean dark face. She found his nearness disturbing and exciting, but most of all he was doing something he really didn't want to do just because she'd asked him. Tears welled within her eyes. "Thank you," she said, then turned and left, not wanting Billy to see her tears. She really didn't know why it meant so much that he go to the party, but it did.

Maybe it was because she didn't want everybody to think that Claire Holladay was a loser. Most people knew that David had broken up with her, however, they didn't know the reason why. She could just imagine the gossip *Por Claire, how is she going to get another man now that David has dumped her?* She was leaving tomorrow, they probably would think that she was sneaking out of town.

Of course, she could tell everyone the truth, but then the party would be more like a wake, and she definitely didn't want that. She wasn't dead yet, nor did she want to be reminded of what September would bring.

For just tonight she wanted to laugh and have fun. And if she was really lucky, maybe she could get Billy to loosen up enough to dance. Then she'd know how it felt to be in his arms. She felt a surge of excitement. Tonight was going to be wonderful.

Billy didn't realize he was still watching Claire walk away until Willie tugged on his hand. Billy reached down and picked Willie up.

"I think Miss Claire likes you," Willie said as Billy lifted him up on the saddle.

"Maybe," Billy said offhand, as he swung up behind Willie.

"Do you like her?"

"Yep. She seems like a nice lady."

"Good." Willie giggled. "Maybe the two of you will get married."

"Whoa, young man. You're thinking way too much. I've been hired to take Miss Claire back to Denver and that's all there is to it."

"Can I go?"

The child's question threw Billy. Why would Willie want to leave a place like this? "That's not for me to say. Who takes care of you?"

"I take care of myself," Willie said, and Billy could hear the pride in the boy as they galloped over the pasture.

"How old are you, Willie?"

Willie held up his hand an extend his fingers. "This many."

"You are only five years old?"

"This many," he held up his hand again and realized that Willie didn't know how to count.

"That is five Willie."

"Can I hold Spot's reins?"

"Sure put your hand right here." Billy placed the little hands in front of his, but he made sure he had a good hold of the reins, too. Glancing back at Firebrand, Billy saw that the stallion seemed contented.

"Like this?"

"Yep, just like that," Billy said. "If you want to turn Spot, you pull the reins like this." He let Willie guide the horse for a little while before Billy finally asked. "Miss Claire told me she found you on the steps of her building. Do you know how you got there?"

"That was last year. Don't know where my ma and pa is. I just remember waking up one morning they were gone. So I kinda wandered around until I found a group of boys. They said I was too little for them, so they took me to those steps and told me to stay there. Then Miss Claire found me and said she was going to take me home with her." Willie sighed. "I like Miss Claire."

"Don't you like it here at Oak Hill?"

"It's all right. I just don't belong."

Billy's heart was twisting. Willie reminded Billy of himself. "How about the other grooms? Don't you sleep with them?"

"Nope. I sleep in the tack room with Floppy."

"And who is Floppy?" Billy was thinking maybe an imaginary friend like he'd had, but Willie completely surprised him by saying, "Miss Claire's dog. She's had Floppy since he was a puppy."

"That's a funny name," Billy said.

"Floppy is funny. He has real long ears and he steps on them and trips. Miss Claire said he's a hound. A basset hound.

"You'll have to show him to me. But hadn't you rather stay with the other boys?"

"They picked on me 'cause I'm little," Willie said matter-of-factly and then he seemed to push everything aside as he changed the subject, "This is fun, Billy. I've never been riding before. How am I doing?"

Billy felt like he'd been hit in the gut. Here this brave little boy was so excited about something small like riding, when his little shoulders seemed to carry a burden. Some unknown feeling was pulling at Billy, and he wasn't sure how he was going to handle the situation. "Do you know that I was once an orphan just like you?"

Willie twisted around to look at Billy. "Really?"

"That right. I didn't have any folks either, so I was living with a bunch of outlaws and, after them, I went to the parsonage to live with five other children."

"And then what? Did you have to find another home?"

"All of us did because the parsonage was closing."

"Your brothers and sisters went with you?"

"That's right. We're a family now."

"Do you suppose I'll have a family one day? I'd like to have somebody just like you," Willie admitted.

Billy was so touched that the child thought so much of him. He hugged Willie. "I promise you, Willie, that one day you will have your own family."

Chapter Nine

Claire couldn't remember when she'd been so nervous.

Tonight, she wanted to leave everyone with a good impression, so they would smile when they remembered her.

It was time to get ready for the party. She sat down in front of her dressing table and brushed her hair. Feeling a tickle in the back of her throat, she grabbed the small, brown bottle and took a sip. She could not cough during the party.

Not tonight.

This night belonged to her.

While she brushed her long wavy hair, Aunt Ute came into the room. "You are ready for me to dress your hair?"

"Please. My hands are shaking so badly that I know I'd make a mess of it."

"Don't worry. We'll have you ready by the time the first guests start arriving, and before your mother starts checking on you."

Aunt Ute took out a box of hairpins, then removed the hairbrush from Claire's nervous fingers. She brushed Claire's long hair until it crackled and snapped. "You really have lovely hair."

"Thank you. Are you going to twist it up in curls?"

"*Ja.*"

"You didn't happen to see Billy when you came upstairs, did you?"

"*Ja,* I did. He was going into his room when I got to the top of the stairs. I haven't had a chance to speak with him yet. He is a fine one, *ja?*"

Claire smiled. "Yes, he is. I'm sorry I haven't introduced him to you. I will do that tonight. However, do not let on that you are traveling with us. Fredrick says Billy will be upset at having another person to look after."

Aunt Ute frowned and looked at Claire in the mirror. "*Nein,* he'll not have to look after me! I've been doing that for more years than he's been alive. And if he gives me any guff, I'll box his ears."

Claire laughed. "I know you'll stand your ground. I just don't want any scenes until we get to the train station," she explained. "So I'm going to keep you hidden until tomorrow. Has Fredrick returned?"

"*Ja.* And the trunks have already been packed in the carriage. So you are all set, young lady," Aunt Ute said as she placed the last hairpin in Claire's hair. "How is that?"

"Lovely." Claire turned, looking at her hair in the mirror Ute held for her. Her tresses had been swept up into a chignon with wisps of hair twirling around her face. Ute handed her the mirror and went to the bed to get her aquamarine gown. So Claire quickly took a sip of cough medicine just to be safe, noticing that each time she took some, it eased her tension as well as her cough.

Feeling more at ease, Claire stepped into her petticoats, and then Aunt Ute dropped the new gown over her head. Claire quickly turned so that she could fasten the long row of tiny buttons on the back.

The gown fit to perfection. The neckline of the bodice was very low, but tastefully so, and showed off her creamy white skin. The pink roses that were nestled in the netting on her décolletage offset the warm glow in her cheeks. Her gown had been designed in the new style of double skirts, both trained, the under one plain, and the upper somewhat shorter and edged with a gathered flounce. The underskirt was of green grenadine and the overdress was of aquamarine.

"You are beautiful, Claire. *So schön,*" Ute repeated in German as she clasped her hands above her bosom and gazed at Claire approvingly.

Claire touched her face. "But I'm so pale."

"Nonsense. Your skin looks like porcelain. That *dummkopf* David will be sorry that he ever let you go. I shall go and get dressed, myself, and I shall see you downstairs."

When Aunt Ute opened the door to go, Claire could hear the voices of the arriving guests in the foyer. She looked at herself once more in the mirror and pinched her cheeks for good measure. And just for safety, she took another swig of cough syrup, feeling wonderful as the medicine warmed her all the way down.

This was her night. She intended to shine.

* * *

"You ready?" Fredrick called as he knocked on Billy's door.

"Come in," came the gruff voice on the other side of the door.

"Whoa!" Fredrick stopped in the doorway before he entered. "Look at you. You look different without a gun strapped to your leg."

"I feel odd." Billy drew his brows together as he looked at Claire's cousin. "I keep asking myself how your cousin roped me into going to this thing."

Fredrick chuckled. "It's called a party. And they're supposed to be fun."

"Yep," Billy said as he adjusted his black cravat. "It feels like I'm going to a lynching. That's another kind of party where I come from."

Fredrick chuckled. "It's hard to resist a beautiful woman, isn't it?" he said as he leaned against the door.

"You might have a point," Billy agreed with a smile. "But I have been known to say no. There is something about your cousin," he paused so he could find the right word, "that is different. I just can't put my finger on what that 'difference' is."

"I agree with you." Fredrick nodded. "Our Claire is different. She's rather like a rare flower that is so beautiful and delicate that you hold your breath, afraid that you'll hurt her in some way."

Billy smiled. "Fredrick, that was plumb beautiful," he drawled. Then he said in a serious voice, "And a nice way to put it."

Fredrick turned a bright red. "Just remember that some of those beautiful flowers have prickly thorns."

"Point taken. I'm sure I'll find a few thorns along the way."

*   *   *

When Billy and Fredrick arrived at the down-stairs ballroom, they paused at the first set of double doors to scan the crowd.

Billy was surprised at how many guests there were. He could count on his hands how many people he knew back home. The Holladays must have invited the entire county. The women were all dressed in very fancy colorful ball gowns. His sisters would die to have dresses so elegant.

"This is something," he finally said to Fredrick.

"Yep." Fredrick nodded. "My aunt always gives the fanciest parties in this part of the country. Just wait until everyone arrives."

"You mean there will be more?"

"Sure. The ballroom and the foyer will be full of people before the night is over."

"So what do we do now?" Billy asked.

"This is pretty much it. Unless you want to go through the receiving line," Fredrick said, then he laughed. "You just stand around and talk, or you could dance."

"Believe it or not, I can dance," Billy said as they stepped out of the doorway into the ballroom. He looked around. "You know there's not a gun in sight."

Fredrick laughed. "My aunt would have fainted dead away if you had worn your six-shooter. However, she will really approve of your clothes tonight. You look like a fancy easterner. You'll fit right in."

Albert strolled over to them. He was dressed the same as Billy, a far cry from the duds he'd had on at the stable.

"Welcome to our party. There are refreshments on a table over there in front of that long set of windows. Please, help yourself or I could find you something stronger, if you'd like?"

"Obliged. Punch will be fine. Don't believe I've ever had any before," Billy said with a nod.

"Fredrick, are you learning the stage coach business from Uncle Ben?" said Albert.

"A little," Fredrick replied agreeably. "Uncle Ben said I have to discover how things are done out there before I can learn anything about the business. I'm going to start driving a stage when we get back to Denver. Uncle Ben says that is learning from the ground up."

"Makes sense," Albert said in agreement. "I had to muck out stables when I was coming up, since I chose the horse business instead of ships. Speaking of stables . . ." Albert turned to Billy—"Thanks for your help with Firebrand. Since we put your pinto in the stall next to his, he's a different horse."

"Firebrand is a fine horse," Billy said, not comfortable with the praise. "He was just lonesome. Let's get something to drink."

"Come this way," Albert said. "I think Heath is over there."

"Great," Billy muttered. Just who he needed to see to top off this boring night.

Claire stood beside her editor, fanning herself with a silk fan that had been a gift from her father on her fifteenth birthday. Glancing around, she noticed that she seemed to be the only one who was warm.

"I thought you didn't like parties," Claire said to Ann.

"I don't. There are usually a bunch of pompous people all trying to outshine the others. I've never understood why people can't be themselves." Ann tilted her head to the side. "There is a good example. Look over there at Lucy Blackwell. See her eyes roaming over the crowd?" Ann said in a low voice. "She reminds me of a vulture looking for its next prey. She's had her head turned toward the door for the last five minutes, so I'll bet she's found the next victim."

Claire followed the direction of Lucy's gawking gaze and discovered the victim at just about the same time that Ann said, "Well, I'll be!" Ann squeezed Claire's arm. "She's going after your cowboy. Yep, Lucy is headed his way."

"You sound like Mother. He isn't *my* cowboy."

Ann leaned back and looked at Claire. "Well, honey, you need to wake up. With a little encouragement, he just might be."

Claire gave a disgusted sigh. "We went over this at the office," Ann said. "*And* I pointed out emphatically to you that you need to give the man a little encouragement. You were the one who told me that you wanted to live life to the fullest. Am I not right?"

Claire knew Ann was right. Claire was acting like she always had . . . prim and proper. "Well, I haven't seen Billy much since we left your office."

"You see him now, don't you?"

Claire nodded.

"It's up to you to flirt with him. Give him a little encouragement."

Claire bit her lip as she watched Billy. "That would be so forward."

"Precisely," Ann agreed.

The music struck up a tune. The crowd backed out of the way as couples took their places on the dance floor.

Ann gave Claire a shove. "Go ahead and ask him to dance."

"He is supposed to ask me," Claire protested.
"Cowboys don't ask. Now go." Ann shoved her toward Billy.

Claire felt light on her feet from perhaps all the excitement. Her head felt a bit fuzzy, but she attributed that to the warmth of so many bodies so close together.

But suddenly she felt very daring. Ann was right. It was time for her to move in on the prey!

Claire could now see Billy clearly as he made his way through the throng of people. He looked magnificent tonight and so different from his cowboy persona, standing tall and proud. You couldn't help but notice him. He was taller than most of the men around him and maybe an inch taller than Heath, who had been considered quite tall before Billy's arrival.

Billy was dressed all in black except for the snow-white shirt which made his handsome face appear bronzed. His coal-black jacket accented his powerful shoulders and the same fabric encased his long muscular legs.

And then there was Billy's face. Claire couldn't draw her gaze away from him. Those dark brown eyes looked enormous and almost predatory tonight. His rich brown hair gleamed beneath the lights and curled just at his neck. No wonder that all the unspoken-for women were gawking and whispering as Claire walked by. She could hear them asking who the stranger was.

She smiled as she noticed that Billy and Heath were talking and apparently getting along, instead of arguing as they'd done most of the time Billy had been in New York.

Then Billy saw her. She knew he did because

something in his eyes changed and Claire's heart leaped. His gaze never left her as she came to him, seemingly drawn by his gaze.

The moment Billy saw Claire, he nearly stopped in the middle of his sentence. He had been telling Heath that he would take good care of his sister, so Heath could rest easy and quit nagging.

The lovely vision that Billy saw floating his way didn't look as though she needed protecting, unless it was from him. Claire was simply stunning. Billy wasn't sure he'd ever seen a woman dressed as beautifully as Claire was tonight. Her dress was low cut, showing the tops of her breasts. She needed a shawl to cover herself, was the first thing he thought but her brothers didn't seem to object, so Billy figured that she was properly dressed. However, if Claire was his, he wouldn't stand for any man gawking at her like he was doing.

Her gown made her eyes shine like rare jewels, but she was still much too pale except for spots of color high on her cheeks. He wanted to see more color in her face. He hoped that her trip out West would restore a healthy glow to her skin. He could picture cornflower blue eyes and golden skin. A tightening in his groin reminded him that he didn't need to think in that direction.

Tonight Claire had an odd look in her eyes—almost as if she were a bit tipsy. Naw, not sweet, innocent Claire.

Just then Billy caught a glimpse of another woman approaching him. She was slightly ahead of Claire, and she was smiling at him as if he was fresh meat. It was no secret what that woman had on her mind.

"Hello, Heath," the woman said when she'd

drawn near. "You must introduce me to your friend. I don't believe I have had the pleasure," she said as she fanned herself.

Heath had a smirk on his face, and he glanced at Billy. "I'd be most happy to. Lucy Blackwell, I'd like you to meet Billy West, a friend from Denver."

"It's nice to meet you, Mr. West. I have an opening on my dance card. Why don't we get acquainted as we waltz?" Lucy said.

"What's a dance card?" Billy asked.

"I'll explain while we dance," Lucy said as she took his hand and led him to the dance floor right past Claire. "Hi, Claire. Nice party." Lucy smiled. "We are going to waltz."

Claire managed a half-smile and nodded to Lucy as she continued on toward her brothers. So much for being forward. Lucy had beaten her to the "prey."

"Hello, puss," Heath said. "You are very pretty tonight and should be dancing, not standing around by yourself. "Shall we?" He held up his arm for her to take. Once she'd placed her hand on his arm, he asked, "How do you feel?"

"Don't start, Heath," Claire warned as she took his hand and walked with him to the dance floor.

Heath swept Claire into his arms and they swayed around the floor to the strains of the waltz. Claire kept catching glimpses of Billy out of the corner of her eye, and noticed that he danced very well. He was also smiling down at Lucy, evidently enjoying Lucy's company, which made Claire clench her teeth.

"I want you to promise me that you'll be very careful and won't do anything foolish," Heath said, drawing her attention back to him. "I instructed Billy to be very careful with you."

She glanced back to her brother, brows raised. "You didn't say anything about my cough, did you?"

"Of course not." Heath looked insulted. "I promised I wouldn't."

"You better not have," Claire warned him.

"I also want you to remember that Billy is a man and you are a woman, and—"

"Heath!" Claire felt as if her body were on fire. "I'm a grown woman. You don't need to explain that to me. If you're going to keep on lecturing me, then you can take me to the refreshment table right this very minute. We're supposed to be having fun tonight." Not *Lucy's* night, she couldn't help thinking with a frown.

"Ah, puss. I just want what's best for you," Heath said as he walked her over to the punch bowl.

Claire could hear Billy's laughter and that didn't improve her mood. She stopped and touched her brother's arm. "Heath, it's time for me to decide what is best for me."

"And you've done that," Heath pointed out. "But it doesn't mean I'm going to stop being your brother, so don't get your hackles up."

Claire realized she was snapping at him. "I'm sorry."

Heath nodded and then said, "Look there."

"Who is it?"

"John Roebling. He and Father must be going to the library," Heath said as he took her elbow and escorted her over to the refreshment table.

"Who?" Claire asked again, knowing she should remember the name, but her brain was fuzzy.

"You've heard us talk about him. Remember the brilliant engineer? I asked him to come tonight and bring his drawings so we can look them over in the library."

"Oh, I remember. He's designing the Brooklyn Bridge."

"That's right. I thought maybe you'd like to see what the bridge is going to look like before you leave."

"Yes, I would." Claire looked at her brother. "Thank you. I just cannot picture such a tremendous bridge," she said as she looked over the crowd. She saw Billy and Lucy coming their way. Lucy was hanging onto Billy's arm, Claire noticed. *Hussy.* Claire touched her lips, thinking that she'd actually said the word instead of thinking it.

"Hello, Claire," Lucy said with a triumphant smile. "I'm not sure you heard me a while ago. Your party is wonderful."

"I'm so glad you are enjoying yourself," Claire said, but then she looked at Billy. "And I'm glad that you *did* come."

"You said that it was important to you," Billy said with a slow smile. "I aim to please."

Claire's breath caught in her throat, and she couldn't find her voice.

"Billy," Lucy broke the silence. "Will you be a sweetie and get me some punch?"

Sweetie? Claire wanted to throw up.

Billy nodded. "Excuse me," he said and casually walked over to where Heath was filling two glasses.

Lucy looked at Claire. "He is so handsome. I hope I get to spend more time with him. I think he likes me."

"Really?" Claire arched her brow, feeling irritated that she was letting Lucy's remarks get to her. "How do you know?"

"It was the way he held me when we danced," Lucy said and then patted Claire's arm. "You'll understand one day when you get over David."

Claire felt her cheeks warm. "I'm over David," Claire said firmly.

Heath and Billy returned with the punch. "I've just told Billy about the drawings, and he wants to see them, as well," Heath said. "Shall we take our refreshments into the library?"

"What drawings? Is there a painting?" Lucy asked, excitedly.

"Drawings of a bridge," Claire explained.

"Sounds boring," Lucy said with a frown. "I think I'll go and say hello to Mrs. Thorndike. Billy, you must save me another dance."

Billy nodded to the flirtatious woman, and then he followed Claire and Heath out of the room, grateful to be away from that woman. She was as pushy as the women back home. He needed to hang a sign around his neck saying "not interested in marriage, so find someone else," in bold lettering.

When they entered the library, the first thing that Billy noticed was the wall of books. He'd never seen so many books in one place, in shelves from the floor to the ceiling. There was a long table in the middle of the room where Mr. Holladay and another gentleman were bent over looking at some bundles of old and curling papers laid out on the long table.

Donald Holladay straightened. "I see my children have arrived. Some of them, anyway. Mr. John Roebling, I'd like you to meet my oldest, Heath, and my youngest, Claire. And this gentleman is Billy West who is going to escort my daughter to Denver."

"Ah, adventure," John said with a heavy accent that Billy hadn't heard before. "That's what life is all about."

Claire spoke first. "It must have been quite an adventure when you came to America?"

"*Ja, Deutschland,* my Germany, is a long way from here. But I've been in this country for many years now."

So, he was German, Billy realized. He'd never met anyone from that country. So far, he had experienced many new things in his short stay in the North. He wondered what else was in store for him.

"Well, we're glad that you came to our country," Heath said. "Or we wouldn't have the hopes of a bridge connecting us to Brooklyn. However, I can't imagine not taking a ferry."

"The bridge will be many years down the road."

Billy glanced down at the drawing. "What is this?" he pointed. "Seems like some kind of rope."

"*Ja,*" John said, nodding. "That is Roebling's wire rope. We make it very strong, so strong that it will support the bridge, making it a suspension bridge."

"A bridge supported by a rope?" Billy shook his head. "Doesn't seem possible," he said.

"*Ah,* I have a skeptic."

Billy persisted. "How do you know it will work?"

John laughed. "I don't blame you for your doubtful look."

"Sorry," Billy said, "I'm just looking at something that doesn't seem possible."

"I know," John said. "I built my first suspension bridge a few years ago in Pittsburgh, and it has worked well. I was impressed. But the Brooklyn Bridge will be grander and will last for a lifetime."

"I'm impressed," Billy admitted. "Maybe when I bring Claire back home, I will get to see the marvel for myself."

"*Ja*, I will take you on a tour myself," John said with a broad smile.

Neither of them noticed that conversation in the room had stilled. Claire could only stare at her father and brother, with stinging eyes that refused to shed a tear.

Secretly, they all knew that Claire wouldn't be returning home.

Chapter Ten

Billy turned and asked Claire if she was ready to return to the party.

Claire managed a weak smile and nodded. She wished she could count on coming home again. Never seeing her family was overwhelming if she thought about it, so she quickly swept those thoughts from her mind so she could get through the night.

They left the study and strolled down the hall back to the ballroom. She almost hated returning to the crowded room, but this was her party and it would be rude to leave her guests so early.

Claire stopped just before they entered the ballroom and looked at Billy. "I want to thank you for coming tonight," she murmured softly, for his ears only.

Billy glanced down at Claire, and he thought she had tears in her sparkling eyes. A look of tired sadness passed over her features and he wondered why, then he passed it off as his imagination. It was her party so there wasn't anything for her to be sad about.

He couldn't help thinking how beautiful she was in this elegant setting. There were many who would love to live in a place such as this one. How would she feel when she had to face the difficulties of the untamed West? The conditions were harsher and many small-boned women, such as Claire, died over the years because they couldn't adjust.

She looked much too serious at the moment so he decided to lighten the mood. "After I went to all the trouble to have this suit fitted, I couldn't very well let it hang in the closet," he said with a grin.

Finally she smiled. He knew she was totally unaware of the captivating picture she made when she smiled.

"You do look handsome tonight," she said.

"Thank you. But shouldn't I be the one complimenting you?"

She took an abrupt step back, then twirled around before meeting his gaze. "If you'd like to."

Claire saw a roguish light in Billy's eyes, when usually she couldn't tell what he was thinking. She found she liked this lighter side of him.

He rubbed his chin. "Hmmm, do I like your gown? How can I find the right words?"

"Well, if it's that difficult . . ." Claire said, vowing she would not beg for a compliment. She looked away.

He reached out and chucked her under the chin, tipping her face up so she'd look at him. "There isn't another woman in that room who holds a candle to you tonight. You're simply breathtaking."

Claire hadn't expected him to be so articulate. "That is the nicest compliment I've ever heard."

"Would you like to dance?" Billy asked.

"I would like it very much, but first I must go to the powder room. Will you wait for me at the refreshment table?"

She watched him walk away from her before she turned and went upstairs.

Once in the powder room, Claire fanned herself. Being close to Billy made her skin flush. She looked around for the attendant, who wasn't in the room. Thankfully, she was alone, so no one could see how flustered she was. It was the perfect time to take another dose of her medicine. Just a little precaution so she didn't start coughing, she kept telling herself. She giggled as she moved over to a special drawer in the bureau. She felt like a little girl about to do something forbidden and she giggled again and then promptly pressed her fingers over her mouth.

"Shhtop it," she warned herself sternly. Then she retrieved her brown bottle and took a sip. She could not have a coughing spell and ruin the magical evening. She took one more sip for good measure before replacing the bottle safely back in the drawer.

Feeling absolutely wonderful, she made her way to the ballroom where she stood just inside the door and scanned the crowd for Billy. She had the misfortune of spotting David instead.

He stood between Lucy and Mary Ann, and they were both laughing at what he'd just said. Then Lucy gestured toward Claire, and David turned and looked her way. He nodded, abruptly taking his leave of the other two women, and hurried toward her.

Claire felt the color drain rapidly from her face. She did not need this. Not tonight.

Her festive mood of a moment ago vanished. David looked every bit the gentleman tonight, but then David had always been the perfect gentleman. Funny, until this moment, she'd never realized how silly he looked. Just like a pompous peacock.

Claire's head swam and she felt light-headed. She wondered why, and then decided she didn't care because the woozy feeling gave her the courage to stand her ground and not flee the room just because David was present.

"Claire, my dear, you do look lovely tonight," David said as he placed a meaningless kiss on her cheek and reached for her hand.

"Thank you," she managed to say without stammering.

"I must admit that I'm surprised you are making such an arduous trip, considering your condition."

"Please do not mention my condition again," Claire snapped and yanked her hand away. "I have told *no one* outside of the family, except you, of my condition, and I trust you to keep my confidence."

David nodded.

"I understand. But could the doctor have been mistaken in his diagnosis? You look anything but sick tonight. You're quite beautiful."

"You act surprised," Claire returned archly. The cad had a smooth tongue, butter wouldn't melt in his mouth. She just looked at him, wondering if he would change his mind about her if she were to tell him that the doctor had indeed been mistaken. Would he tell her he'd made a mistake and still want to marry her?

As she gazed into David's eyes, she saw him in a

new light. She saw him for what he was . . . shallow. What a shame she'd never seen it before. He'd never loved her as a person. He'd loved her as one would a trinket, something pretty that he could show everybody.

"There is no mistake," she said.

"I see," he returned, stiffly. "I heard you were traveling out West. Do you think that wise?"

"Why wouldn't it be?" she fired back, growing more irritated by the minute.

"Well, you know—" David stammered, looking extremely uncomfortable.

He still couldn't talk about her sickness. It was as if it were an issue that he couldn't accept. "I've done many things that were not wise, but my trip isn't one of them," she said.

Irritation shone in his dark eyes. Good, she thought with satisfaction. He understood her sentiments exactly.

"I'm sorry if I hurt you, Claire, but I couldn't marry you. I'd get used to having you around, and then you'd be gone."

Wonderful! Now he was pitying her. Claire could feel unbidden tears stinging her eyes. "I would so hate to inconvenience you."

David reached out and touched her arm, but Claire shrugged him away. "You're upset," he said. "In time you'll get over me."

She thought with fearful clarity that she'd almost married this cad standing in front of her. She had already gotten over him. However she did need more time to get over the embarrassment of ever believing she had been in love with him in the first place. David needed to be taken down a notch. She longed to slap the smug expression off his face, but instead she decided a good barb would work just as well.

"I already have."

Billy had just taken a bite of a small cake when his gaze settled upon Claire. Some dandy had stopped her as she entered the ballroom, and she obviously wanted to get away. Who was the man that kept reaching out and touching her arm? Whoever it was, the look on her face told Billy that the man was upsetting her.

"Hello, Mr. West," a female voice sounded from behind him. He turned and was relieved to see it wasn't Lucy. "Do you remember me?"

"Yes, I do. The lady from Claire's publishing house."

"That's right. I'm Ann, Claire's editor."

"I'm pleased to see you again," Billy said with a frown.

"Then why are you frowning?"

Billy nodded toward Claire and the dandy. "That fellow over there seems to be upsetting Claire."

"Where?" Ann turned to see where Billy was looking, "I was looking for her so I could say good-bye before I left," Ann said as she spotted Claire. "That's David Ader. No wonder she's upset. She and David were once engaged. I don't know what she ever saw in the man, but I'm glad he broke it off. He's so shallow."

So that was the fool, Billy thought. "She looks none too happy to see him."

"Can you blame her? He humiliated her in front of all her friends. Perhaps we should rescue her."

"I'm with you," Billy said.

"Claire," Ann said when they reached her friend. "I'm afraid I must leave, and I want to say good-bye." She spared a brief glance for David. "David," she said curtly, and then she turned back to Claire. "I look forward to your first article." Ann touched Billy's arm. "I'm sure you'll be safe in Mr. West's company."

"I should have known that you were encouraging her," David snapped, glaring first at Ann and then Billy.

Billy knew he didn't like the son-of-a-bitch right away. And Claire was so nervous it made him think that she still cared for David. Mixed feelings surged through him, and he had to fight the urge to punch David in the face.

Claire had never been so delighted to see anyone as she was to see Billy and Ann. She smiled brightly. "I'm looking forward to my adventure. I shall write you often and let you know everything that is going on."

"I'll count on that," Ann said. She embraced Claire warmly and whispered, "Take care of yourself, and remember, don't hold anything back. Ask for what you want."

Claire nodded, then watched Ann leave. A lump formed in her throat. She turned to Billy. She was afraid to trust her voice.

"Would you care to dance, Claire?" David asked, taking her elbow.

"I believe the lady has promised me the next waltz," Billy interrupted in his deep manly voice as he held his hand out to her. She pulled her elbow from David's grasp and took Billy's hand.

David shot her a look of furious contempt as she

took Billy's hand. David didn't want her, nor did he want anybody else to have her. He looked at Billy. "Who are you?"

"Does it matter?" Billy swept Claire into his arms.

The music seemed to surround Claire as she whirled about the ballroom. Now that she was away from David, she began to relax. She was amazed at how smoothly they glided around the dance floor. Having taken so much laudanum, she felt as though she were floating in a dream as the music drowned out everything around her. All she could see was Billy. She didn't realize just how strong that medicine was, but she was fully aware of Billy, his warmth, his strength, his masculine essence. Something within her glowed.

Looking into Billy's eyes, she said with a smile, "You dance divinely, sir."

"You mean, for a cowboy," Billy said with a smile as his arm tightened on her waist.

"You don't look much like a cowboy tonight. As a matter of fact you are quite dashing, but—" Claire's voice was shakier than she would have liked.

Billy arched a brow. "But?"

Claire gave him a sly smile. "I like you better in your ordinary clothes because that's who you are," Claire told him, the effects of the strong medicine making her speak her mind without holding back. His strong arm fit around her waist snugly, and Claire could feel his taut muscles beneath her fingers. He tightened his hold, and she figured that Billy had liked what she'd just said.

His gaze lazily appraised her. "I don't pretend to be other than I am."

"I know," she said in a breathless whisper, and then she stumbled, but his tight grip kept her from falling, and once again he pulled her closer . . . much closer than was proper. Claire became extremely conscious of Billy's virile appeal.

"Are you all right?" There was concern in his voice. "You can't possibly be tipsy."

"I'm just a wee bit dizzy," Claire said, fanning herself with her hand. "Do you mind if we step out on the veranda for some fresh air?"

"Not at all," Billy said as he took her elbow and guided her through the double glass doors that led to the veranda. They drifted toward the far corner where a large tree limb swept down over the porch.

The air was just a bit crisp, and the breeze felt good on Claire's skin. She turned to face him. "This is much better. Thank you."

Billy leaned against the white rail, seeming quite at home there. "Mind if I smoke?"

"No."

He reached into his pocket and withdrew a cigarette he'd evidently rolled earlier. She studied him as he struck the match and bent his head to light the tip of his cigarette. Then he straightened to his full height and blew out a breath of white smoke. It formed a little ring as it drifted through the air. Billy West looked so powerful and strong in his black jacket. Nothing like the dandies she'd known around New York.

Billy's brows lifted a fraction. "Something wrong?"

The texture of his voice was so deep, so rich, that she could listen to him forever. And at the moment all she could think of was kissing him. Of course, she couldn't tell him that, so she said, "I like watching you smoke."

I like everything about you. She left those unspoken words hanging in the air.

"Glad that I can please, ma'am." Billy chuckled. "Are you ready to travel?"

She nodded. "Everything is packed and ready. Will you be glad to be going back home?"

Billy nodded. "You'll see why as we travel. The country out there is so wild, untamed, and simply beautiful."

Much like you, Claire thought. "Are there many people there?"

"In some places. Nothing like New York City. Sometimes you can go for miles without seeing a dang thing." Billy looked down at her and smiled. "And you definitely won't need a dress like this one out there."

"You don't like my gown?"

"On the contrary, you are very beautiful in it tonight, as I told you earlier," Billy said. He paused, and Claire could see hunger in his dark eyes. She tried to deny the pulsing knot that had formed in her stomach as his galvanizing look sent a tremor shuddering through her. "The color of your gown makes your eyes look like rare gems."

Her heart lurched madly as she tried to suppress all these new feelings that sent dizzying currents racing through her. He'd said that so seriously that she wasn't sure how to take it. Did he truly mean it? His bronzed features were so earnest and his voice had been so devastatingly honest that Claire found herself in waters she'd never ventured in before. "Thank you," she whispered.

A noise sounded behind her. She turned as David stepped through the open doors. He stopped and looked around.

Claire didn't think. She simply reacted and threw herself into Billy's arms, causing him to drop his cigarette as his arms instinctively came around her.

"What's this, sweetheart?" Billy asked. "A little forward, wouldn't you say?"

"David just came through the door. Please kiss me," she said, tilting her face upward toward him. "For just a moment, pretend that you care. At least, until he goes away."

Billy was stunned. He couldn't react. It was as if his dreams had come true. Here was the beautiful woman he'd been thinking of just moments ago exactly where he wanted her.

"Please," she begged when he didn't respond.

Her soft plea was Billy's undoing. He glanced down into her pleading, blue eyes. His arms encircled her, one hand rested in the small of her back, and then he whispered for her ears only, "It's my pleasure."

"Claire," David called from somewhere behind them.

Billy could not care less who was there as he succumbed to temptation and lowered his head. His warm lips covered Claire's and the rest of the world disappeared as he pressed against her yielding lips. She responded by parting her lips slightly, letting him seek the warmth and promise of passion as yet unleashed. He wasn't disappointed as her passion seemed to grow stronger.

His tongue plunged and caressed her mouth as he felt her fingers slide through his hair. God, she was sweet.

"Claire Holladay, you didn't wait very long before you threw yourself at someone else." David's accusing voice was closer.

Neither Claire nor Billy bothered to respond.

Claire had forgotten that this was supposed to be a chaste kiss to show David she was over him. She was so shocked at her own eager response to Billy's touch that she couldn't remember anything.

David who? her subconscious asked as reality slipped away through her fingers and in its place fiery passion burned deep in her, a passion that she didn't know she possessed until tonight. True she'd been kissed before, but never like this.

Nothing like this.

She didn't know that a man's touch could feel so wonderful.

Her hand shifted across Billy's back as her lips moved against his. She wanted to give him as much pleasure as she was receiving. She followed his lead and realized she was doing something right when he drew her closer and moaned.

He tore his mouth away from her, and she knew that she didn't want him to stop. He placed soft kisses on her throat until she heard herself moan as she dissolved right in his arms. She would have collapsed in a heap on the ground if he hadn't been holding her so tightly.

He lifted his head, and she felt as if she were staring at a dark sea of chocolate. His eyes were so dark and round. Claire thought she saw passion, but she wasn't sure. All she knew was that she felt a new kind of dreamy intimacy between them, something she'd never experienced before.

She felt for the first time something she'd never felt before, something she'd never expected to feel . . . regret that they had to stop. What scraps of sanity remained within her told her they couldn't start the long trip ahead like this.

This was a business relationship. Billy wouldn't even be here if he'd not been sent to do a job.

What was he thinking about?

Was he regretting the kiss? Was Billy as confused as she?

Claire couldn't tell by the serious expression on his face. He looked more like he was in pain instead of experiencing a pleasureful moment.

She hoped at least he'd enjoyed the kiss.

It was evident that one of them needed to say something, so she started. "Thank you."

Billy looked a bit confused. "Thank you?"

"For the kiss. I didn't want David to think that I was still pining over him when nothing could be farther from the truth."

Billy glowered at her. "So you used me?"

"Well I wouldn't like to think of it that way. It was quite enjoyable," Claire said. She cocked her head to the side and smiled. "Wasn't it?" He was acting peculiar.

"Don't you know?"

"Of course it was for me, silly," she said a little aggravated that he wouldn't answer the question. "But what about you?"

"Sweetheart, it was wonderful. Magnificent. Do you think we convinced David?" Billy's voice was so husky that Claire shivered, and then she realized that her arms were still wrapped around Billy's neck.

"Yes," she said in a breathless whisper. She felt Billy stiffen and something in Billy's expression had changed, a muscle flicked angrily at his jaw. What had happened? She let her arms slip down and stepped back away from him.

As Billy's senses returned, he realized that he

had indeed been used. It didn't matter that his mind had turned to mush and he'd jumped at the chance to kiss her. It was the fact that she wanted to make David jealous and Billy wasn't sure he liked knowing that small fact.

He wanted Claire to kiss him because she desired to . . . not to impress David, who she apparently still cared for, or she wouldn't have gone to all the trouble to convince him she didn't care.

And the thought that she did care for the pompous coyote was like throwing salt into a raw wound. The harder he tried to ignore the truth the more irritated he became. He was attracted to the lovely Miss Holladay. He'd admit that. Where in the past he had been able to resist such females, all this one had to do was ask in that soft voice of hers and he forgot everything else. He was both surprised by his behavior and angry with himself. He must remember he was no better than hired help.

His mouth spread into a thin-lipped smile just before he said, "I'm glad I could be of service to you. But don't you ever use me again, Claire Holladay or you'll live to regret it."

Claire watched Billy's back as he disappeared into the ballroom, leaving her all alone. She never realized that a simple kiss would make him so angry.

She didn't move for a long while as her jumbled thoughts replayed in her mind.

Billy was right.

She had used him and for nothing more than to save her pride. She had found pleasure and sadness all in the span of a few moments, and she ached to go back and undo the last few minutes.

But she couldn't, she thought as she moved to the door. This wasn't the best way to start her trip. What would tomorrow be like?

It would be a long trip with neither of them speaking.

Chapter Eleven

The next morning when Billy went downstairs, he expected to find Claire waiting for him in the foyer. Of course, he was learning that Claire didn't always do or act as he thought she would.

Last night was a perfect example. Hadn't she fallen into his arms and demanded that he kiss her? He couldn't predict what this woman was going to do next! And to further confuse him, she'd kissed him far more passionately than he would have expected from a shy virgin. She had used him for her own purposes. And as much as he'd enjoyed the kiss, the reason for it made him damned mad.

As Billy paced back and forth in the foyer, muttering to himself, Margaret joined him. She told Billy that Claire had taken the carriage with her luggage to the depot and would be waiting for him at the station. Then Margaret, who had tears in her eyes, excused herself, telling Billy that she'd be right back.

He felt sorry for Mrs. Holladay. It was difficult to

let her daughter go and he could see that she loved Claire very much. He wondered what it would be like to have a parent's love. Claire was so lucky. *But* she was also hardheaded. That brought him back to his anger.

Billy was still frowning when Fredrick joined him, smiling and clearly looking forward to the trip. Until he saw Billy.

"What's wrong?" Fredrick asked.

"Your cousin. Seems she has taken matters into her own hands and has already left for the train station without letting us know."

Fredrick rubbed his chin. "Maybe she thought that it would save you the trouble. You know women; they don't travel light."

"That's not the point, F. D.," Billy snapped. "I'm responsible for each of you, therefore I need to know where you are and what you're doing at all times. There will be no wandering off on your own. Have I made myself clear?"

Fredrick held up his hands. "Hey, you need to tell her that, not me."

Billy knew he was taking out his frustrations on Fredrick but he was there—*she* wasn't. "Rest assured that I will speak to the lady just as soon as I see her."

Margaret came back into the foyer with a basket of food on her arm. "I can see that you are both ready to leave. Here are some goodies to eat on your trip," she said as she handed Billy the basket.

"Thank you. I assure you this . . ." Billy held up the basket. "Will not go to waste. I'm surprised that you are not at the station."

"I have already said my goodbyes, as hard as they were," Margaret said in a tired sounding voice. "Claire didn't want any crying or carrying on at the station—not that I would have, mind you, but she didn't want to take any chances. My daughter is a very headstrong person, which you will find out once you get to know her."

"I'm already finding that out," Billy grumbled.

Margaret looked at her nephew. "Your visit has been much too short, my dear. You must not stay away so long."

"I won't," Fredrick said as he hugged her.

"And promise me you'll report on how Claire is doing."

Fredrick raised his right hand. "You have my word that I will give you a full report."

Margaret turned to Billy. "Now, Mr. West. . . ."

"Billy," he corrected.

Margaret gave him a smile. "Billy, then. It has been a pleasure to make your acquaintance. I shall confess that I feel much better knowing that you're looking after my daughter. I'm afraid that we've protected Claire far too much, but we've had our reasons. So please be patient with her and don't let her do anything foolish."

Billy smiled patiently. The entire family had given him instructions on how to handle Claire. And now her mother didn't want Claire to do anything foolish. This trip she was taking was probably the first of many foolish things Claire would want to do, and he wondered how he would be able to handle her. After last night, he knew he needed to keep his hands off the woman. She was much too tempting, though at the moment, he thought Claire could use a good spanking. But he wouldn't dare say so with her mother standing in front of him with trust in her eyes.

"She'll be safe with me," Billy promised.

Margaret folded Billy into a warm embrace, taking him by surprise. "You'll soon find out how special Claire is. If I could pick the perfect son-in-law, he'd be just like you."

Billy smiled, but thought to himself that she'd change her mind as soon as she found out that I have no money. Hell, he didn't even have a normal family. He had no idea what kind of people his parents were, and he'd learned a long time ago that he was better off not knowing. Anyone who'd throw his or her child away was rotten to the core as far as he was concerned. Billy could never give Claire the things that she was accustomed to, and he'd never ask her to live with less.

Whoa! How did his train of thought gallop down the road to marriage? It wasn't a road he was ready to travel with any woman, no matter how tempting she was. Especially not Claire.

"My goodness, young man. What a frown on your face. Is the idea of marriage that distasteful?" Margaret laughed.

"Now don't go marrying me off, Mrs. Holladay," Billy joked. "I'm just not ready yet."

Margaret reached out and squeezed his arm. "My dear, none of us are ever ready for marriage. Remember, the love we give away is the only love we keep. Love creeps up on us when we are the least prepared for it. But don't worry, marriage is the farthest thing from Claire's mind as well. So you're safe."

Billy flashed her a relieved smile. He liked this woman, and she really didn't have to worry. Her daughter would be safe with him—but was she safe *from* him—that gave Billy concern. "Is Mr. Holladay here so I can say goodbye?"

"I'm afraid Donald has already left for the city. He told me to convey to you that he was happy to have had you as a guest in our home, and that you're welcome to come back to visit us anytime. And. . . ." she paused, "as a token of our appreciation for taking care of our daughter, he has given you Firebrand. I believe you admired the horse yesterday?"

"No, ma'am. I can't take Firebrand." Billy shook his head emphatically. "He is a beautiful horse, but that is too much."

"Nonsense." She held her hand up to stop him. "We insist. Besides, Albert said since your little pinto has been in the stall near Firebrand, he's turned into a different horse. When you take your horse away the grooms are afraid that Firebrand will go back to his wicked ways."

"Thank you," Billy finally said, reluctant to owe so much to the Holladays. Of course, controlling their headstrong daughter might be worth two horses. He looked at Fredrick. "Do you have all your gear ready, F. D.?"

"Who?" Margaret asked.

"Yep, I'm ready," Fredrick answered Billy, then looked at his aunt to explain. "Out West they call me F. D."

"For heaven's sakes! Why?"

"It's a long story, Aunt Margaret, and we really must be going," Fredrick said as he hugged her one last time. "I'll write to you."

Aunt Margaret pulled Fredrick aside and whispered something as Billy turned toward the door.

Once outside, Fredrick glanced at Billy as they hurried toward the stables. "If my uncle gave you a horse, you've got yourself a real prize. He handles only the best horse flesh in the country."

"I know. Wait until you see the stallion," Billy said as they walked toward the stable doors.

When they reached the barn, Albert was leading Firebrand and Spot out of the stable. We have them all ready for you," Albert said at about the same time Heath walked out with Fredrick and Claire's horses.

"Obliged," Billy said.

"He's some horse," Fredrick said as he rubbed his hand down Firebrand's flank. The horse side-stepped. "He's a bit skittish."

"Not as bad as he used to be," Heath said. "Seems as if Billy has a way with horses."

Billy glanced at Heath. "Thanks for the compliment."

Heath grunted. "You just make sure that you take damned good care of our sister. Be gentle. Don't let her do anything foolish. If anything happens to her, you know who I'm coming after."

Two days ago, Billy would have been angry with Heath's remark. Now Billy realized that Heath was just being Heath. Billy stopped stroking Spot's muzzle. "A compliment and a threat. Both in the same breath. Should I say that I'll not miss you?"

Fredrick chuckled as he checked the cinch.

Heath chuckled also. "Now you have hurt my feelings."

"I'm sure you'll get over it," Billy said as he shook Albert's hand. "I really appreciate Firebrand. Maybe you can come out West and visit once I start my ranch?"

"It's very different from here," Fredrick offered. "But I think you'd both enjoy the wide open spaces."

"I just might do that," Albert said. "I'm going to sound like Heath. Be patient with our sister. She's special."

"Since I've now heard the same thing for the

third time this morning, believe me, I will give
Claire special care. I must admit that I've never
seen such a loving family. She will miss all of you,
I'm sure. However, Claire and I need to have a talk
and establish a few rules."

"Good luck," both her brothers said at the same
time, then laughed.

Billy mounted Spot and took the reins for
Firebrand. "Good to meet both—" Billy paused
and cut his eyes at Heath. "Well, at least one of
you."

"Go to hell," Heath said, and then he slowly
smiled. "Don't look too smug. I just might take a
trip West myself. Maybe drop by and see you."

"Just let me know that you're coming, so I can
be out of town," Billy said with a grin, then added,
"We better get going. Where is Willie? I want to say
goodbye."

"Willie went with Claire to the station," Heath
told him.

"I'll see him there," Billy said. "And I promise
I'll send your sister back safe and sound, if she
isn't happy," Billy said as he took up the reins and
pulled to the right to turn his mount. But the sad
look that slipped unknowing over Heath's and
Albert's faces surprised Billy. Did their sister mean
so much to them that they couldn't bear to see her
go away for a few short months? Strange, he
thought.

Claire had instructed the porter to load her luggage and told her driver to wait for Willie. Then
she sat down on one of the long wooden benches
that flanked the train platform. Aunt Ute sat be-

side her. She had already pulled out her knitting and was busy with the ecru-colored yarn. Willie sat at her feet, playing with her dog Floppy.

Since everyone was occupied, it gave Claire a moment to rest and think. This morning had been so busy taking the trunks out to the carriage and checking to make sure she hadn't forgotten something, she hadn't thought of last night at all.

She had thought that going ahead would be better for all concerned. And she'd kept her mother so busy there was no time for tearful goodbyes. At the same time, she wasn't looking forward to seeing Billy after last night. Waiting at the station gave her the time she needed to think about what she was going to say. She hoped Billy had cooled down by now. But she also knew that if he'd come downstairs to find that Aunt Ute and Floppy were also traveling with them, he would have made a scene. If she'd confronted him at home, the rest of her family would have joined in the fight, and she didn't want them any more upset than they already were.

She was an adult, as much as they'd coddled her, and she could handle her own battles. However, if she could avoid one battle, she would. She wasn't sure how Billy was going to react about anything this morning since he'd been so angry at her last night.

Last night . . . Claire sighed. If she closed her eyes and thought about his kiss, she felt warm all over. And she was pretty sure he had felt something, too.

David had ruined everything. She hadn't wanted to have that confrontation. Of course, she wouldn't have been kissing Billy if it hadn't been for David behaving like a fool. She sighed again as she watched the steam hissing out from under the locomotive. Billy was right, of course. She had used him, and she was not proud of the fact. But she'd wanted to kiss him long before David had walked out onto that veranda.

Perhaps, this morning she'd pretend that nothing had happened last night, and when Billy was in a better mood, she would apologize to him.

"You think Floppy will like riding on the train?" Willie asked in a sad voice.

"I hope so," Claire said with a smile. She hated leaving Willie since she'd been the one who always looked out for him, but she couldn't risk having him being left alone once she died. That wouldn't be fair to him. He would grow up thinking that all adults abandoned him. Maybe her brothers would take special care of Willie.

She looked around and wondered why it was taking Billy and Fredrick so long to reach the station.

Billy was quiet as they rode to the train station. Now that he was on his way, he realized that in these few days he'd come to like the Holladays. He would miss them. True, he wanted to return to his home, but he wouldn't have any strong objections if he had to bring Claire back home so he could visit again.

When he looked up, he could see the train station in the distance. They turned toward the cattle cars where the horses would be kept.

They dismounted and unsaddled the horses, choosing not to leave the care of their animals to others. Billy now owned some very expensive horseflesh, and he wasn't chancing their safety to some young kid who didn't know beans about them.

Billy led Spot in first, and then made sure that Firebrand was settled in the next stall. Fredrick followed and took care of his horse and Claire's.

They headed for the passenger platform. The station was a brown oblong building trimmed in white. There were four hardwood benches: two on one side and two on the other, and he could see several people seated and a few more groups standing around waiting to board.

"If we're lucky, this will be a smooth trip with no problems," Billy said. He glanced at Fredrick. "What did Mrs. Holladay whisper to you back there, and don't tell me it was to take care of Claire."

Fredrick laughed. "Nope. She was very disturbed by the name F. D. She said I should live up to my name instead of changing it. That people who respect the person will respect the name. And I guess she's right."

"Yeah, she does have a point. She seems like a smart woman to me," Billy said.

Fredrick looked up ahead of them. "Claire is probably wondering what is keeping us."

"It's good for her. She needs to learn some patience. Maybe then next time she'll let me know her intentions," Billy said. "I'm sure, as concerned as everyone is over her safety, the driver and Willie will not leave until we arrive." Hopefully, she's wringing her hands with worry, Billy thought to himself. Maybe it would teach her a lesson.

"When they reached the square platform behind the depot, Billy saw Claire sitting on one of the long benches. She didn't look in the least bit worried. As a matter of fact, she appeared contented. She leaned over, caressing a long-eared hound, and talking to Willie who was down on his knees, petting the dog.

She was the perfect refined lady, dressed in a dark blue traveling dress, he thought as he approached.

A rather large-boned woman sat next to Claire. Billy didn't recognize the woman, and assumed she was a servant from the house or possibly another passenger resting while they waited to board the train.

Billy stepped in front of the small group. All eyes shifted his way, but it was Claire's vivid blue eyes that Billy focused on.

"Good morning," Claire said in a chipper tone. "Did you sleep well? You look a little grumpy this morning."

"I slept fine," Billy said, his gaze never leaving her face. "It was when I woke up that the grumpiness, as you put it, set in."

"Really?"

Billy nodded.

"And why is that?" she persisted. "I would have thought that you'd be happy to be getting underway."

Billy felt his jaw tightening, and he had to keep himself from lashing out at her. She looked so completely innocent. "When I was informed that you'd struck out on your own, my mood went South fast," Billy clipped.

"For heaven's sake, why? I can't see that it is anything to get upset about, but apparently you do." She shrugged. "I thought to save you the trouble. As you can see," she waved a hand, "all my trunks have been loaded and I'm just fine."

Damned hardheaded woman. "Let's get one thing

straight. Where we are going, your life could very well depend upon you following my instructions and doing everything I say. Not heading off on your own."

She had the nerve to cut her eyes up to the sky and appear as if he were bothering her. "That may be true, sir. But I assure you that I am quite capable of taking care of myself."

Billy leaned over and looked her straight in the eyes. "Maybe I should make myself perfectly clear. If you wander off again without my knowing where you are going and when you'll be back, I will tie you to your seat and make your life damned miserable."

Willie tugged on Billy's breeches. "Are you angry at Claire, Mr. Billy?"

Billy glanced down at the child. "No. I'm just trying to get my point across."

"Billy is right," Fredrick added. "It's dangerous where we are going. It is nothing like this part of the country."

"You've made your point," Claire said as she got to her feet. "And I suppose that I'm sorry for saving you the time and trouble, if it will make you happy. We are ready to go."

"We?"

Claire turned that innocent expression on him again, which he was learning meant that she was up to something. "I must have forgotten to mention that my Aunt Ute will be traveling with me as well as my dog, Floppy."

The woman Claire spoke of slowly got to her feet. "So you're the young man that Claire has been telling me about."

"Wait a minute," Billy said. "This wasn't in the

bargain. I was supposed to bring one person to Denver."

"You don't think you can handle the task?" the bigger woman asked.

Billy straightened. At least the woman wasn't on eye level with him. "Of course I can."

"Then what is the matter? I assure you that I have traveled more than you, young man. I came here all the way from *Deutschland,* and can probably show you a thing or two. It isn't proper for a young woman to travel alone, as you should well know."

Billy had no doubts that the woman could take care of herself. Aunt Ute would make any man back up and cower in fear.

"And the dog," Claire added.

Billy felt as if he were being hog-tied. Floppy looked up at him. He didn't even bother to pick up his head; he just managed to arch his brows. The soulful look was so sad that Billy said, "All right, he can come."

Claire smiled. "Good."

"Bye, Floppy," Willie said with a pat on the head. He turned and looked up at Billy, then reached out his little hand. "I wish I could come with you."

Billy saw the tears gathering in the child's eyes. He ached for Willie and, worse, there wasn't a damned thing he could do about it. Reaching down, he helped Willie to his feet. "Come and take a walk with me."

Porters were rushing back and forth, pulling carts piled high with trunks and barrels. Boy, these people had a lot of stuff when they traveled, Billy thought. All his possessions were in a saddlebag.

Willie held onto Billy's hand as they moved away

from the others. He wasn't sure how he was going to handle this goodbye. True, he'd just met Willie, yet he felt a certain bond with the child.

"I sure have enjoyed getting to know you," Billy finally said.

Willie sniffed. "Me too." Without warning Willie stopped and wrapped his arms around Billy's legs. Willie's voice quavered. "I like you—you're different."

Billy scooped Willie up in his arms and hugged the child. He could feel the small arms around his neck, hanging on for dear life. Willie sniffed.

Billy felt as if his heart was breaking as he said in a tight voice, "I like you too." This was harder than he thought it would be. Billy took a deep breath, and set Willie back on his own feet.

Billy knew what he must do.

Take A Trip Into A Timeless World of Passion and Adventure with Kensington Choice Historical Romances!
—Absolutely FREE!

Enjoy the passion and adventure of another time with Kensington Choice Historical Romances. They are the finest novels of their kind, written by today's best-selling romance authors. Each Kensington Choice Historical Romance transports you to distant lands in a bygone age. Experience the adventure and share the delight as proud men and spirited women discover the wonder and passion of true love.

4 BOOKS WORTH UP TO $24.96— Absolutely FREE!

Get 4 FREE Books!

We created our convenient Home Subscription Service so you'll be sure to have the hottest new romances delivered each month right to your doorstep—usually before they are available in book stores. Just to show you how convenient the Zebra Home Subscription Service is, we would like to send you 4 FREE Kensington Choice Historical Romances. The books are worth up to $24.96, but you only pay $1.99 for shipping and handling. There's no obligation to buy additional books—ever!

Save Up To 30% With Home Delivery!

Accept your FREE books and each month we'll deliver 4 brand new titles as soon as they are published. They'll be yours to examine FREE for 10 days. Then if you decide to keep the books, you'll pay the preferred subscriber's price (up to 30% off the cover price!), plus shipping and handling. Remember, you are under no obligation to buy any of these books at any time! If you are not delighted with them, simply return them and owe nothing. But if you enjoy Kensington Choice Historical Romances as much as we think you will, pay the special preferred subscriber rate and save over $8.00 off the cover price!

We have **4 FREE BOOKS** for you as your
introduction to
KENSINGTON CHOICE!
To get your FREE BOOKS, worth up to $24.96, mail
the card below or call TOLL-FREE 1-800-770-1963.
Visit our website at www.kensingtonbooks.com.

Get 4 FREE Kensington Choice Historical Romances!

♡ **YES!** Please send me my 4 FREE KENSINGTON CHOICE HISTORICAL ROMANCES (without obligation to purchase other books). I only pay $1.99 for shipping and handling. Unless you hear from me after I receive my 4 FREE BOOKS, you may send me 4 new novels—as soon as they are published—to preview each month FREE for 10 days. If I am not satisfied, I may return them and owe nothing. Otherwise, I will pay the money-saving preferred subscriber's price (over $8.00 off the cover price), plus shipping and handling. I may return any shipment within 10 days and owe nothing, and I may cancel any time I wish. In any case the 4 FREE books will be mine to keep.

Name_____

Address_____ Apt._____

City_____ State_____ Zip_____

Telephone (____)_____

Signature_____

(If under 18, parent or guardian must sign)

Offer limited to one per household and not to current subscribers. Terms, offer and prices subject to change. Orders subject to acceptance by Kensington Choice Book Club.
Offer Valid in the U.S. only.

KN113A

Chapter Twelve

Willie stared up at Billy, his brown eyes brimming with tears. They were so trusting, so young, and God knows the child needed someone. It was as if Billy could see himself in Willie, and that made his heart ache.

Billy touched the top of Willie's head. "Do you think that you'd like to live with me?" he asked.

Willie eyes widened, and the puddled tears slipped unchecked down his plump little cheeks as he cautiously asked, "Are you funning me?"

"Nope," Billy said with a shake of his head. "I'm dead serious."

"You mean you want me to work for you?" Willie asked.

"No. I want you to be part of my family, seeing as you don't have one of your own. I kind of grew up the same way as you, so I figured we should throw in together."

"Really? You'd be my pa?"

Billy wasn't sure he was ready to be a father. He

hadn't thought that far ahead. Hell, he hadn't even thought about getting married. But he had to give Willie some kind of safety to hold on to, so he thought of a compromise. "How about brother?" he suggested.

Willie wiped the tears from his cheeks with the palm of his hands. "Brother," Willie tested the word. Slowly he smiled, his forlorn face brightening. "I'll work hard, you'll see. You won't be sorry."

"Never figured I would be," Billy said. "If you want, I'll take you with me and you can meet the rest of our family. They're all just like you and me. None of us had any parents. Besides, I'm going to need somebody to take care of Floppy and Spot. Now that's a big job. Are you up to it?"

Willie grinned. His eyes shone bright with happiness as he motioned for Billy to lean down. When he did, Willie threw his arms around Billy's neck. "I love you, Billy. I really do. You won't be sorry."

"I love you, too," Billy told him, realizing he'd never said those words to anyone. He ruffled Willie's brown hair. "Welcome to the family. And you're not a hired hand, so you are not expected to work for your keep every minute. Your duties will be like everyone else's. Now I'd better go and buy a one-way ticket for you."

Willie's brow furrowed. "I don't have any money," he said.

Billy gave him a smile. "You don't need any money, Willie. You're family now. I'll take care of it."

As soon as Billy had walked off, Willie ran over to Claire. "I'm going to get to go, too, Miss Claire. Me and Billy are going to be brothers."

"That's wonderful, Willie," Claire said, delighted. Then she leaned down and hugged the child. It seemed that Billy West was full of surprises. Who would have thought that a rough cowboy would take a child under his wing? Claire's heart swelled with happiness. She had taken care of Willie while he was at the stables, but with her leaving, there would be no telling what might have happened to him. Willie would have a chance now, with Billy to guide him.

"Floppy wouldn't know what to do without you to take care of him," Claire said as steam began to hiss from beneath the train's engine.

"All aboard," the conductor called.

"Shall we go?" Claire said.

"Not without Mr. Billy," Willie said. "He's getting my ticket."

Billy had just left the ticket counter, when he stopped and looked at the group sitting on the bench. He could do nothing but stare at his small group. While he'd been sent to bring back one person, he now had Claire, her big German Aunt, and a hound that was moving as slow as molasses, and last, but not least, Willie. And of course, Fredrick.

Billy gave a half-smile. He couldn't believe he'd just adopted another brother.

How had things gotten so complicated?

Hell, he didn't know why he hadn't asked Claire's brothers to come along, too, and then they could all be one happy traveling family.

Hell. Billy shook his head. What was done was done.

"All board," the conductor called again as the large coal locomotive steamed and hissed as if it were impatient to be on its way. The coal smell from the engine floated in the air along with a few cinders. As Billy looked at the train, he couldn't help thinking this was the future. One day, the train would replace the stagecoach line.

When Billy reached the group he said, "Let's get this trip underway." He glanced down at the dog. "And that means you've got to get on your feet, Floppy." When the dog did nothing but look at him, Billy looked at Claire and arched a brow. "He does move, doesn't he?"

"Of course," she said but she looked at the dog as if she had doubts. "Floppy is just thinking about what he wants to do. He likes to weigh his options."

Willie ran over and grabbed Floppy's leash and pulled on it. Again, Floppy raised his eyebrows, but nothing else moved. "Come on boy, we've got a new home. We're going to be together forever."

Great, Billy thought. I've got to ride herd on a finicky woman, and now her pet who doesn't take instructions any better than she does.

Evidently, Floppy had finished weighing his options because he finally moved. Or maybe Willie had managed to jerk him up onto his feet.

"See," Claire said. "It just takes him a little while." She stood and followed her pet. Butterflies fluttered in her stomach. This was the biggest thing she'd ever done in her life. She was now on her own, and she was going to make the best of it no matter how scared she was. Besides, what did she have to be frightened about? The worst thing that could happen was she'd die a little earlier than expected.

What little future she had lay ahead of her. She was both happy and sad as she realized she would never see her family again. She shoved those thoughts to the very back of her mind, knowing that she was doing the best thing for all of them. Her family needed to remember her the way she was now: living and breathing. She did not want them hovering over her when she took her last breath.

Claire felt someone behind her. Then she heard Billy whisper, "Change your mind?"

She jumped. She hadn't heard him coming. She took a deep breath to compose herself. Finally, she turned and smiled. "Not on your life, Billy West. You're stuck with me all the way to Denver."

Her remark left Billy speechless.

"Come, Claire," Aunt Ute said before disappearing into the train. "I am very ready for this adventure. We will see things we've never seen before."

"All Aboard," the conductor called from the bottom of the steps. He was dressed in dark blue with a big bow tie and brass buttons with gold braid to match the buttons, and he looked very official.

The group started toward the passenger cars, where the conductor had placed a small wooden footstool on the platform.

Claire stepped up and entered the car. She stopped when she reached the top step and turned back to look at Floppy, who had stopped and was seated on the platform beside Willie. "Come on," she called to her pet.

The dog looked up at her as if she were absolutely crazy.

"It's a bit high for Floppy," Claire concluded, and looked hopefully at Billy. "Floppy might need a boost. Maybe I should come back down and help him up."

Billy held up his hand. "Never mind," he said. "I'll get him."

"Need some help? Fredrick asked."

"I think I can manage one flea-bitten hound by myself. Go ahead and get our seats," Billy said then turned his attention back to the furry nuisance. "Come on, Floppy. Put your feet on the step," he instructed as he patted the stool.

Floppy raised one brow, but nothing else moved.

"He must be weighing his options again," Billy muttered.

"A little cooperation would be nice," Billy told the dog, who must have understood him because Floppy finally moved toward the stool, stumbling on his ear when he stepped on it, but instead of stepping up on the stool he bent down and sniffed Billy's hand.

"Come on, Floppy, it's easy," Willie said as he stepped up on the stool. "See, just like this." He climbed into the railcar.

"Jump!" Billy commanded in what he thought was a very firm voice.

Floppy rolled his eyes up at Billy, but didn't budge an inch.

"He doesn't jump," Willie explained.

"Apparently, Floppy doesn't do much of anything," Billy grumbled. He'd had enough. He reached down, wrapped both arms around the fifty-pound hound and lifted him into the car. "You could have done this yourself," he told the ball of fur who gave Billy a big lick across his cheek.

"Basset hounds are a bit different from other dogs," Claire said as they moved down the aisle.

"How so?"

"They have to weigh their options."

"What in the hell is that supposed to mean?" Billy asked.

"Your language could improve," Aunt Ute reprimanded from her seat.

Claire turned around and looked at him before she took her seat. "They don't get in a hurry, they don't fetch, and they don't jump. And they are very adept at playing dumb," she said.

"So what good are they?"

Claire sat down and smoothed out her skirts. "They are bred for hunting rabbits as long as you're not in too big of a hurry. But they are lovable. Just look at those big, brown eyes." She rubbed Floppy's head as he settled by her feet. He did look up at Billy, and gave him a 'don't-you-love-me?' look. "You'll see, once you and Floppy become friends."

Billy arched an eyebrow. "I don't think so. But I can see how he got his name."

Willie sat on the floor next to the dog. Billy and Fredrick took their seats facing Aunt Ute and Claire.

The car filled fast as the rest of the passengers came on board and found their seats. There were hushed voices all around them. A woman with four children was sitting on the other side.

"Tickets," the conductor called as he strolled the isle taking up tickets.

Aunt Ute handed him the tickets for everyone. "I believe you'll find the correct number, sir."

"Yup, everyone except the dog." The conductor chuckled. He's so cute we'll let him ride free. Where are you folks headed?"

"Missouri," Claire said, and then threw a question back at the conductor. "Have you been working for the railroad a long time?"

" 'Bout ten year," he said. "Why do you ask?"

Claire straightened in her seat, trying to look

professional. "I'm a reporter for *Harper's Weekly.* I'm going to write a few columns for the paper about traveling West. I'd love to ask you some questions later when you have the time."

"Sure thing. Name's Randall Carlson." He lifted his hat, then added, That is R-a-n-d-a-l-l," he spelled out the name. "We'll talk more later. You know it won't be long before you can ride the train clear to California. Now that will be one whale of a story."

"I agree," Claire said with a smile. Now she had her first article. Her editor would be pleased.

"Better get the rest of these tickets collected," Mr. Carlson said before he moved on.

Claire noticed that Billy was staring at her in a peculiar way. "What?" she asked.

"You knew all along your aunt was traveling with us, yet you never bothered to mention the fact to me," he stated, his tone challenging.

"You work for my uncle. I really didn't see the need for you to be informed about it. I am paying her way and she is a grown woman."

"Next time, let me be the judge of what I should or shouldn't know," Billy told her.

"Entschuldigung sir mir. Don't go getting excited, *junger Mann,"* Aunt Ute said, calmly. "I've traveled more than you ever will. You might even come to like me just a little."

"I don't dislike you—ah, Miss—"

"Just call me Aunt Ute like everybody else. *Ja?"*

"Thanks, ma'am. I don't dislike you, Aunt Ute. I don't even know you. It's just that I don't care for surprises. Surprises can get a man killed out there." He jerked his head in the direction of the head of the train.

Aunt Ute had taken out a handkerchief and was

wiping the soot off the window. When she finished, she looked at Billy, and said, "Since we are traveling companions, tell me a little about yourself."

The last thing that Billy wanted was to talk about himself. He didn't much feel like talking at all, but every eye of the small group seemed to look intently at him, waiting for his reply. And since this was going to be a long trip, he'd best be cordial. What was done—was done. And it still stung that Claire had made a point of reminding him that he was an employee. That was a point that he shouldn't forget.

"Not much to tell. When I'm in Denver, I pretty much work all the time, riding shotgun on the Holladay stages. How about yourself, have you been in this country long?

"*Ja*. About two years."

"What is Germany like?" Fredrick asked.

"There are many mountains where I come from. That is probably what I miss the most about my country."

Billy smiled. "Then you're going to like Denver. It's in the middle of the Rocky Mountains."

"*Ja*. So I've heard."

"I'm so glad that you came with me," Claire said as she put her hand on Ute's arm.

Ute glanced at her niece with affection in her eyes. "You needed me, so I came."

"Needed you?" Billy questioned.

Claire realized that her aunt had slipped. "It's improper for a lady to travel alone."

Billy stared for a moment before he said, "There isn't much propriety out where we're going."

A few cinders flew in the window accompanied by the strong smell of smoke. Claire started to answer, but began to cough instead. Drawing out a dainty white handkerchief, she held it to her mouth as the bout of coughing continued.

Efficiently, Aunt Ute drew out a brown bottle of medicine and gave it to Claire who promptly took a swig then crinkled her nose. She coughed a few more times then said, "Water."

Billy reached down and retrieved a canteen from beneath his seat, thankful that he'd filled the thing before the trip began. "Here's some water," he said as he handed her the canteen.

"Thank you."

When she had finished drinking and her coughing had stopped, Billy said. "Your cough doesn't seem to be getting better."

"Actually it is," Claire lied. "The doctor said it would take some time for the cough to go away completely. And the ash from the steam engine tickled my throat."

"I see," Billy said.

The way Billy was staring at her, Claire didn't think he believed a word she had said, but he'd have to accept what she said until—or if—she was willing to tell him the truth.

Everyone grew quiet as the train got under way and the countryside rolled by the window, giving Claire her last glimpse of New York. She hadn't allowed herself to think about what had happened between her and Billy last night. She was so confused it gave her a headache. Why couldn't she have met Billy as a normal person? Someone with a future.

She wouldn't allow herself to fall in love with him, but she was going to experiment with her feelings. As Ann had pointed out, she needed to experience life and not have any regrets. Claire didn't think that she'd ever regret kissing Billy.

And she most certainly didn't want to die a virgin after saving herself all this time for a future husband . . . that she knew now she'd never have. She wanted to experience the physical side of love, if only for a little while.

"Fredrick, where is Claire?" Billy asked as he watched Fredrick splash water on his face, a ritual usually done in the morning. However, it was way past noon.

"I'm not sure," he said as he reached for a hand towel. "I've been playing cards in the smoking car."

"I can tell you've been doing something," Billy said sarcastically. "You're supposed to help me keep an eye on Claire."

"Yeah, I know." Fredrick finished drying his hands. "But what can happen to her on a train? She's a grown woman. And I know for a fact that she hates having people watch over her all the time."

"I don't care what she hates. I was hired to bring her back to Denver safely. Once she gets to Denver then she can do whatever she wants, but until that time, I need to know where she is."

"Do you want me to look for her?' Fredrick asked.

"No. I'll find her. Go back to your cards or, better yet, get some sleep. You look like hell."

Fredrick started to go, then turned and said, "She's probably interviewing someone."

"No doubt," Billy snapped as he started through the passenger cars. It seemed as though Claire had interviewed every damned person on the train. It was dusk when Billy left the second car and was headed for the third when he came face to face with Claire. She paused on the small platform that linked the swaying cars.

"Where are you going?" she asked.

"If I had been going someplace, I would have let you know where I was going," Billy snapped, then added. "If I could have found you, that is."

Claire could see that Billy was angry. She also realized this was the first time they had been alone since they'd boarded the train three days ago. She looked at him and tried to read his thoughts, but she could see nothing. "I think you are trying to make a point here," she said with a smile.

"Damned right! What have I told you about letting me know where you are going?"

"If I had been leaving the train, I would have. But how far can I go on a train?" Claire laughed. The man got upset over the least little thing! "I finally got a chance to interview the conductor," she said, hoping Billy would understand.

His expression didn't change one bit.

"I have a job to do," she said, "and I'm going to tell you that I'm through having people telling me what to do every minute of the day. I am an independent woman, and I can look after myself. And that includes you!" She poked him in the chest.

Billy grabbed her wrist. "You can be as independent as you'd like, Miss Holladay, once I deliver you safely to Denver," he growled. "But until that time, do not push me, or I'll—"

"You will what?" Claire asked, glaring up at him.

Billy heard her challenge but somehow his eyes were focused on her lips . . . those soft, pouty lips that he remembered all too well. "Or I'll—," he started his sentence again, but never finished it because the train lurched and Claire tumbled into his arms.

If he were anything close to a gentleman, he'd set her up straight, and get the hell out of there. Instead, he pulled her closer.

Claire did nothing to stop him.

Damn it all, she could, at least, slap his face or something.

But she didn't.

And he seemed powerless to resist as he lowered his mouth to temptation.

Just as his mouth closed over hers, he heard a small sigh from Claire as if she'd been waiting for him to kiss her all along. Her arms went around his neck. The fact that she'd wanted this kiss just as much as he did should have sent alarms off in his head.

But Billy West wasn't thinking with his head.

Hot pleasure coursed through him. He parted Claire's lips, sliding his tongue inside to explore her sweet mouth. Passion radiated from the core of her body. The thought barely crossed his mind before an unwanted picture of Claire in David's arms entered his mind. He didn't like that picture. Had she been passionate with that stiff-shirt? How could she have been?

Billy's mouth plundered hers causing her to shiver as she collapsed against him. He wanted to wipe out all thoughts of another holding her. Damn the others. His was the only kiss she should ever remember.

Claire felt weak all over as she experienced the most wonderful sensations, much like she had the first time Billy had kissed her. Billy shifted. His mouth moved in a different direction as he began to kiss her neck, slowly, and softly. His tongue moved slowly up her neck to flick at her ear lobe before he kissed her ear, softly.

Claire felt as if she'd just melted into a puddle of water and if Billy hadn't been holding her, she'd surely have fallen off the platform and onto the tracks. She was a little shocked at her own eager response.

"Oh, Billy," she said in a breathless whisper. "You don't know what you do to me."

"I can imagine," he murmured in her ear making her shiver again.

His hand moved up to Claire's breast where he began to rub his hand gently, back and forth across the soft mound. A spurt of hungry desire spilled through her. She jerked at first, but then settled down when Billy started to murmur words in her ear.

The door opened behind Billy, jerking him to his senses. He pulled away from Claire with a curse.

"Oops," Fredrick said from behind Billy. "I see you found my cousin." Fredrick smiled like a child who'd been given a stick of candy.

Billy turned slowly keeping Claire behind him. He felt like punching Fredrick in the nose. "Yes, I found her," Billy snapped. "Is there something else you wanted?"

"No—No. I'll go back to the smoking car." Fredrick held his hands up in a gesture of surrender. "They are probably getting ready to start another poker game. Since I've rested, I'm ready to go again. Care to join me?"

"Fredrick!" Billy warned.

"I'm going," Fredrick said with a smile. "I can

see you have things well in hand." He turned to leave, but not before Billy heard him chuckle.

Fredrick couldn't have said anything farther from the truth. Billy didn't have anything in hand. As a matter of fact he felt as if his entire world were spinning out of control.

He should be pushing Claire away from him, not pulling her closer. Yet, as he gazed down at her, all he could think of was finding some private place so that they could continue what they had started.

"Billy," Claire said, making his name sound like a caress. "I want to apologize for using you at my party the other night. You were right. I was wrong."

Billy's gaze lingered on Claire's kiss-swollen lips. "You still care for that cad, don't you?"

"No. I did what I did out of pride. Not because I wanted to make David jealous, as you thought."

"So you're not trying to impress anyone this time?" Billy asked as he brushed a few strands of hair away from her face.

"Only you," she said in such a soft voice that he wasn't sure he'd heard her.

It was a good thing that they were not alone on this train. Billy thought, because he wanted this woman so much.

As he stared down into the wonderful blue depths of Claire's eyes, Billy realized that he should assure her that this wouldn't happen again.

But why lie?

Chapter Thirteen

The morning started off well enough, Claire thought, her mind still reeling from what had happened last night. And what had not.

They had just finished their breakfast in the eatinghouse. It was a routine that Claire was learning. The conductor called them Refreshment Saloons. Every fifteen miles, the train would stop, all the doors were thrown open, and the passengers rushed out and went straight to the Refreshment Saloon where tables were available for eating. The food was pretty good—pies, patties, cakes, hard-boiled eggs, ham, and custards. An hour later a bell would ring letting everyone know that the train was getting ready to depart.

Claire followed the others as they returned to their seats in the passenger car. Fredrick had gone back to get something from the sleeper car, and Willie rubbed his eyes sleepily as he settled into one of the seats next to Floppy. He curled up with the dog and went to sleep.

Claire glanced out the window while the rest of

her companions talked. Coal smoke drifted by the windows as the train rumbled down the track. She was used to the swaying of the train now, and she enjoyed watching the countryside as they passed through it. How much it had changed from that of New York! The farther she traveled from her home, the cruder the buildings outside became. The fine, silken dresses worn by the passengers in New York had also disappeared, she noticed when the train stopped in a small town. She supposed the women out here had no use for such finery.

Claire was determined to act as normally as possible today—as though Billy had never kissed her. She certainly didn't appreciate the silence he had maintained so far this morning. Was he always going to have regrets after they kissed?

At least he hadn't become angry this time. She wasn't too sure what she was doing wrong. Obviously, she wasn't doing something she should, or Billy wouldn't be so withdrawn. She would love to ask Ann, but of course, Ann was hundreds of miles away. Perhaps she wasn't very good at kissing and Billy was simply disappointed.

Something was certainly bothering him this morning, and Claire was sure he wouldn't tell her what it was, even if she asked.

She frowned. Ann had said to go after what she wanted, but Ann hadn't told her what to do if the man she wanted wasn't cooperating.

When she couldn't stand the stony silence any longer, she asked him, "How many days until we get to Independence?"

"Tired of traveling?" Billy asked, his brow raised with an I-told-you-so look. It was the first time he had spoken this morning.

"Did you sleep with a burr under the cover?"

Claire snapped back. "I was simply asking a question."

"I don't have any idea what you're talking about," he said.

No, you probably wouldn't, she thought to herself. Why were men so difficult to understand? Or was it just *this man*? Claire turned to Aunt Ute. "Tell him how grumpy he is this morning,"

Aunt Ute looked from one to the other. Something was going on between these two. She could see it in the way they looked everywhere but at each other. The funny part was they were not fooling her. She hadn't been born yesterday, and she knew physical attraction when she saw it. *Ja*, these two had it bad. They just didn't know it. "Maybe he doesn't know when we'll get there," she said.

Billy frowned at her. He must have thought she was criticizing him, Ute thought.

"We will be in Independence some time tomorrow," Billy replied. "From there, we will take the Overland Stage on to Denver."

Claire looked at him. "Let's hope that trip will be as pleasant as this one."

"It will be a little harder," Billy said, trying to soften his voice. He realized he'd been snarling at Claire and he really wasn't sure why, other than he'd gotten very little sleep. Every time he shut his eyes, her face floated through his mind, and he couldn't seem to stop it.

"It will be a lot more confining from that point on. We have plenty of room to walk around on the train. However on a stagecoach, there is nothing to do but sit and stare out the window."

"Will you be riding in the carriage or on your horse?" Aunt Ute asked innocently.

Billy's brow arched. "I'll probably ride to give

you more room in the coach. Or I might ride shotgun if I'm needed."

"Surely the stage will stop some," Claire reasoned.

"Billy didn't mean to make it sound like the
stage never stops. It stops every fifteen miles to
change horses, so you'll have a chance to get out
and stretch your legs," Fredrick supplied as he sat
down with them. "You're going to like the landscape once we board the stage. That part of the
country is very different from what you've seen so
far."

Fredrick and Claire continued talking about the
trip, so Billy tried to relax. He sat back. He was a
little worried about Claire. He hoped the dust
wouldn't cause her to cough more. Sometimes it
could be pretty bad even inside the stage.

Now was bad enough. She seemed to have a
coughing spell once or twice a day. Day before yesterday, she'd had such a bad spell that she'd had to
lie down. And it worried him. She had told him,
herself, that the doctor said she would be getting
better. If this was better, he wondered what it had
been like before. No wonder she was so pale and
thin. The woman needed sunshine and good food
that would stick to her bones. Maybe if he could
get her healthy she would survive the harshness.

He watched Claire as she talked to Fredrick.
Billy hadn't known Claire very long, but he had
known her long enough to know that there was
something exceptional about her, and the harder
he tried to ignore the truth the more it persisted.
Claire Holladay had come to mean something to
him. He just wasn't ready to explore what that
something was.

A noise sounded above Billy's head. He glanced

toward the roof of the car. Had he just heard foot-steps?

The train started to slow and then the engineer hit the brakes. The train hissed to a sudden halt, throwing the passengers forward. Claire landed in Billy's lap. Fredrick wasn't as lucky when Ute landed in his lap.

"What's happening?" Claire asked as she pushed her hair out of her eyes, and leaned back so she wouldn't be in Billy's face—the temptation to kiss him was too great.

"I don't know, but it isn't good," Billy replied. "Are you all right, Willie?"

"Yep, me and Floppy are fine, but what happened? And why is Miss Claire sitting in your lap?"

"Let me help you back to your seat," Billy said to Claire, both of them ignoring the child's comment.

Claire really didn't agree, but she knew she couldn't stay in his lap. She was, after all, a lady.

As she straightened her skirt she realized that everybody was chattering, wondering what could be wrong. She drew out her pad and starting jotting down notes.

"Are you thinking what I'm thinking?" Fredrick asked Billy.

Billy nodded slowly. "Be ready."

Claire didn't understand what they meant, but before she could ask, two men dressed all in black burst into the car. They had black handkerchiefs tied around their necks and their guns were drawn and pointed at the passengers. Children cried and women gasped as if they were going to faint.

"Sorry for the inconvenience, folks, but this here's a holdup, and we're here to relieve you of your coins and valuables. We expect your full co-operation. Put your coins and jewelry in the bag Bitter Creek's carrying 'round," the taller of the two said.

Billy recognized the tall one. He was Grat Dalton, one of the members of the infamous Dalton gang. After all these years, Billy recognized him. He was one of the gang that had done away with the gunslingers Billy had lived with. He should probably thank Grat because he would have probably turned into a gunslinger, too, if he'd stayed with the other men. He realized that they must have had at least an ounce of decency because they had let him live that day instead of shooting him, too.

But at the moment Billy wasn't in a thankful mood. His hand hovered near his gun.

Grat stood guard while the other fellow produced a small black sack and started down the aisle.

"Are you really train robbers?" Claire turned and asked.

"Well we ain't Sunday school teachers, ma'am," Grat replied.

"You don't have to be snide, sir," she informed him.

"Be quiet, Claire," Billy warned.

She glanced at Billy. "I will not." She turned her attention back to the man standing. "Mr.—"

"The name's Dalton. You'd best remember it."

Fredrick drew in his breath behind her. Claire wondered why. "As I was saying, Mr. Dalton. I am a reporter for *Harper's Weekly,* and I'd like to ask you a few questions for an article that I'm doing on the West."

"Jesus Christ, lady. We're trying to rob you,"

Dalton snapped. "Just put your valuables in the bag and shut up."

"It's very obvious that you are robbing us, but—" Claire stopped as the other man reached for her hand. She tried to jerk it back. "You can't have my mother's ring, sir."

Aunt Ute whacked Bitter Creek's hand with her umbrella. *"Dummkopfs."*

"Jesus," Bitter Creek swore and snatched the umbrella away, still holding onto Claire.

Billy jumped to his feet. "Get your hands off the lady, or I'll put a bullet through you."

Bitter Creek immediately dropped Claire's arm and pulled his gun, but Billy was faster. "Now why don't you both drop your guns?"

"Billy, you're going to get yourself shot," Claire fussed as she stepped out into the aisle and tugged on his sleeve. "You should sit down."

"Be quiet, Claire," Billy warned.

"I'm tired of hearing that," Claire snapped. After all, she was trying to save him. She could probably reason with the men. She'd promise them fame, and then they would forget about taking these good folks' money.

"If you'd just take a few moments to answer my questions." Claire stepped toward Dalton as she spoke. "It would help my article a great deal and make you very famous. What made you turn to a life of crime?"

Dalton jerked Claire in front of him. "Maybe you'll calm down now that we have your lady," he growled as he eyed Billy. "Drop your gun, or we'll put a bullet in her head."

Claire gasped. "You do, and you'll go to jail."

"Don't hurt her," Willie begged from the floor.

"Shut up, kid."

Billy really didn't see that he had a choice. He had no doubt that Dalton would carry out his threat. Reluctantly, Billy lowered his gun.

"Drop it," Dalton ordered.

Billy did, and Bitter Creek kicked the gun aside, then started backing up toward Dalton. "You could be in one of those dime novels, Grat."

"Maybe I'll talk to her," Dalton said. He sounded as if he were mulling over the idea.

Another man entered the car dressed just like the other two. "What the hell is taking you so long?" Bill Dalton said. "We've already busted open the safe." His gaze shifted to Claire. "Who's she?"

"Some reporter."

Billy took a step forward. "Get your hands off her."

"I don't think so," Grat said. "Maybe we'll get her to write a story about us. She may come in useful after all." He looked at Billy. " 'Sides, we need a little insurance that you are not going to follow us, 'cause if you do, you know what will happen to her," he said, jerking Claire off her feet.

"You mean, you are going to give me an interview?" Claire said as her hopes built. She could see her article in the magazine now. "Train Robbers and Why They Turned to a Life of Crime," by Claire Holladay.

"That's right, lady," Dalton said. He tightened his grip around her middle, almost cutting off her air supply as he pulled her backward with him. They inched their way to the door and backed out of the car and off the train. Dalton looked directly at Billy. "If anybody comes out that door in the next few minutes, we'll shoot her."

"Don't worry. He isn't serious," Claire tried to

assure Billy. She didn't want him to do anything foolish—like getting shot. "I'll be fine. I just need to get my interview." And with that she was gone.

Once they were outside, Claire demanded. "Could you please get that gun out of my back, sir!"

"Honey, you seem to be right bossy. You're our hostage now. You don't make demands."

"Hostage? No," Claire said, shaking her head. "That would mean that you're going to keep me. I'm just going to ask you a few questions, and then we can be on our way," Claire told them.

Bill looked at Grat. "She ain't from around here, is she?"

Grat just shrugged, then said, "Lady, we just robbed a train. And now you think we're going to stand around and chew the fat with you? You're plumb loco."

"Shit, lady you're coming with us," Bill Dalton said. "Throw her on a horse, Grat, and quit arguing with her. Time's a-wastin'."

"No. No. You can't take me!" Claire protested, suddenly alarmed. Now that she realized that they meant to take her with them, she began to struggle. "I need to get back on the train. My medicine is on the train."

Somebody slapped her on the face, hard. Claire was too stunned to react, so they shoved her on the horse, up in front of Bitter Creek, who wrapped his arm around her much too tight. She tried to scream, but his next words stopped her.

"You scream, and we'll have to gag you," Creek told her. "You know you're a right soft little thing. You just might provide a little fun."

Cold chills raced through Claire's blood. A little too late she realized that she was dealing with unreasonable men who were nothing like the men back home. Even common thugs at home held on to some shreds of decency. These men appeared to have none.

What had she gotten herself into? She wasn't afraid of dying. Pain, on the other hand, was something she had no tolerance for. She wasn't willing to go through hell before dying. And being tortured by these men would certainly be that.

How was she going to get out of this mess?

And then Claire knew the answer. Billy would come after her.

She took a deep breath. Now all she had to do was keep her wits about her and stay alive until he found her. How hard could it be to outthink these dull-witted men?

The woman didn't have a brain in her head, Billy thought with a pungent curse.

He sank down to the seat and tried to figure out what to do. He couldn't believe what had just happened. He'd lost the boss's niece! Hell, if he'd only just lost her, it wouldn't be near as bad. But he'd let her be taken by train robbers. And worse, he couldn't go charging after them for fear that they would kill Claire, and he didn't even want to think of what they could do to her before they killed her. His stomach felt like it had been tied in knots.

He had to do something. He had to reach her before it was too late.

"We must go after her," Aunt Ute insisted and headed up the aisle. "I'll get those *Dummkopfs* and make *Schnitzel* out of them."

Damn, Billy thought. Was everybody in the family plumb crazy? "Wait," he said, reaching for Ute's arm.

"What will they do?" Ute asked. "Is she in much danger?"

Fredrick answered. "Claire is with a bunch of ruthless outlaws, Aunt Ute. There is no telling what they'll do."

Ute fidgeted with her gray traveling suit as if she were nervous, then she looked directly at Billy, refusing to sit down. "What are you going to do?"

"If Claire had kept her mouth shut when I told her to, we wouldn't be in this situation," Billy grumbled as he raked a hand through his hair. And her aunt wouldn't be worried to death at the moment. He glared at Fredrick. It didn't help that Fredrick had painted the woman a real picture. "I'm going to go after them."

"How?" Willie asked from the floor. "Do you want Floppy to track her? He has a real keen sense of smell."

Billy would have laughed if the situation hadn't been so serious. He'd be lucky to get Floppy off the train under his own steam, much less give chase. "Thank you, Willie, but Floppy doesn't move fast enough. I have to get going so I won't lose the trail."

Billy looked at all the concerned faces and kept his next thought to himself. *I hope I can find where they have taken Claire.*

"I want you and Floppy to stay with Aunt Ute and continue on to Denver without me. I'll meet you there," Billy instructed.

Willie got to his feet. "But how will you find us?"

Billy turned to Fredrick. "You go to Mr. Holladay's office once you reach Denver, and explain what happened." He just hoped the hell that Ben wouldn't kill him when he got back. "He can arrange a place for Aunt Ute, Willie, and Floppy to stay until I get there."

Willie looked down. "He'll put me in some orphanage," he said dully.

Aunt Ute touched Willie on the shoulder, and he looked up at her. *"Nein,"* she said. "I will not leave you until Mr. Billy arrives. You will be safe."

Willie glanced back at Billy with a crestfallen look before staring down at his boots again.

Billy grabbed his hat. "I will find you; you'll not be alone anymore. Do you understand? You're never going to be alone again," Billy said over his shoulder as he headed for the door. Once there he stopped and looked at the child.

Willie nodded and gave him a small smile.

"Good. Fredrick, you are in charge," Billy said. "I'm going to fetch my horse. If I'm lucky, we'll meet up with you at the stage, but don't wait if we're not there. If it takes longer, we'll ride to Denver and meet you there." Billy put on his Stetson. "Fredrick, you can explain to Ben what has happened. And when Ben quits cussing, tell him I *will* bring her back."

Fredrick hurried behind Billy as he strode to the cattle cars.

They leaped up into the car, and Billy wasted little time finding his saddle and getting ready to go. While he was saddling Spot, Fredrick dropped the walkway for the horses to walk down.

"Are you going to take Claire's horse?" Fredrick asked as he wiped his hands on the back of his pants.

"No. Her horse isn't used to this part of the

country and would slow me down. I'll steal a horse when I find her," Billy said as he tightened the cinch.

"They hang you for horse thievery," Fredrick pointed out.

Billy smiled. "Not if it's thieving from outlaws."

Fredrick turned somber. "Do you think they'll kill her?"

Billy stopped. He felt those now familiar knots forming in his stomach at the thought. He turned from Spot and stared at Fredrick. "I don't know. She will have seen their hideout. I can't imagine them letting her go. But she is smart. If she keeps her wits about her, she'll be fine."

The train whistle blew, and Billy knew the engineer had cleared the tracks and was ready to get underway. He led his horse out of the car, then blew out a disgusted sigh as he mounted. "You'd best get back on the train before it pulls out. The train's way behind schedule as it is. Watch out for Willie, Fredrick."

"You can count on me," Fredrick said.

Spot was prancing, ready to stretch her legs, and Billy was anxious also.

Fredrick turned back toward the passenger car, but stopped and looked back over his shoulder. "Take care of yourself."

But Billy had already ridden off.

As Billy rode he kept his gaze on the ground as he tracked the bandits. Two of their horses were missing shoes, so that helped. It would slow them down some, and it would be easy to tell where they went if they crossed paths with other horses. He did take a brief moment to look up to the sky and say a small prayer. He was going to need all the help he could get.

* * *

Claire wasn't sure how long they had been riding. It felt like days. She was sore in places she hadn't even known she had, and she was real sick of this Creek person trying to squeeze her bosom every chance he got.

At the top of a hill, they paused for just a minute. Down in the valley, surrounded by trees, sat a small brown cabin, which Claire assumed must be the gang's hideout. She was so glad to see a place to stop, she almost cried with joy.

They rode down to the cabin after getting a signal from one of the gang below. The moment they stopped and Creek loosened his grip, Claire slid from the horse and immediately crumpled to the ground. Her legs had gone to sleep and offered no support. And worse, the dust she'd stirred up drifted into her nose and made her cough.

Crumpled in a heap on the ground, she coughed and coughed while she frantically went through her pockets, searching for the little brown bottle she always kept there.

"What's the matter with her?" Grat asked Bill.

"Damned if I know."

"Well, somebody drag her into the house. I'm ready for some grub."

Claire was still coughing as she tried to get the bottle out of her pocket. She managed to reach her handkerchief, just as she had a deep retching cough, and she held it to her mouth.

Creek reached down and jerked her to her feet so she couldn't get the bottle. When she removed her hankie from her mouth there were small specks of blood on the white cloth. It was proof that the cough had caused some of her lung tissue to hemorrhage. A long time ago, Doc Worden had warned her about coughing so hard. Claire took a deep breath and started to tell the man she needed her medicine, but before she could get the words out, she blessedly fainted and the world went black.

When Claire awoke, she was disoriented, having forgotten what had happened. Then everything came flooding back to her in a rush. She struggled to sit up on the small bed and managed to squeak out, "Water."

The three men sitting at the table turned. But no one moved.

"Please," she begged.

Grat got to his feet. "I'm going to get her some before she starts that hacking again." He walked over to the sink where he dipped some fresh water out of a brown wooden bucket. Moving back over to the bed, he offered Claire the dipper.

She took several sips of water, and it helped relieve her parched throat. "Thank you," she said, but his next words wanted to make her take them back. "Get some rope so we can tie her up," Grat said to Bitter Creek.

Claire knew she couldn't stand to be tied, so she had to think fast. "If you tie my hands, I'll not be able to write my notes about all of you. You do want to be in the magazine, don't you? Or maybe you don't want to be as famous as Billy the Kid?"

Thankfully, she saw their eyes brighten with interest. "We're twice as mean as The Kid," Grat informed her.

"Well, I'm sure no one back East knows that," Claire insisted. "I've seen lots written about Billy."

She paused so her words could sink in. She started to say article, but assumed that they wouldn't know what she was talking about. "Don't believe I've ever heard anything about the Duttons."

"That's Dalton, lady. And we're getting ready to tell you a thing or two," Grat said.

"At least tie her feet to the chair. She can sit at the table to write," Bill said.

"Who in the hell are you giving orders to?" Grat snapped at the other man. "Get off your ass and help me tie her."

Bill shoved back his chair. "Sometimes, Grat, this house ain't big enough for the two of us. If you wasn't my brother, I'd probably put a bullet in you."

Splendid! This was all she needed, Claire thought. She was very tired and grumpy as well. She didn't need any more fighting.

She pulled out the pad and pencil which she'd stuffed in her other pocket before they'd so rudely dragged her off the train. She also had a charcoal pencil. She placed the paper on the table, then ran her hands over it to smooth out all the wrinkles. When she was ready, she looked up at the three men sitting across from her. She wished her editor could see her now.

"Tell me something about yourselves," Claire said when no one volunteered to speak. It seemed the men had lost their voices and needed coaxing.

"Like what?" Grat asked.

"What did you do before you became robbers?"

Grat and Bill laughed and looked at each other.

"You tell her," Bill said.

Grat grinned and then said, "We were Deputy Marshals."

Claire couldn't hide her surprise and she chuckled. "You might say that you went from good to bad. But why? What made you turn your back on the law?"

"I don't know about that good and bad," Bill said, pursing his lips. "We like to think of it as going from poor to rich."

Claire jotted down her notes before looking up. "Other than money, was there something else that made you turn?"

"Yup," Bill nodded. "You might say it all went South when Grat, here, got accused of stealing."

Claire shifted her gaze to Grat. "And did you steal something?"

"Maybe a horse," Grat said with a grin.

"Isn't that a serious charge out West?"

"You're not exactly out West, yet." Bill pointed out. "Heard a city slicker once say that the Missouri River is the dividing line between the East and West. A man with a chunk of land on the East side is a farmer; on the West he is a rancher. A cow on one side is milked; on the other it's punched."

Claire chuckled. "I like that. I believe I'll write that down." She scratched a few notes on the paper, then looked up. "Now back to the story. Were you guilty of taking the horse?"

"Hell, yes," Grat stated. "But the law should carry special privileges," he justified. "Anyway, when they threatened to lock me up, I knew it was time to hightail it and look for another line of work."

"And you couldn't find work?"

"Sweetheart, robbing trains is hard work. Takes lots of planning, and it's right dangerous, too. Could get your ass shot off real fast," Grat said, then caught himself. "Sorry, ma'am."

"Thank you." At least she had them being polite. "Now can you tell me, what was the one job that you remember most?"

"Hey, you going to mention me? I'm part of this here gang," Bitter Creek protested.

Claire felt as if she were working with children. But she also knew that these were violent children. So she would have to make them feel that they needed her. "Of course I'm going to mention you. Tell me where you came from and how you joined the gang."

"Let's see." Creek rubbed his jaw. "Came from Fort Scott, Kansas. At the age of twelve I started working on a ranch."

"What about your parents?" Claire asked.

"Who do you think sent me out to work? Anyhow, I grew bored with working for nothing, and several years later I stumbled upon these two, and I kind of improved the gang. I got brains, you see." He tapped a grubby finger to his head.

"Are you finished?" Bill asked.

"Yup."

"Good. Now what our biggest job was . . ." Bill tapped his finger against the table and looked at Grat. He nodded. "Probably was our job that wasn't," he said with a chuckle.

"You'll have to explain that," Claire said.

Bill reared back in his chair, balancing on the back two legs as he prepared to tell his story. Claire assumed that this was going to be a good story by the way he was smiling.

"Somewhere around June, last year, we went to the Red Rock train station. We positioned ourselves and waited for the train to come along. When the train got to the station, the coaches were dark. It didn't look right, so we let the train go on unmolested. Suddenly, a second train appeared, and as it slowed at the station we boarded it and proceeded to rob it. Turned out to have a measly fifty dollars."

"Yep," Grat agreed. "But we was right to be suspicious of the first train. Heard later that it was full of loot to the tune of seventy thousand dollars."

"That must have made you sick," Claire said, not bothering to look up as she wrote. She had some good stuff here.

"Well it did and it didn't," Bill stated. "We come to find out, it did have seventy thousand dollars, but it was also full of armed guards, y'see."

"So that could have been the end of everything."

All three men nodded, but Bill said, "Like to have thought we'd out-foxed them, but we'll never know."

"Are you planning future holdups?" Claire asked.

"You betcha," Bill said. "We're planning to rob two banks in the same town at the same time. Ain't never been done before."

Claire didn't bother to hide her surprise. "When are you going to do that?"

"In a couple of days. We'll have to decide what to do with you first."

Claire laid down her pen. "If you hurt me, you will not get your story printed. It all starts with me."

Grat stood and looked down at her. "I guess we'll have to think about this problem and see what's worth having . . . gold or a story," he said, and this time he wasn't smiling. He was dead serious.

Claire didn't say anything. She just hoped that if

they killed her, they'd do it quick. She'd miss her last few months, but she wasn't going to be scared.

On the other hand, if she'd just keep her mind sharp and convince them that she could make the Dalton gang as famous as Billy the Kid, she might be able to wiggle out of this mess.

And in the meantime, she'd pray that Billy would find her.

But with every day that went by without Billy coming to her rescue, Claire's hope faded little by little.

Chapter Fourteen

Billy had ridden for two damned days.

It had taken him half a day to figure out that he'd taken the wrong trail, so he had to backtrack and pick up the tracks of the gang, hoping all the way that the trail had not grown cold.

Fortunately, it hadn't.

Billy was thankful Thunder had taught him to track, or he would have still been on the train, in a world of trouble from having lost the boss's niece.

Now as he sat atop Spot looking down into a craggy ravine, he knew he'd found the outlaws' hideout. The rudely built cabin was well hidden in the trees. Only someone well trained in tracking would have spotted it. There was an outhouse and a corral over to the side of the cabin, and he recognized one of the horses there as one he'd managed to glimpse from the train window.

Watching the small brown house, he couldn't see any movement, but that didn't mean they weren't there. Their horses were in the corral, so they had to be close. Billy counted five horses, which meant he was outnumbered. That in itself wasn't so bad, but he couldn't ride in firing for fear of hitting Claire, or worse, one of the Daltons might shoot her before Billy could get to her.

His stomach tightened into one large knot at the thought. His life used to be so simple. Strange, he hadn't felt this way in a long, long time. Hell, when you had nothing to live for, there was no reason to fear dying. And it wasn't fear for himself that he felt, but fear for Claire. Not knowing whether she was dead or alive was eating a hole in his stomach. If she'd only kept her mouth shut, none of this would have happened.

But then, that wouldn't have been Claire.

He reasoned that she had to be alive, but he didn't know if they'd molested or beaten her. The thought of all the things they could do to Claire made his stomach turn and his blood run cold.

Billy had lived with outlaws when he was a boy, and he knew full well that most of them didn't have a thread of decency. How many beatings had he suffered at the hands of drunken outlaws? More than he cared to remember. There had been times when he'd thought he would never be able to get up from the floor again.

Slowly, he drew out his Colt .45 and opened the revolving chamber to check the load. There were six bullets: one for each man and an extra, just in case. Grimly, Billy flipped the chamber closed and twirled it before replacing the gun in its holster.

He waited for the right moment. There wasn't much movement down below, and that gave him time to look over the compound. The first thing he needed to do was sneak down to the corral and get a horse for Claire. They wouldn't get far riding on one horse, not with the others hard on their trail. He just hoped she could ride with a western saddle instead of one of those fandangled, ladies' saddles.

He'd never seen any of that kind around these parts. Claire had brought her own sidesaddle but, of course, it was on the train. It wouldn't do her much good now.

Hell, if he could do nothing else, he'd throw her over the saddle and give her riding lessons later. One way or the other, she was coming out of there. Or he'd die trying to get her out.

Billy tied Spot to a tree, and then made his way to the corral. He moved very quietly so not to alert anybody in the house.

Once he reached the corral he glanced around. He was in luck—nobody was watching the horses. Evidently, they were not worried about somebody tailing them.

Looking over the horses, Billy selected a mare from the group, thinking it would be better suited for Claire. After saddling the horse, he left the gate open so the other horses could wander out. If he scattered them now, it would be the first thing the gang noticed once they came out. And he didn't want a gun battle. Claire could get hurt.

He led the mare back to where Spot was munching on grass and tied her. Already one of the horses had wandered out of the corral, looking for greener grass.

Now to rescue Claire.

Billy crouched low and made his way slowly down the hill. The cabin door opened and Billy froze. Two men came out dragging a big black Wells Fargo box behind them. They placed it a good twenty feet from the house.

"This is the damnedest box I've ever seen," one

of them muttered. "Maybe a few bullets will help open the cussed thing," the man said. Billy recognized him from the train. He thought he remembered the Daltons calling the man Creek.

"I'll go first," Creek said, then drew and fired at the box. The bullet ricocheted off the box, and both men had to duck to keep from getting hit.

Billy smiled at the idiots. He recognized one of the Dalton brothers. The cabin door opened again, and two more men shuffled out. "What in the hell are you doing, Creek?"

"Aim was a little off," Creek said. "I say, we try it again."

"Have at it," the other said.

While they were busy, Billy seized the opportunity to make his way down the hill to the back of the cabin. When he got there without incident, he breathed a sigh of relief. There was a window in the back, and it was half open. He smiled. Luck was on his side.

Now to rescue Claire, who was probably scared to death and wishing she'd listened to him, Billy thought. After he made sure she was safe, he'd make her beg for forgiveness to teach her a lesson.

Claire was exhausted.

The novelty of having a reporter around seemed to have worn off and the men were not as eager to talk to her as they once were. Even her freedom to move around the cabin was being curtailed. They had started tying her to a chair, and she could barely stand the confinement. And she hadn't eaten anything but a biscuit in two days. She was past the point of being hungry, but she couldn't bring herself to eat the filthy stuff her captors had offered her. Two more gang members had arrived, but they had left her alone, so far.

She had tried to convince the Daltons to release her, so she could get her story out to the magazine, but they wouldn't let her go.

Oh, they wanted their story told. Of that, she had no doubt. They had even let her sketch them, but they had indicated they were afraid that she'd bring somebody back to their hideout. She'd tried to assure them that was a most ridiculous notion. She wasn't even sure what state she was in, much less the exact location. Leading somebody back to this place would be an impossible task. However, she hadn't been able to convince them.

Claire thought they might be thinking about letting her go if she had many more of her coughing spells. But every day they said no. Creek had been eyeing her in a way that made her very uncomfortable for days, and she was beginning to think he might try something.

She had to get away.

At first, Claire had been certain Billy would come from her. But that hope had dimmed several days ago. Too much time had passed. If he were coming, he would have had plenty of time to find them by now. And the more she thought about it, the more she realized she had no idea how he could have possibly found her out in the middle of nowhere. It wasn't as if there were signs pointing the way. She didn't know how anybody knew where they were in this part of the country. It was all so empty.

The morning had started off like all the rest. After the men had tied her to the chair, Claire watched them take the strongbox outside. She felt completely helpless, but there was no one to help her, so she had to do something for herself. She struggled with the ropes binding her hands.

Bill stood at the door watching the other men, who were evidently shooting at something, Claire deduced from the sound. Now, while they were distracted, was probably her best chance to get away.

Somebody must be smiling down on her today, she thought as the ropes finally loosened from around her wrists. Now she only had one outlaw to contend with, and he wasn't paying attention to her as he watched the men outside.

Now was her chance.

She worked at the rest of the knots until the ropes fell away, and her hands became free. Bending over, she struggled with the ropes around her ankles and was finally rewarded for her efforts when the ropes came loose. She left them around her ankles to give the appearance that she was still tied.

Glancing around the room, she saw a partially open window. That was how she'd make her escape. She wasn't too sure where she'd go once she was free, but it was certainly better than sitting here and waiting to see what fate might bring her. After all, she knew what the worst could be.

The bullets were still glancing off the box, so Claire knew her captors were still occupied. Except for Bill. As if Bill could read her thoughts, he turned and looked at her. Apparently he didn't see anything suspicious, so he turned back to the excitement outside. After another minute, he succumbed to the temptation and joined the others out front.

Thank God, Claire breathed. She raised her eyes heavenward. Now was her chance.

Quickly, she kicked off the ropes and started for the window, but she stopped when she remembered her papers. Grabbing the papers and slipping them into her pocket, she ran to the window. There wasn't any way she was going to leave her article, not after what she'd been through to get it.

She took a deep breath and ducked through the half open window.

She was just about through when someone caught her and began to pull. Oh no! Had someone realized what she was up to . . . someone like Creek?

She opened her mouth to scream, but a hand covered it. So she did what any woman would do . . . .

She bit him.

"Shit!" Billy swore next to her ear. "You bit me."

"I didn't know it was you," Claire said defensively.

"Shh," he hissed. "I'm trying to get you out of here."

"It's about time you showed up!"

Billy looked at her as if she'd lost her mind. "Come on." He tugged her hand. "We've got to get out of here, before they discover you're gone."

The gunfire sounded in the background and covered their crashing through the leaves and sticks as they rushed through the woods. Billy hadn't let go of her hand as he dragged her behind him.

By the time they reached the horses, the firing had stopped.

"Hurry," Billy urged, grabbing her and shoving her up into the saddle. "You'll have to ride astride."

"I'm fine, thank you," Claire said, then snatched the reins from him. The sorry rascal hadn't even bothered to ask if she was all right.

Billy couldn't help but smile once he'd turned away from Claire. He liked her spunk, but he wasn't going to let her know it. "Follow me. The strongbox will only keep them busy for a little while."

He had no more gotten the words out of his mouth when the sounds of shouting drifted up to them from below. "The horses are loose! Somebody help me," Bill shouted.

"Let's ride!" Billy nudged his horse with his heels and they were off. He wished now he'd scattered the horses earlier. He wouldn't normally have been so careless, but this last week he felt as if he'd left his mind back in Denver.

He took the lead, and Claire followed as they galloped across an open field. Every time he glanced over his shoulder, Claire was right with him. She handled a horse better than most men. An odd feeling of pride stirred within him that she could keep up.

When they reached the other side of the field, Billy pulled up and looked behind them. He could see the tops of the outlaws' heads as they crested a ridge. "We're going to have to cut through the woods to lose them. Keep low so you won't run into any low hanging branches and get knocked off your horse."

Claire nodded and did as she was told.

As they raced through the woods, the trees seemed to be a blur. Finally they reached a stream. They galloped right through it. Then Billy swung back and retraced his steps into the river. He was glad to see that Claire still followed him.

They trotted along the winding stream, staying in the water. Once in a while Billy would ride up the bank and then back down again. Claire wondered if Billy knew what he was doing, but she supposed he did. His actions seemed deliberate. If they weren't, then she was in a lot of trouble.

After what seemed like an hour, they emerged from the woods and stopped. Billy turned, and, shading his eyes with his hands, he scanned the dark woods. He seemed to be listening, as well.

"I think we've lost them," he finally said. "It's getting late, but we'd better ride a little farther before we make camp."

"Where are we?" Claire asked.

Billy chuckled and shrugged. "I wish I knew."

"That wasn't the answer I was looking for," Claire said in a weary voice.

Billy smiled, reached over and patted her hand. Then they started riding.

When they stopped again, it was late afternoon. The sun was low in the sky, but they still had a good two hours more of daylight. They could probably ride farther, but Claire was ready to get to town so they could find a nice hotel and a hot bath. She looked around. She had to admit this was a lovely place. It was a grassy spot nestled in a clump of cottonwood trees near a lazy brook. It would be a wonderful place for a picnic, Claire thought. Of course, that would require food. "How much farther to town?"

"I have no idea," Billy said as he dismounted.

"You know that is the second time you've said that. It's especially distressing since you're leading," Claire told him as she leaned on the pommel. "Where are we going to spend the night?"

"Right here," Billy replied as he took Spot's reins and led her over to a tree.

Claire looked around. "But I don't see a house."

Billy turned and looked at her, and then drawled, "Don't reckon you do. Have you ever slept outside?"

"Of course not," Claire replied primly as she slid from her horse and walked, rubbing her sore bottom, to where Billy was undoing the cinch of his saddle.

"Then tonight will be a first, sweetheart," Billy said, lifting the saddle from his horse. He hefted his saddle to the ground, and then turned to Claire. "Here. Let me unsaddle your horse."

Claire could see that he was laughing at her, and she didn't appreciate it one bit. She was tired, she was hungry, and she was in no mood to be laughed at. "I can do it myself," she snapped.

Billy said nothing as he untied his bedroll from his saddle and dropped it on the ground.

Claire snatched the saddle from her horse and very nearly collapsed from the weight of it. She staggered, but managed to drop it at her feet. It was heavier than she'd anticipated.

Billy stepped in, and picked up the saddle and tossed it next to his. "Here. You take the blanket and spread it out on the grass while I build a fire."

Claire did as he told her. She watched him out of the corner of her eye. He was ignoring her. Didn't he care? Of course he didn't. Why should he? After all, she was just a job to him. But he could at least ask how she felt or something.

Billy was busy gathering small stones, which he brought to the edge of the grass. He arranged them in a circle and then went back and started picking up dried branches and small limbs.

Claire turned toward the babbling brook. What a wonderful sound it made, and it looked so refreshing. Today had been hot, so the water looked very inviting. She'd never in her life bathed out-doors, but she felt so grimy, she'd do anything to feel clean again.

Hadn't she said she wanted to do things she'd never done before? She'd never thought she'd be doing anything like this, however. The cool water was calling her. So far, she'd left home, ridden a train, spent time with outlaws, so what difference would bathing in a creek make? She smiled.

"I think I will go to the stream and bathe," she found herself telling Billy.

"Wait a minute," Billy said. He walked over to the saddlebag. He reached in and pulled out a white cloth, which he handed to Claire.

"What's this?" She started unwrapping. There in the middle was a big cake of white soap.

"Oh my goodness," Claire exclaimed. "It's the answer to a prayer." She sniffed at the soap. It was nothing fancy, there was no scent, but it was precious to her.

Billy grinned. "I thought you'd enjoy your bath more with that. You can leave the cloth and the soap on a rock, and I'll wash up after you do."

"Thank you," she said and started for the river. Funny, she'd thought he would have said something about her bathing in the creek, but he acted as if it was something he did all the time. Did this mean there were no bathtubs out here? No, that couldn't be. Women wouldn't stand for cold baths all the time. She was sure there would be a bathtub where she was going. At least, she fervently hoped so. If there weren't, she'd rectify that right away. In the meantime, she'd worry about the problem of bathing in a stream. Outside. Where anybody could see her.

How wicked, she thought.

When she reached the water's edge she found a spot with a sandy bank located near some scrub bushes. The creek tumbled over several layers of jutted and round boulders, then fell a short distance into a small pool at the base of the waterfall.

Heaven. Surely she'd found a little bit of heaven. This place was beautiful and seemed unspoiled by human hands. Her own little Garden of Eden.

Claire stepped out of her gown, took out her little brown bottle and looked at it. More than half of the medicine was gone, but she'd have to make it last until she rejoined Aunt Ute.

Claire shook her dress out in front of her to rid the garment of the dust from travelling. She sneezed as the gray cloud rose in the air and tickled her nose. This dress would never be the same again, after all the abuse it had received in the last week. Oh, how she'd love to wash it, but then she'd have nothing to wear but her underclothing, and that wasn't the proper thing to do. So she tossed the garment on one of the bushes so it could at least air out while she bathed.

As she stepped out of her many layers of petticoats, she decided she wouldn't need all of them since she would be sitting astride to ride, so she'd use one as a towel.

She started to remove her chemise when her hand stopped. No, she couldn't undress completely. She did have a little modesty, so she'd just wear the chemise into the water. It would get clean as she washed herself. Then she'd hang it near the fire to dry.

The lye soap smelled so fresh as she bathed, and it felt wonderful as it glided over her skin. She ducked under the water to wet her hair. Taking the bar of soap, she began lathering her long, damp tresses.

A shot rang out. Claire jumped and nearly lost her footing in the water. Had the outlaws found them? No, there would be more shooting if that were the case. But what in the world could Billy be shooting? Another snake? Billy could handle a weapon, so once she got over the initial surprise, she felt very safe. A wicked smile touched her lips. Just the thought of Billy West gave her goose bumps.

Such a silly reaction, she fussed at herself. Wading over to the waterfall, she let the water rinse the suds from her hair, but that didn't stop her from thinking about Billy.

When she was around him, she tended to forget what lay ahead of her and the problems she had. *She felt normal when she was with him, and she liked that.* Contentment along with several strange feelings confused her when she was near him. It was nothing like what she'd felt for David. And she had thought she loved David. Hadn't she? Now she wasn't at all sure. She rarely thought of him anymore, and she thought that was strange. For three years her whole world had been David, and now she didn't give a fig for what he was doing.

Shutting her eyes, she enjoyed the cool water slipping over her head as she pictured Billy kissing her like he had at the party. Even the thought of the kiss made her tingle all over. It was like an itch that needed to be scratched.

Realizing she'd wasted enough time, she stepped out of the cool water. She must have been imagining it, but she was certain she smelled something cooking. Her mouth watered. It sure smelled good. Her stomach grumbled as she wrung the water from her hair. The white chemise clung to her wet body and made her look almost naked. She peeled it off so she could hang it up to dry.

It sure was taking Claire a long time to get clean, Billy thought as he turned the rabbit over on the fire. His experiences from the wagon train had served him well.

He figured Claire would be starved. He was. He'd heard her stomach rumble a couple of times. She'd be surprised that they were going to have some meat. He glanced toward the stream. But what was keeping her?

He could always join her in her bath, he thought.

No. That would be dangerous, he cautioned himself. Hell, he didn't even know if the woman could swim. He hadn't asked. What if she'd drowned? He shook his head, disgusted with himself. Now he had to go and check on her.

He strode over to the high bushes where she'd hung her dress. Peeking around the bush, he saw Claire as she rose from the water and waded toward the bank.

He damn near stopped breathing.

Her chemise was molded to her wet body and left nothing to the imagination. Her breasts strained against the clinging material, and he could see her nipples were tight against the fabric. As she emerged further he could see the dark triangle between her legs, and he quickly jerked away and made his way back to the campfire.

"Just go ahead and shoot me now," he mumbled.

'Cause there wasn't any way he was going to make it through the night.

Chapter Fifteen

Smoke curled up from the pit, drifted over the meat, as it rose lazily into the dusky air.

Billy turned the rabbit so it wouldn't burn as he waited for Claire to return. A sizzling hiss came from the coals as the fat dripped onto the hot embers. The wonderful aroma surrounded the campfire, making his stomach growl. He couldn't remember when he'd last eaten. He'd been so focused on finding Claire that he hadn't stopped to eat.

A few minutes later, Claire returned to the campfire. Billy forced himself to look at her. At least she'd put on her blue dress. It looked different, though. It hung straight to the ground where before it had been fuller. The image of her in her white chemise still burned in his mind, and his body hadn't yet calmed down.

"I didn't know that a bath could feel so wonderful," Claire said, holding out a damp piece of flimsy material.

Her chemise. Billy gritted his teeth. The images in his head would not go away.

"I need to hang this near the fire to dry," she said as she shook out the garment.

"Go find a tree limb," he snapped.

A few minutes later, she returned with a three-pronged limb. She planted it in the ground and then carefully draped the white material over the branches. After accomplishing her task, she sat down on the grass near him and began to dry her hair by rubbing it with a piece of cloth.

Her skin looked pink and soft . . . and so very touchable. *Enough,* he told himself sternly . . . *get your mind back to the rabbit.* "Where did you get the cloth?" Billy asked her.

"From my petticoat. I decided that so many petticoats would just get in the way when I'm riding. And it's apparent that I'll be riding for a while." She shrugged. "So I tore it in half. I left the other half by the stream for you."

"Thanks," he said gruffly. Realizing he was taking out his lack of control on Claire, not that she seemed to notice, he softened his next question. "Are you hungry?"

"Starved. They gave me very little to eat," Claire said. She stopped drying her hair and looked at the animal spitted over the fire. "What is that, and where did you get it?"

"Rabbit. He made the mistake of crossing my path. At least we'll have something to eat now. However it will be a far cry from what you're used to eating," Billy said as he stood up. "How about turning the meat every so often so it won't burn? I'm going down to the creek."

Claire looked at the rabbit and the fire, before

looking back to Billy. "You're pretty resourceful, Billy West." She gave him an approving smile.

"I try to make the best of what I got," Billy said, intending to go to the creek and wash any thoughts of her out of his mind and body. But he made the mistake of looking at her. Their eyes locked, and he saw a longing expression in their depths. He couldn't draw his eyes away.

That scared the shit out of him.

Finally, he forced himself to turn and start toward the river. He hoped the water was good and cold because he needed something to cool the burning urge roaring within him. He could do it one of two ways. He could sink into Claire's warm body and die happy. Or he could drown himself in the water . . . he chose the latter.

Dusk had finally settled in and the campfire burned with an orange glow as Claire combed her fingers through the long strands of her hair. It was almost dry. The roasted rabbit smelled good as it sizzled over the fire, and she was more than ready to eat. She'd never eaten rabbit. She was doing many things she'd never done before, and each new thing was more exciting than the one before.

The familiar tickle started in the back of her throat. Grabbing the bottle of medicine from her pocket, she took a small sip. This time she received instant results.

Billy came strolling up. He had her torn petticoat in his hand, and he looked refreshed from his bath. His damp hair glistened black in the firelight and his skin appeared much darker than normal. Billy West looked dangerous, and she felt drugged by his clean and manly scent.

"Are you hungry?" Claire asked Billy.

"Starved. I only have one plate, knife, and fork, but we can make do," Billy said as he produced each item from a saddlebag. "Here is a canteen."

Billy removed the rabbit from the spit and placed it on the plate Claire held. "Ain't no delicate way to do this," he said, cutting the meat. It was so tender that it fell apart. "Give it a minute to cool, then dig in."

She took a small bite, and chewed for a moment before murmuring her approval, "This is so good."

"Glad you like it, but I reckon you're just too hungry to care. Wish I could offer something else to go with it," he said, and then he took a piece for himself.

Claire chuckled and Billy glanced at her, puzzled.

"What?"

"I was just thinking about what my mother would say if she could see me eating with my fingers." Claire rolled her eyes. "I can hear the lecture now. But you know, it's fun doing things you're not supposed to."

"I take it you've always done everything the right way." As far as Billy was concerned, rules were made to be broken.

Claire smiled. "Pretty much."

He reached for another piece of meat and shrugged. "Sometimes you learn from doing things the wrong way."

"But I've never been given the chance," Claire said. She licked the grease off her fingers, and then wiped her mouth delicately with the piece of petticoat. "Are you going to teach me the things I need to know?"

Her voice was so soft that Billy found himself

looking at her mouth and saying his thoughts out loud. "I'll teach you anything you want to learn."

Her eyes glistened. "Anything?"

"Anything," Billy replied.

Good, Claire thought. She just didn't know how to ask him to teach her how to love, and she had no idea how to seduce him. Just the thought of Billy holding her in his arms sent a shiver of anticipation skipping over her body. Flustered, she dropped the plate and the bones scattered over the ground.

"I've made a mess," she said and began to pick up the bones to cover her agitation. Thankfully, Billy didn't comment on what she'd said, and the sensual spell was broken.

While she cleaned up, Billy put more wood on the fire. Soon the flames leapt high, bathing them with warmth. Even though the days had been warm, the nights turned cool once the sun set.

"Where do I sleep?" Claire asked.

Billy had just sat down on the blankets. "Right here beside me," he said as he removed his boots.

She supposed she should have protested, but she didn't. With a shudder of anticipation, Claire slipped off her shoes and joined him on the blankets. She faced him and folded her arm under her head. She wanted to see his face while they talked.

"Tonight will get even colder," Billy said. "The fire will keep the animals away, but we'll need to share our body heat to keep warm."

"Animals?" Claire asked, a smidgen of alarm skittering through her. She slipped closer to him without realizing that she had.

Billy chuckled. "You probably don't want to

know the many animals that lurk out here. But I'll protect you."

She smiled at him, wondering if he felt this intense physical awareness that she did. "I'm counting on that."

"I guess we should get some sleep," he said finally. "Morning comes early."

That wasn't what she'd hoped he'd say, but Claire snuggled closer. Here she was, sharing body heat, and all Billy could think of was sleep. Maybe she wasn't as appealing to him as he was to her. Ann would surely flunk her at seducing Billy. She obviously had as much effect on him as a pesky fly.

Here they were all alone out in the middle of nowhere, and he wasn't taking all the hints she was throwing his way. Was she doing it wrong, or did he just not desire her? Claire had no idea what would happen once they reached Denver, so she decided that now was the best time to give it one more try. She reached out and touched his hand.

"I'm not sleepy. Let's talk for a while," she said in a husky tone.

He tightened his fingers around hers. For a long moment, Claire felt as if she were floating as she stared into Billy's strong face and compelling eyes, trying to communicate her desires to him. She knew she didn't want this moment to end.

Billy felt as though he was cornered in a dead-end canyon without a gun. He was responsible for keeping Claire safe, not violating her. He had to figure out how to keep his mind off what he really wanted. Maybe talking would help. He swallowed and tried to moisten his dry mouth. "What would you like to talk about?"

Claire looked as though he'd hit her, but he

couldn't think like that. After a moment, she recovered. "Tell me about your family," she said. "What do they do now?"

"They have a cattle ranch named The Wagon Wheel. Thunder is also a lawyer. Doesn't practice much, though."

"Why didn't you stay on the ranch and help?" Claire asked as she watched Billy's face. She wanted to learn everything she could about him. Maybe then she'd know how to reach out and make him understand.

"I did for a while, and then I thought it was time to strike out on my own. At first I made a real mess of things. I realized I was going down the wrong path, and was more likely to wind up in jail than make something of myself. Then I met Ben. Actually, Thunder introduced us. I went to work for your uncle and found I liked the stage line."

"But I thought you wanted to start a horse ranch?"

"I do. That is my dream," Billy said, his voice distant. "But dreams cost money, and that is something I don't have."

"What about your family?" Claire asked, wanting to reach out and touch him, but still unsure of herself. "Don't they have money? Won't they help you?"

"They do, but that's their money. I want to make something of myself on my own."

"You are a very proud person."

"Where I come from, pride is important to a man. Without it, you're nothing."

"I could lend you the money," she said softly.

Billy stiffened, then he reached over and touched the side of her face. "You are so sweet. But this is something I have to do for myself. Your uncle is paying me handsomely to bring you safely to Denver. That will be my start."

"So I'm nothing more than a job to you?" Claire asked, feeling completely rejected. Had she read more into Billy's actions than was really there?

He stared at her for a few moments, then he cleared his throat. "At first that was the case," he said huskily. "But now . . ."

"Well, don't stop there. You've already insulted me."

Billy placed his hand on Claire's. "But now . . . I don't know how to explain it. Before I met you, you were just a name. Now, I have met the person that goes with the name and you've become—" His eyes were dark as he stared down at her, and they seemed to bore right into her. Claire wished to God she could read his thoughts. "I care about you, Claire."

Claire's heart began to beat faster. Her pulse raced. Had she heard him correctly? He cared about her.

She couldn't move.

She couldn't think.

He cared about her! His eyes held a warm intimate look as he lay there watching her reaction.

This was a big moment, Claire realized. And she usually said the wrong things at times like this. Such an attraction to this man could be perilous. Yet, she was certain it could be wonderful as well.

The old Claire would think she should wait. But, she reminded herself, she had nothing to lose. Nothing could ever be perilous for her now. She wanted to experience what she only dreamed of having before, and she wanted to experience it with somebody she loved. She knew now that what she felt for Billy was much stronger than anything she'd ever felt for David. Her heart ached with what she could and couldn't have. She might not have forever, but what if she could have her heart's dream for just a little while. What if she took the chance?

She reached over and placed a hand on his chest. "I care about you, too," she said softly.

Billy made a noise, a groan that sounded as though he were in pain, before pulling her to him. For a moment, he just held her, and Claire knew she'd found heaven. Her head fit perfectly in the hollow between his shoulder and neck.

"Claire, we are from two different worlds," he murmured into her hair.

"Should that change the way we feel about each other?"

"In the long run it will."

She drew back and looked at him. "Billy, tomorrow may never come. Some of us don't have tomorrows. I know how I feel right this very moment, and I want you to make love to me."

Billy couldn't take any more temptation. He looked into Claire's deep blue eyes and saw that she meant what she said. The desire that he saw scared him. A man could get lost in those eyes. Then he felt what little sanity he possessed slowly seeping out of his body. What would one little kiss hurt? "You were not in my plans, Claire Holladay."

"For tonight, forget about past, present, and future and be here with me," she whispered.

Billy brushed his lips against her cheek and then ever so slowly he moved up to her earlobe, where he placed tender kisses as he whispered in her ear, "We shouldn't be doing this. I have nothing to offer you. Send me away."

Claire shivered in his arms. Her soft curves

molded perfectly to the contours of his lean body.
"You have yourself, Billy. That's all I want. Make
love to me."

She didn't have to ask again.

His mouth found Claire's, and he took what
he'd been craving. This soft willing body, pressing
so urgently against him, sent him right over the
edge. It didn't help that he actually felt something
for her . . . something he didn't want to feel. As
her arms went around his neck, she returned his
kisses with all the eagerness a man could want.
After that, all Billy's logical thoughts ceased to
exist.

His lips pressed on hers, and she parted her lips
as if she knew what he wanted. He delved into her
warmth, savoring the taste of her as his demanding lips caressed hers.

Finally, he pulled back. "You have on too many
clothes," he told her while he unhooked her dress.

She didn't flinch or bat his hand away. Instead,
her eyes never left his face, as if she were trying to
memorize it. The trust he saw in her eyes humbled
him.

He slipped the gown from her shoulders and
discovered that she had nothing on underneath.
Her skin looked like ivory. Billy's breath caught in
his throat as he stripped off his own clothes while
feasting his eyes on Claire's beautiful body. She
was perfection.

"Come," he said as he reached for her and
pulled her into his arms, dragging her fully against
his body. She fit him perfectly.

His arms encircled her, and he placed one hand
on the small of her back. He drew her face to his as
he pressed kisses on her cheeks and then to the
pulsing hollow at the base of her throat. Then he

found what he truly wanted. His demanding lips caressed hers. He wanted to know every intimate detail of her.

Claire now knew what physical love was. She was shocked at her own eager responses to the touch of his lips. His moist, firm mouth demanded a response. She felt transported on a soft and wispy cloud of pleasure. She couldn't believe that she was letting him do such things to her. But it felt so right that she was powerless to resist. His mouth opened over hers with such a fiery demand that her whole body responded. She tried to get closer to him, and when she did, she felt his rigid arousal pressing urgently against her. Instead of scaring her, as it should, it fired her blood.

Claire needed Billy West more than she had ever needed anything.

Slowly, she parted her lips and let him kiss her intimately. When she responded with her own tongue, she heard him moan.

Billy's mouth left hers, and he began to trail kisses down her throat, but he didn't stop there. He kept moving down her chest until he found her rose-tipped nipples. He licked circles around the tight nubs, then captured one trembling peak in his mouth. He teased it to the hardness of stone. She gasped as he suckled at her breast. Her quick intake of breath pleased him.

With his other hand he rubbed her body with agonizing slowness, teasing her, taunting her, as he moved further down her body. He parted her legs and found the tempting throbbing spot deep within her that she offered him. With little coaxing, she instinctively parted her legs, and his fingers slid through the curls down to her moist warmth.

His fingers burned into her tingling skin. Claire jerked. She wanted to pull away, yet at the same time, she wanted more. As he moved his fingers within her, he kissed her taut nipples, rousing a melting sweetness within her. She arched her back in surrender, and all the while his hands were moving, teasing her, making her ache for something more.

Billy rolled her on her back and positioned himself between her legs. He saw the passion in her eyes and knew that she felt the same things he did. He eased into her little by little. God she was tight. He didn't want to hurt Claire, but there was no other way. He took a deep breath and drove into her.

Claire cried out. She didn't realize it would hurt so much. She struggled to get away from him, but he held her tight.

"I'm sorry. I hurt you," he whispered in a choked voice. "The pain will ease in a moment, sweetheart. Do you want me to stop?" Billy asked. He lay very still and after a moment her body adjusted. If she said yes, he'd probably die right here. He couldn't remember when he'd wanted somebody as much as he did this woman.

"No," she said in a faint voice.

Slowly, he started to move again, feeling her tightness surrounding him. She was driving him crazy with desire. Her arms tightened around him, and she began to move with him.

His shoulders and arms were taut with the strain of holding back, but as soon as she began to match his rhythm, he could hold back no longer.

After the pain eased, Claire enjoyed the feeling of Billy within her. The dormant sexuality of her body had been awakened and she craved the unknown as she moved with him, searching for something more. When he thrust deeper, she felt an awakened response from deep within her. The flames of passion burned and her body began to vibrate with liquid fire.

Together they found the tempo that bound their bodies as one as they both found bliss. A burst of sensations made tears spring to her eyes.

Claire knew the flooding of uncontrollable joy when she saw stars bursting into a bright light before her eyes.

Without a word and wrapped in a blanket of contentment, she snuggled within Billy's arms and fell fast asleep.

The next morning just before daybreak, they lay in each other's arms. Claire had never felt so contented and safe. A gentle breeze blew over them, cooling her heated skin. The fire still kept the area bathed in a soft orange glow. She turned to face Billy.

He reached and brushed the hair clinging to her cheeks away from her face. "You are so beautiful," he whispered. "Did you sleep well?"

"I've never slept better," Claire admitted.

Billy took a deep breath, "Claire, I shouldn't have made love to you."

"I didn't please you?" she asked. She didn't try to hide the disappointment in her voice.

"Hell, yes, you pleased me. I feel like I've died and gone to heaven," Billy paused. "Here in front of me is an angel, an angel I don't deserve."

She took his hand and pulled it to her lips to kiss his palm. "You put yourself down, Billy West. You deserve anything you want."

He stared at her for a long moment. "You don't

understand. I'm not the marrying kind, Claire," he blurted out.

Claire wasn't sure what to say. Maybe Billy didn't want her, and this was his way of telling her. But then again she had no intention of marrying, either. After a long moment of silence she said, "Good. Neither am I."

Billy wasn't sure what he expected, but it definitely wasn't the answer he'd just received. He'd expected a little disappointment on her part— maybe a tear.

He received neither.

And the damn part about it—he experienced a stab of displeasure and he had no idea why. Wasn't her answer what he wanted? Hadn't he said he didn't want to get saddled with a woman?

Without thinking what he was doing, he pulled her closer. "I'm sorry I hurt you last night. I would never hurt you."

She looked up at him. "Are you sorry we made love?"

"No," Billy said huskily, taking her hand. "It was wonderful. You sorry?"

"Not at all." She kissed his chin. "Thank you for showing me what love could be like."

This was the damnest conversation he'd ever had. Hell, he normally didn't talk at all. He just got up and left. So why did he find the need to explain himself? The only answer he came up with was that he didn't want to hurt Claire. After making love to her, he felt like he had a part of her and in a way he did . . . she had given him something special. Something no one else could ever have given him.

He kissed her gently and then he deepened the kiss briefly, until he realized that he wanted her just as badly now as he had before. Nope, that was wrong—he wanted her more now than he had before.

Pulling away, Billy wondered what to say as she looked at him with such dreamy eyes. "We should be going," he finally said.

"Before we do," Claire said. "Let's not question what has happened between us. Life is so short. I could have stopped you, and I didn't. I don't want you to feel guilty."

"What's done is done," Billy said and moved away from her. He pulled up his trousers. Why was this woman agreeing with him so damn irritating? "What if I wanted to marry you? Does that mean I have no say so?"

She started to get up. "Turn your back, please."

"For heaven's sake, why?"

"Because I ask you to," Claire said.

Grudgingly, Billy did as she requested. He could hear her slipping on her clothing.

Then she spoke. "You just told me more than five minutes ago that you were not the marrying kind."

"That's right," Billy admitted, then found that he wasn't happy to be right as he turned back around.

She threw her hands out to the side and ask, "So what do you want, Billy West?"

Billy raked a hand through his hair and then looked at her. Damned if he knew what he wanted, but he wasn't going to tell her that. "Get your horse."

Chapter Sixteen

And so their morning started.

What had been the most wonderful, exhilarating experience of Claire's life faded to dull gray as the sun began to rise. Had she made a mistake? Only time would tell.

She watched Billy's rigid back as he broke camp, and she wondered if last night had been only a dream. The only thing she knew was that taking the chance of making love to Billy West hadn't provided the answers she'd wanted. After making love to Billy, she'd thought that she wouldn't think about him in that way anymore . . . he would be out of her system.

However, after experiencing the wonderful pleasure of love and seeing a tender side of Billy she hadn't known existed, she wanted so much more.

Claire didn't bother to say another word to him. After a series of one-syllable answers, she'd finally understood. He didn't want to talk to her this morning, even if she did want to talk to him.

She dressed and saddled her brown horse. She paused to rub Spot's muzzle and whisper in her ear, "Your master is very ornery, but then I guess you already know that."

Finally they were under way. Claire followed behind Billy, wondering if he knew where they were going. Far be it from her to ask.

She studied the land, noticing how brown and dry the countryside seemed. The green grass or pretty trees were found only in patches. It made her miss her green pastures back home.

About midday she could see a river up ahead, and the land began to change from mottled brown to a rich, verdant green. She decided to break Billy's stony silence because she was tired of staring at his stiff back. She kneed her horse into a trot and rode up beside Billy. "What's that?" she asked, pointing to the river.

"It's the Missouri," Billy said. "We should be in Independence shortly."

"Good," Claire said. "At least you know where you're going now."

He frowned. "I knew where I was going all along. I just didn't know where I was for a while."

Claire smiled at that. Sure sounded like lost to her. "I need to finish my article and mail it to my editor," she said, though she doubted he cared one way or another.

Billy grunted his reply.

So much for conversation, Claire thought. She couldn't figure out why he was acting so grumpy. She couldn't seem to make him happy no matter what she did. Hadn't she agreed with him that she didn't want marriage? Maybe he had been disappointed with her last night, and he didn't know how to tell her. However he hadn't seemed disappointed at the time, but then she hadn't had any experience in that area, so she had nothing to compare it with. Billy had her totally confused. She had tried to puzzle it out so much that her head hurt and she was no closer to knowing than she'd been when she started. She needed to get her mind on something else, and planning out her article seemed as good a way to distract herself as anything.

Shifting in the saddle, she tried to find a comfortable position. That was getting hard to do because she was so sore, and that brought her mind right back to what had happened last night. How did she feel about last night?

She considered the question for a moment, and just the thought of the passion they'd shared made her body grow warm. All right, she'd admit that it had been wonderful. There was no other way to describe making love to Billy. She liked the way he held her, and when he'd kissed her—well, she liked everything. She knew she should have regrets, but she didn't.

And the worst part was, she wanted more. It was rather like tasting candy . . . One piece just wasn't enough. She almost laughed at herself.

She was hopeless.

Smiling, she watched the object of her affection who was once again riding in front of her, his back straight, the sun bringing out the red in the ends of his brown hair which hung beneath his Stetson. Claire sighed. He was so hard to figure out and even more difficult to get close to. However, she was glad that she had chosen Billy. Ann would be proud of her for taking a chance and getting to know him.

Billy didn't pretend to be anything other than

what he was . . . a cowboy. And who would have thought that type of man would have appealed to her. Definitely not her mother, who would have chosen a businessman, someone like David, and now Claire knew exactly what kind of man David really was.

During the noon hours, they rode along the wide Missouri River. Billy might have gotten them to the river, but they still had a long way to go before they reached civilization. "Why does the river look so brown?" Claire asked.

"The Missouri is too thick to swim in and not quite thick enough to walk on," Billy said with a hint of a smile. "By daylight, the broad current is repulsive looking, like flowing brick-colored mud."

Claire nodded. "I think I have to agree with your description. It does look disgusting."

Some time past noon, the town of Independence appeared in the distance, and Claire breathed a sigh of relief. She was very tired. She had ridden horses all her life, but never hour upon hour and, she also realized, her last year of staying indoors had cost her a great deal of strength. But she would never complain. She didn't want Billy to think of her as some helpless female.

They rode slowly into town, and the first thing Claire noticed was that this town was bigger than some of the others she'd seen. There were no large brick buildings as there were in New York, only wooden, sun-washed buildings constructed on both sides of the street with wooden walkways in front of most of the buildings. The streets were dirt, with hitching posts in front of each building for the animals.

It was a bustling little town full of buckboards and covered wagons. Independence was the starting point for many wagon trains heading West, so there were twice as many wagons as there were people, or so it seemed.

Little puffs of dirt scattered from their horse's hooves as they trotted down what Claire assumed was Main Street. There were no well-dressed men and women, only people dressed in crude work clothes. Everything seemed to be clothed in varying shades of brown.

As they passed the last building, which was trimmed in fading red paint, Claire glanced up to see two women dressed in what appeared to be their underclothing. She gasped and looked quickly away.

Billy hadn't been paying attention to the surroundings. He was intent on their destination. He was about to turn down a side street when he heard Claire gasp. He swung around in his saddle and looked at her. "What's wrong?"

"Those women back there were in their unmentionables," Claire said, looking appalled.

"Don't mind them. They're just the local whores," Billy said, then pulled his mount to a stop in front of a large black gate. He didn't say anything more as he slid from his horse and stood in front of the gate.

Claire wondered why they had stopped here. The gate was in the middle of a long brown wall that seemed to be encasing something. She looked through the black bars and saw a water fountain with a very large live oak in the center of the yard. There were buildings around the yard, the doors of the rooms left half open and apparently unoccupied. The yard was scattered with rubbish and leaves. It appeared that no one had lived there for a long time. There was also a bigger building that resembled a church. But there was no cross, so she wasn't sure.

"This isn't the hotel, is it?" Claire finally asked. She hadn't expected fine hotels like back home, but she was hoping for something decent. "This place looks deserted."

"It is," Billy said in an odd-sounding voice. He sighed and then remounted his horse. He looked at Claire. "This is the parsonage where I used to live with the other children."

"I see," Claire said quietly. She could see that revisiting the place had upset Billy. "It appears that it once was very lovely. Was that big building a church?"

"Yeah, that was where Father Brown preached. He was a nice man, and he was good to me," Billy said. Then he looked earnestly at Claire. "You know, I didn't think that seeing this place would have any effect on me. I always swore up and down that I hated it here, but now . . ."

"But what?" Claire prompted. It was evident that Billy needed to talk.

"But now I realize that this really was a home. It looks so much smaller than I remember, though," he said absently. "It was a place where I was safe and had a bed to sleep in. And I had some good times here," he said in a very low voice.

Billy sounded so sad that Claire reached over and touched his arm. "Sometimes we don't appreciate things when we have them. It's only after we lose them that we realize how much they meant to us. And it probably looks smaller because you were younger at the time so everything looked big to you then. I imagine you have a lot of memories of this place both good and bad. That's something that no one can take away from you. Memories last a lifetime."

"Guess you're right," Billy agreed as his eyes met hers.

Claire gave him a reassuring smile and then he surprised her by leaning over and kissing her. The kiss was so soft that it felt like butterfly wings barely touching her lips. Then he straightened and she glimpsed a heart-rending tenderness in his gaze before he masked his feelings again.

For just a moment, he'd shared a part of himself with her, something Claire sensed he never did with others. She wanted to sigh at the tender moment, but she could see that the moment was over and Billy's no-nonsense personality was back in its place, leaving her to wonder if he'd always regret kissing her.

He reined his horse around and started down the alley without saying another word. Claire wanted to scream. How could he be so tender one minute and a stranger the next? The very next time he wanted to kiss her, she was going to tell him no. "Where are we going now?" she asked.

"I thought maybe you'd like to sleep in a hotel tonight and have a hot bath."

She nudged her horse forward and trotted up beside him. "I cannot deny that I'm looking forward to a warm bath to ease my aching body. However, I did enjoy last night and sleeping under the stars. It was very special."

Billy turned to her and to her surprise said, "I did, too."

Well, at least it was something, she mused. But she still wasn't going to let him kiss her again, no matter what.

* * *

Billy left Claire at the hotel while he went to the stage office to see what had happened to Fredrick, Ute, and Willie.

Claire had said that she needed to finish her article for *Harper's*, so she could get it in the mail by this afternoon, and then she was going to take a hot bath.

Billy figured he'd buy them some new duds and clean up before dinner. For now, he needed to check in at Holladay's Stage office, so Ben would know they were alive.

He walked into the small building which was half the size of the office in Denver. Billy had never made this run, so he didn't know the people who worked here.

A tall, thin man with spectacles perched on the tip end of his nose looked over his glasses as Billy approached the counter. "May I help you, sir?"

"I'm Billy West. I work for the stage line."

"Ah, Mr. West." The man nodded. "Nice to meet you. I'm Too Tall Sam," he said. Then he stood and moved to the counter to extend his hand to Billy. "You can call me Sam."

"I can see where you got your name," Billy said. The man had to bend over to look through the window at Billy.

After they shook hands, Sam returned to his desk and sat down. "Mr. Holladay will be relieved that you have arrived. I assume you have his niece?"

"Yes, I have her," Billy replied.

"Good." Sam nodded then leaned back in his chair. "We have received a telegram every day from Mr. Holladay wanting to know if you had shown up."

"I'm going to send him a telegram as soon as I leave here," Billy said, leaning on the counter and looking over for something to write on. "Do you know if Fredrick and his party made it safely to Denver?"

"Yep. Him and that funny talking woman arrived in Denver day before yesterday."

"And the child?"

"Yep. I remember a little one. He had an odd looking dog with him. The dog didn't move much."

Billy smiled. "That would be Floppy."

"Name suits 'im. Everything on that dog flops."

Billy snatched a sheet of paper and started writing out his telegram. "I guess we need to book passage on the next stage," Billy said when he finished.

Sam started laughing. "Mr. Holladay is sending in a special coach for his niece. He dispatched it yesterday, so I guess he reckoned you'd find her. Said he wanted something special for her."

Billy raised his brow. "And did Ben happen to say anything about me?"

Too Tall Sam gave Billy a sly smile. "Said if you didn't bring his niece home safely, he'd personally nail your hide to the nearest tree."

Billy chuckled. "Well, as long as he wasn't angry." He turned to leave. "Where was the stage coming from?"

"Not sure, but it wasn't Denver, 'cause the telegram said to expect it tomorrow."

"I guess we'll see you tomorrow morning," Billy said. "Do you know who the driver will be?"

"Didn't get that kind of information. But as you know, all the drivers are good."

"Ben wouldn't have it any other way," Billy said as he shut the door behind him.

He stopped by the telegraph office and then

made his way back to the hotel. A hot bath was going to feel mighty good to him. After he bathed, they could mail Claire's letter and have a nice dinner.

When he walked past the Emporium, he remembered that Claire could use a fresh dress since all her clothing had been sent ahead. He turned into Mr. Gardner's Dry Goods store. He could remember coming in here when he was little and begging for a stick of candy.

The bell over the door jingled as it always had, and Mrs. Gardner looked up from where she was working behind the counter. She didn't recognize Billy as she greeted him, and he wasn't about to bring up the past. He'd be in here the rest of the day answering questions. Instead he simply described Claire to Mrs. Gardner, and she helped him pick out a new frock and hat. He let her pick out the underthings. Since he was in a buying mood, Billy splurged and bought himself a red shirt, and then he wondered why. He wasn't much on clothes.

Back at The Brown Hotel, Billy knocked on Claire's door. His room was next to hers . . . a safe distance to protect her reputation.

"Who is it?" came the feminine voice from the other side.

"Billy."

She opened the door wrapped in nothing but a sheet. Her hair had been pinned up and little wisps of damp hair hung down on her bare shoulders. Her dewy skin looked creamy and inviting, so much so he couldn't remember why he'd come to her room.

When he didn't move, Claire said, "Come in so I can shut the door. I'm not decent."

No shit! It was like inviting the lion into the den.

He moved like a puppet as she pulled on his hand, his eyes burning holes in her. "Sweetheart, that is an understatement."

"I've just gotten out of the bath water, and I couldn't bring myself to put on that dingy dress just yet."

Billy finally snapped out of his stupor. "I hope that you wouldn't answer the door like that for just anybody."

She gave him a disgusted look. "Of course I wouldn't. If you remember, I asked who was there first."

"Thank God for small miracles."

"Quit looking at me like I've committed a crime. I grew up around three brothers so I'm not very modest. Besides, after last night . . ."

She blushed. He liked it when she smiled and blushed.

"Would you like to take advantage of the hip tub they have set up in the small alcove? The water is still very warm, and I have an extra bucket of hot water beside it." Claire pointed.

"That does sound inviting, but maybe I should just go to the bathhouse," Billy said as he shifted the brown paper bundle in his arms.

Claire took a step closer. "Billy West. Are you afraid of me?"

"Yes, ma'am," he said with a grin.

Claire laughed. "That's what I thought. What's in that package under your arm?"

"Oh, I forgot. It's the reason I knocked on your door in the first place. Here," he handed her the package wrapped in brown paper tied with string. "I thought you might like a new dress and some underthings."

Claire took the package to the bed and quickly untied the twine. She was amazed that he'd been so thoughtful when he'd acted like a grumpy bear most of the day.

There in the brown paper was a light blue dress. It was simple but very pretty with a touch of lace around the collar. She couldn't believe it. Now she didn't have to wear those dirty clothes again. She turned back to Billy and threw her arms around him, giving him a quick kiss on the lips, "I love you."

She started to move away from him, but his arms tightened, preventing her from turning. "You came too close to the beast, sweetheart," Billy said in a husky tone.

Claire gave him a slow, sassy smile. She kind of liked this flirting, and she knew that Ann would approve. "How do you know that I didn't set a trap for the beast?" she said as her arms slid around his neck and the sheet came loose and puddled around her feet.

The touch of his lips on hers sent a shock wave through her entire body. She had turned into a shameful hussy, she thought as her arms slipped around his neck.

Then she remembered she wasn't going to kiss him.

Well, maybe just once more, she reasoned as her lips brushed his gently. It didn't take Billy long to respond and she returned his kiss with wild abandon.

His tongue moved inside her mouth, deepening the kiss, making her burn as her body rubbed against his.

Billy broke off the kiss. "If I'd known that I'd get this kind of reception, I would have brought you something a long time ago," he said and held her away from him. "Now put on some clothes before I forget everything that needs to be done."

Claire was a little disappointed as she moved away and snatched the sheet around her. Hadn't she just said that she wasn't going to kiss him anymore? Well, this time she meant it! No more! Maybe she should give up trying to seduce Billy. She evidently was good at flirting, but lacking in everything else.

And evidently sex didn't agree with him or he wouldn't be so grumpy.

She slipped on her old chemise and then wrapped herself in the sheet so she'd be covered, while she laid out the new clothes. "What needs to be done?"

Water splashed behind her. She jerked around to see Billy's head resting on the back of the tub.

"I see you decided to take me up on my offer," Claire said with a smile.

"Yep, at least one of them," he said. "I figured it would save time, and you're right. The warm water is great."

Claire shook out the dress and Billy's shirt. "I like your red shirt," she said.

"I thought it would brighten my brown and black wardrobe," he teased.

"I do notice that brown and black are very popular colors around town," Claire commented. "This dress is lovely, thank you," she said again. When he didn't answer, she turned to look at him. He was lathering his arms, and looking sinfully delicious.

But she wasn't going to kiss him.

"You're welcome," Billy said finally. "I thought it matched your eyes."

At least he had noticed something, she thought with a wry grin as she watched him trying most unsuccessfully to lather his back.

"Here, let me help you," Claire said as she approached the tub. She got down on her knees and took the sponge from him and lathered it with soap. Then she began to scrub his back. Her hands slid wantonly over the wet, bronzed skin. She loved his dark skin, his strong shoulders. She noticed a purplish-red spot on his right shoulder. "What's this?"

"I was shot."

"Shot. Why?"

"Well, just like the trains, we have robbers who want to rob the stages. My job is to make sure that they don't succeed, and sometimes I don't see them coming quick enough to get out of the way."

"But you could get killed," Claire protested as she poured hot water over Billy's back.

"Sweetheart, things are different out here. You can get killed crossing the street."

"But I don't like the idea of you being shot," she said.

Billy leaned back in the tub and watched her. When he didn't say anything, Claire began washing his chest, letting her hands glide over his warm skin. Her own body was beginning to warm also.

Billy couldn't believe the woman was kneeling by the tub, washing him. She showed none of the shyness that most women would. Yet he knew first hand, that she had been a virgin until last night. And that thought made his blood heat. He never wanted anybody else to touch Claire. Reaching out he took her arm and pulled her into the tub on top of him.

"What are you doing?" she squealed.

"Enjoying my bath," he said as memories of last night returned and made him stir. Her body slid over his until she was lying on top of him. Her chemise clung to her breasts and appeared much too inviting. "This could be the most delightful bath I've ever had," he said.

"I—I shouldn't be doing this. We're going to get water on the floor," Claire protested.

"Shhh," Billy whispered as his lips met her inviting throat. He placed soft kisses on the pulsing hollow at the base of her throat as he whispered, "You're so beautiful."

He wanted more and pulled her up toward his mouth until he had a tempting wet breast to nibble upon, but the chemise was getting in his way. He tore it completely off then drew her nipple into his mouth and sucked hard until he heard her moan. "Hold yourself up for me."

Claire's blood pounded through her. But she did as he asked, placing her hands on each side of the tub to free Billy's hands. She looked down and watched as he feasted on her breast, sucking and pulling with just the right pressure to drive her wild. With his right hand he massaged the other wet breast until both her nipples were throbbing and her arms grew too weak to hold herself up.

She collapsed on him, sending water sloshing over the rim of the tub, but by now she was beyond caring. She wanted to kiss him and she didn't wait for him to go first. She placed wet kisses on his face before finding his lips and taking what she wanted. Her tongue moved inside his mouth while her hands roamed over his body, sliding along his wet skin. She arched against him wanting to feel all of him.

Billy's quick intake of breath caught her attention before she felt his hands go around her waist, lifting her up and then pulling her down on his arousal.

She gasped as he entered her swiftly. Her eyes sought his, and he saw the blazing passion he was promising her.

"Does it hurt?" he asked, his voice husky. "You are still tight around me and it feels good, but I don't want to hurt you."

She shook her head. She didn't want him to stop. She wanted to move.

"Tell me, Claire. How does it feel?"

"Wonderful," she breathed in a hushed whisper as she began to move.

"Sweetheart, you're driving me crazy," Billy said as he gripped her hips and began moving her up and down, faster and faster, until they exploded in an outpouring of fiery sensations.

She melted against him, once again wrapped in that warm glow.

The letter to her editor was all but forgotten. There would always be tomorrow, but for now Claire had what she wanted.

Chapter Seventeen

Claire was still basking in the glow of their afternoon bath when suppertime arrived.

They walked down to the local eatinghouse. There was a big sign with a rose painted on it and the lettering said "Rosa's." Billy told her that the place used to be called Sam's.

The restaurant consisted of one large room with many tables scattered about it. The tables were covered with red and white gingham and there were gingham curtains over the front window as well. It appeared clean and homey, Claire thought, as they entered the place.

She had to smile when she thought of what her mother's expression would have been. However, Claire wasn't as critical as her mother and the place looked good to her, much better than a campfire and a rabbit. Of course, she'd enjoyed her time with Billy, but tonight she was famished and wanted real food.

If the number of hungry diners was any indication, the food must be good. There was only one table left, so she followed Billy to it. Once she was seated, she leaned over and whispered to Billy, "Have you eaten here before?"

"Can't say that I have," Billy said as he looked over the menu, which was a one page handwritten sheet.

"But you used to live here."

He lowered the menu and peered at Claire over the top. "It takes money to eat in here and that was something we didn't have. Besides, we had a cook until she quit."

"Oh," Claire said, then looked back at the menu. She couldn't imagine not having enough money to eat, and the way Billy was frowning at the menu, she hoped that wasn't a worry now. "Well, I have money if you need it."

"Claire." He said her name as if he were speaking to a bad-mannered child. "That was then. I can buy you dinner now."

"Fine," she said, wondering why he couldn't see that she only wanted to help. Money seemed to be a very touchy subject, and she hadn't meant to insult him.

A waitress approached their table. She was a young girl with long blonde hair. "What can I get you folks?"

Claire looked at Billy and asked, "What do you suggest?"

"I'm going to have steak and potatoes," he told the waitress before looking at Claire. "What about you?"

"I'll have the same," Claire said and handed the menu to the waitress, who, Claire noticed, was smiling at Billy more than she should be.

"Our steaks are the best," the waitress said to Billy. "I'll have them fix yours extra special."

Claire couldn't blame the girl for flirting. Billy looked so dark and devilish tonight. His red shirt added even more color to his tanned face and made his eyes appear black and dangerous.

The front door opened and a fatherly-looking gentleman strode in. He was a good six feet tall and possessed the powerful build of a bull. His clothing was like most of the men's; he wore brown homespun trousers with a gun strapped down to his leg. But there was something about him that suggested kindness.

"What has drawn your attention?" Billy asked when he noticed that her eyes were focused over his shoulder. When she didn't answer him, he turned and looked toward the door. "Well, I'll be damned," Billy swore. He stood and started toward the man.

"Ward Singer," Billy said as he reached the big, blond-haired man.

The larger man looked stunned for a minute before a flicker of recognition lit his eyes, "Are my eyes playing tricks on me?"

"Nope," Billy said with a smile. He grabbed Ward's hand. "Come on over and sit with us. We just ordered dinner."

As they approached the table, Claire saw Billy smiling. It was different from any smile she'd seen before. This was a true smile that came from within, and it made Billy look so much younger. Evidently, this man was someone Billy knew and liked.

"Ward Singer, I'd like you to meet Claire Holladay."

The waitress interrupted long enough to get Ward's order. She flashed Billy another smile, then left.

"Ma'am," Ward said with a nod. "I just knew you were going to say this pretty young thing is your wife."

"Afraid not," Billy said. "I'm not the marrying kind. I was hired by her uncle, Ben Holladay, to escort her to Denver."

Claire felt Billy's stinging remark and had to say something. "Billy is perfectly safe with me."

Ward chuckled.

Billy glared.

Then Ward asked, "Denver, so that's where you live now?"

"Yep."

The conversation was going so fast that Claire was getting lost and feeling left out—but being the reporter that she was, she had to know everything. "Wait," she said to gain their attention. "First, it is nice to meet you, Mr. Singer."

"Ward," he corrected.

"Ward." She smiled. "How do you know, Billy? Are you from the parsonage, too?"

Billy laughed. "Not hardly. Ward is the wagon master that was in charge of our wagon train. He's the one that took us out West, and Thunder Bradley was the guide for the wagon train. I'm sure our family was a challenge to Ward."

"That was one wagon train I won't forget," Ward admitted. He paused as the waitress returned with three piping-hot steaks.

Claire's mouth watered. She noticed that Billy was served with the biggest steak. The waitress was trying to please him.

"Tell the cook, thank you," Billy said.

"A moment, please," the waitress left and returned with a Mexican woman.

Billy stood and placed his napkin on the table. "I don't believe it, Rosa! This must be your place."

"Señor Billy," Rosa said with a smile. "You've turned into a man since last I saw you."

"A lot has happened since the last time you saw us at the parsonage, Rosa. But we are all doing fine and it appears that you have done well for yourself."

"Sí. I now work for myself. Tell me, did Brandy ever learn to cook?"

"Heavens no. Ellen and Mary took over the job or we would all have starved."

Rosa laughed. "I will let you get back to your guest. Enjoy your dinner, it's on me. Be sure to tell everyone hello for me."

"I'll do that, Rosa." He sat down and picked up his fork. "She used to do the cooking at the parsonage for us," he explained.

After Ward had taken his first bite of steak, he looked at Claire and said, "That group of kids didn't know one darn thing about a wagon when they started on the trip. I gave them only three-to-one odds that they'd survive, but they proved me wrong."

"We didn't have much of a choice," Billy fired back. "We had Thunder, who pretty much made sure we did what was expected."

"This steak is mighty good," Ward said, placing another juicy slice in his mouth. "Probably be the last one I get for a while. I'll be heading out day after tomorrow. It's going to be my last trip."

Billy smiled. "Can't say that I'm sorry I won't be on the train—it's so slow. What are you going to do after you retire?"

Ward looked at Claire. "What I've been doing is looking for Brandy and Thunder."

Claire wiped her mouth with the napkin. "You didn't know where they were?" she asked.

Ward took a sip of sarsaparilla. "I left them at Ft. Laramie, but when I came back to check on them the next time through, they were gone." Ward looked at Billy. "Now I want to know what happened."

"It's a real long story. The man who Brandy thought was her fiancé turned out to be a wolf in sheep's clothing. It seems Sam ran a hog farm."

Claire frowned. "He raised pigs?"

"No." Billy laughed. "It's the name of a house of ill-repute."

Ward looked stunned for a moment, then said, "You're kidding."

"Oh my goodness," Claire added.

Billy nodded as if he were remembering it all. "It was terrible, and we had no one to turn to."

"I shouldn't have left you kids before meeting the man," Ward said.

"You had no way of knowing. 'Sides, you had a whole wagon train full of travelers who probably wouldn't have liked the delay," Billy said, then continued with his story. "It seems Sam wanted Brandy as one of his girls instead of his wife like he led her to believe.

"Ward, you'd have been proud of Brandy. She stood up to Sam and refused to be a part of his bevy of ladies. But Sam demanded payment of the money he'd sent to her, and he was furious that she had brought five children with her."

"Sounds like Brandy is a spirited lady," Claire commented, completely caught up in the story. Until this moment, she had never realized how simple her life had been.

Billy grinned. "Brandy is determined, no matter

what she does. Anyway, she agreed that we would work to pay off our debt by cleaning and taking care of the animals. And so we did. We lived in the wagon next to the barn.

"Have to admit it wasn't bad. I'd hunt for food, and the girls cleaned the house. But one day Sam had been drinking and attacked Ellen."

"Did he hurt her?" Claire was horrified. She placed her fork down on the table.

"Brandy arrived before Sam could ravish Ellen," Billy said, glancing at Claire. "Then Sam turned on Brandy and she shot him. After that she was arrested and taken to Denver to stand trail for murder."

Ward shook his head. "I had no idea."

Claire realized that she was really glad to learn a lot about Billy as he spoke to Ward. These were things that Billy might never have told her, and now she was getting to see where he came from and what had made him the man he was. He definitely hadn't had an easy life.

"Everything turned out all right," Billy said with a smile as he leaned back with a cup of coffee. "Thunder showed us what a great lawyer he was by getting Brandy off with self defense."

Ward leaned forward on the table. "Well, did they ever get married? Never seen two people who couldn't live with or without each other. I couldn't believe Thunder rode off and left her in the first place."

"Yep. Thunder did the right thing by her. He bought a ranch for them. You'd never believe what happened next."

"There's more," Ward said.

"Remember that heavy chest of Brandy's that Thunder complained about being too heavy?"

Ward nodded. "Sure do. I still can't believe he allowed her to take the trunk all the way with her."

"Well, it was heavy for a reason." Billy chuckled. "Seems the bottom was filled with gold bricks."

"Damn," Ward swore, then apologized to Claire. "You were rich all the time—just didn't know it."

"Ironic, isn't it?" Billy said with a frown. "There was a time when I thought our only home would be a covered wagon, and Brandy had been sitting on a fortune the whole time."

Claire thoroughly enjoyed this conversation and the meal. Satisfied at last, she sat back and asked, "So why haven't you started the horse ranch you want?"

Billy glanced at her. "That's Brandy's money. I will make my own."

"Do you know anything about horses?" Ward asked her.

"Yes, I do. My family has had a horse farm for many years."

"Maybe you and Billy are meant to be together, since you have the same interests and all," Ward suggested and then smiled at the glare that Billy sent his way. He could remember Thunder looking at him in exactly the same way.

Billy decided the subject needed to be changed quickly. "Have you heard from the MacTavishes? I always liked them. They sure made the journey nicer for my whole family."

"Who are they?" Claire asked.

"A couple of Scots who traveled with us on the wagon train. As a matter of fact, they adopted my youngest sister, Amy, who was three years old. Amy loved Nettie MacTavish from the start, and we wanted her to grow up having two parents. It was too late for the rest of us, but she had a chance at a normal life."

Ward leaned back in the chair and folded his hands across his belly. "I saw them the last time I was in Oregon. Of course, they wanted to know if I had found out where you folks had gone. To be truthful, I think they kind of adopted all you kids. They both have big hearts."

Billy set his coffee mug down. "How are they doing?"

"I don't think they particularly like Oregon. I'll tell them where Brandy is and maybe they can travel down to see you folks. I think they would be a lot happier being around somebody they knew."

"Gosh, we'd love to see them. I'll be sure to tell Brandy when we get back home," Billy said. He pushed his chair back and stood. "It was good seeing you, Ward. You will have to promise to come and see us when you're finished with this wagon train."

Ward stood, too. "I'll do that. See you folks, then," he said as he walked around the table. Glancing at Claire, he said, "It was mighty nice meeting you, ma'am. Look forward to seeing you when I visit in September."

Claire rose from the table and gave Ward a smile. She really liked this man. "I hope I'll be there," she said, but the month of September held dread for her.

The next morning, Claire woke up feeling a little sad that Billy hadn't come to her room last night, and then she scolded herself for such foolish thoughts.

They were not married.

They were not really anything. Claire sighed as she sat down to brush her hair. She couldn't ask for more, but she wouldn't lie to herself, either. She cared for Billy. She hadn't intended to let her emotions get involved, but somehow she had.

She put the brush down and went to a small table. She pulled her pad of paper in front of her and started writing to Ann. Claire poured out every detail of what had happened between her and Billy so far, and then she ended the note with—What should I do next?

Claire sighed as she folded the letter. She felt much better sharing her feelings with her editor. Ann had always been there to give Claire advice and guide her.

A loud rap sounded on the door and drew Claire away from her thoughts. She knew it was time to leave. She went to the door and opened it. "Good morning."

Billy looked refreshed from a good night's sleep. "I trust you slept well in your nice soft bed?"

Claire gave him a slow smile as she stared longingly at him. "I preferred the night before."

Billy reached out and softly touched the side of her face. "You shouldn't look at me like that. You're much too tempting."

"Does that mean that you are going to kiss me good morning?"

"I'd love to, but we must get moving. Are you ready?"

"Yes," she said, a little disgusted with herself. She swept by him. If he'd wanted to kiss her, then he would have. She most certainly wouldn't ask again.

* * *

When they reached the Overland office, she noticed that a stagecoach was there waiting for them. A man leaned against the stage, his foot propped against the sidewalk as he drank a cup of coffee. He had thick white hair and his whiskers were pepper-colored. He turned as they approached.

"It's about gol-danged time," the man said to Billy.

Billy laughed as he reached for the man's hand. "What are you doing here?" he said, pumping the man's arm up and down.

"Figured it was the only way to get you back on the job. You can't seem to find your own way home," he said with a grin. Then he looked at Claire. "Is this her?"

Billy nodded. "Yep. Claire Holladay, I'd like you to meet Rattlesnake Pete. He is one of your uncle's drivers."

"It's nice to meet you," Claire said with a brief nod of her head.

"You're a right pretty little thing," Pete said as he grinned at her. "Are you ready to make the ride, little lady?"

"I guess so. I need to have somebody mail these letters for me, though," she said and left them to give her letters to the gentleman behind the counter. After thanking him, she went back to the stage. "Are there other passengers?"

"Nope. You'll have the whole place to yourself," Rattlesnake said as he opened the door.

She glanced at Billy questioningly, before climbing into the stage. "Are you riding with me?"

"No, sweetheart. I'll ride up top with Rattlesnake as shotgun. Remember? That's my job."

Claire had seated herself when she mumbled, "I thought I was your job."

When she looked up, Billy was leaning into the stagecoach door. He gave her a smile guaranteed to make her toes curl, and then he said, "Sweetheart, I'm not sure what you are anymore . . . but I wouldn't say job." He shut the door.

Claire stared at the closed door and whispered to herself, "Then what am I?"

———

Chapter Eighteen

A few days later, they were finally nearing Denver. Claire felt like she'd been through hell. She now knew she'd truly left civilization behind her when she'd gotten off the train.

On the first day out, Rattlesnake received word that Indians were attacking anything that moved, so he and Billy made the decision to ride straight through, stopping only to change horses and take care of necessities such as eating.

Claire had started the trip content in the luxurious coach, which she learned belonged to her uncle. And it was nice. The seats were blue velvet, and the cushions were quite comfortable. At least, they had been at the beginning of the trip. They had grown uncomfortable by the second day. The windows had leather curtains that she could pull when the dust became too much, and there were lamplights on both sides of the stage to light at night.

Everything seemed perfect when they began the journey. Claire occupied herself by writing in her journal about the people she'd met and the towns she'd seen. It had seemed a pleasant enough way to pass through the countryside.

They stopped every fifty miles to change horses. The stations were all the same: a one-story hewn cedar log house with one to four rooms. A muslin curtain separated the kitchen from the dining area.

By the time they reached a station, Claire was so glad to get out and stretch her legs that she didn't much care that the stations were plain. However, she was going to mention to her uncle that the places needed to be spruced up.

The meals that each station served were always the same: bacon, eggs, biscuits, and coffee.

She had a hard time comprehending the fact that there were no towns beyond Independence, Missouri. The land was wide open, and she now saw why they called this country the Wild West.

On one particularly bad day, when it was dusty and hot, and she longed to escape the coach, which she now thought of as a prison, she began to cough. When she reached for her medicine, she found the bottle was completely empty. She had thought she had a few drops left, but as she turned the bottle up nothing came out. She had to endure her coughing spell until she fainted.

When Claire came to she found herself on the stage's floor, feeling extremely sore from all the bouncing around. She climbed back onto her seat and dusted herself off. She was very glad that Billy hadn't seen her disgrace herself. Now she was anxious to reach Denver and her medicine.

On the second day out, they were attacked by a small band of Indians. When she heard the gunfire, she stuck her head out the window to see what was going on. She caught a glimpse of Billy, climbing on top of the stage with his rifle, but she wanted to see what was going on so she leaned out farther.

She turned her head and saw four half-clothed men on dappled ponies galloping behind them. Their faces were adorned with paint of different colors and they looked very fierce. They carried lances decorated with colored ribbons and feathers. An arrow flew at her and stuck into the door.

Billy shouted for her to get inside. As the stage picked up speed, she was bounced around like a sack of potatoes, but she did what she could to hold on.

When the stage finally slowed to a normal pace, she assumed that the danger had passed, and they would stop the stage to check on her, but she was mistaken.

Finally the stage did stop at a way station to water the horses. But before she had a chance to tell Billy that she was all right he began to lecture her on the foolhardiness of sticking her head out the window when there was gunfire.

It was probably the most he'd spoken to her in two damn days. She wanted to scream that no, she wasn't all right. She was tired and bruised from the wild chase and very irritable. All she wanted, at the moment, was to sleep in a bed.

But the I-told-you-so look in Billy's eyes made her determined she wouldn't complain even if her life depended on it. So she drew in a deep breath and merely said. "I'm fine, thank you."

Once they reached the Colorado territory, the landscape began to change, and the air changed too. It was easier for Claire to breathe.

Now as the stage barreled down the streets of

Denver, her sleep-deprived body leaned against the side of the stage. She gazed wearily out the window.

Main Street was wide and dirty just like everything out here, Claire thought. Denver was bigger than the other towns they had been through. It appeared a little more civilized, but it was still a far cry from New York City.

There were covered wagons pulled by oxen and buckboards pulled by horses. Some lumbered down the street while others were tied in front of buildings. There were several in front of the Rocky Mountain Emporium. They rolled past Capital Bank and several restaurants before reaching a two-story building where the stage finally pulled to a stop. A huge sign overhead indicated that they had reached the offices of US Overland Dispatch.

Thank God, they had finally arrived! Claire sent up a small prayer. She didn't wait for someone to open the door for her and to exit in a lady-like manner, as she should. After all, she hadn't had a bath in a week, so she didn't feel much like a lady as she came bursting out of the stage and right into Rattlesnake.

"Whoa, little lady," he said as he settled Claire back on her feet. "Welcome to Denver. I hope yer going to like our right nice town." He hooked his thumbs under his red suspenders and rocked back on his heels. "I told you I'd get you here safely."

Claire was tired and irritable to say the least, so the idea of being polite and nodding never entered her mind. "What you didn't tell me was I would be held prisoner in that—" she said pointing to the stage, "that uncomfortable box."

Rattlesnake didn't look the least bit offended. He spat out a wad of something dark and disgusting, then grinned at her. "Billy," Pete yelled. "I think we got us an unhappy customer, and yer in charge of complaints."

Billy jumped down from the stage with a leather mail pouch thrown over his shoulder. He ambled over and came to a halt in front of Claire. She looked madder than a wet hen, and her appearance was so disheveled that Billy couldn't help smiling. She was covered in alkali-dust, her hair had escaped its pins and was hanging in limp strands around her face, and her clothes were rumpled and dirty. Yep, disheveled was a good word to describe her. Then he looked closer and noticed a bruise on her forehead. He frowned.

"What happened to your head?" he demanded.

"I hit it on the floor of the coach while you were evading wild Indians!" she snapped. "But I could just as well have died in there, and neither of you would have noticed."

"Rattlesnake, I told you not to take that hard turn," Billy snapped. "That must have been when Claire hit her head."

Rattlesnake gawked at Billy as if he were loco. "Well now, I didn't have time to ask those Indians to get out of the way. Not that they would have, mind you. And I figured the little lady would like to keep her scalp, so a little discomfort didn't seem to matter none."

Claire reached up and touched her hair. "Keep my hair?"

"Yep, the Injuns would have liked to have your scalp."

Billy noticed that they had started drawing a crowd with their arguing, and he didn't want everybody to think that passengers usually arrived in the condition of the three of them.

"Let's go inside," Billy said as he reached for Claire's elbow.

"Billy West!"

Billy turned to see who had called him. He'd just turned back when Mandy threw herself into his arms. He couldn't do anything else but release Claire and put his arms around his former girlfriend. This was just what he needed right now.

Claire looked at the young, blonde woman who was draped around Billy's neck, kissing him. She noticed that he wasn't kissing this woman like a sister, so Claire figured it must be the fiancée that he'd mentioned.

Disgusted, she walked past both of them and into the building. Evidently the woman didn't know that they were not engaged. Or perhaps, Billy had lied to her. Well she didn't care. It was none of her business.

She approached the counter just as a sensation of intense sickness and desolation swept over her. She bit down on her lower lip. She would not embarrass herself by crying over something that had never belonged to her. But she had to say something to the man behind the counter who was staring at her in an odd way.

"Can I help you?"

"Where is Mr. Holladay's office?"

"It's upstairs, miss."

"Thank you," Claire said. She turned and headed for the stairs. She passed a mirror on her way and came to understand why the man had looked at her so strangely. She could do nothing but roll her eyes. Her appearance left little to be desired, and that was an understatement. She looked like something an animal had dragged in.

"You can't go up there," the little man said as he

started out from behind his counter. "Mr. Holladay don't see nobody unless they are announced first."

Claire didn't bother to stop as she climbed the first flight of steps. "I'll announce myself."

"It's all right, Fred," Billy said as he marched into the building and started up after Claire. "The lady is with me."

That's what he thinks, Claire fumed to herself. He was with her! And he would do well to remember that.

When Billy reached her, she informed him, "You didn't have to come."

"I was hired to deliver you to your uncle, and I intend to do so and finish my job," he teased.

Claire wasn't in a teasing mood.

Once they were in the upstairs hallway, she turned on him. "I realize now that I'm nothing more than a job to you. No matter what you say. Go back to your lady friend. I'm sure she wants your company more than I do." She swung around to walk away.

"Wait," Billy said, reaching out and grabbing her arm. He then pushed her against the wall.

"Wait for what?" she whispered, not wanting her uncle to overhear them arguing.

"I was teasing," Billy said, then he let out a long, deep sigh. "We've been through this before." He placed his hands on the wall on either side of her head as he leaned closer. "I don't deny that you were a job, but that was in the beginning. Somewhere along the way you have became more than just a job," he said huskily as he leaned closer. "I'm not sure what you are to me, Claire, but I'd like to find out."

He tried to place a soft kiss on her lips, but she held out her hand and stopped him. It had been days since he'd shown her any kind of attention. "I'm not going to kiss you anymore, Billy West."

"And why is that?" he asked with a lopsided grin.

"Because every time I kiss you, you turn into a grumpy old bear. Therefore, I conclude that you don't enjoy kissing me as much as I do you."

"What a stupid notion," Billy grumbled as he leaned a little closer. "Claire Holladay, you'd drive a man to drink. First, I do enjoy kissing you. Almost too much. You're a distraction to me—one I don't need," he told her. At the same time, his actions betrayed his words as he pressed a kiss on her forehead, and then another on her cheek. "But if you don't want me to kiss you. . . ." He left the thought unfinished, then kissed her other cheek.

Claire felt as though her bones had melted. "What about that other woman?"

"She means nothing to me. Mandy started the rumors that we were engaged, so she'll have to tell everyone that she lied."

Claire touched the side of Billy's face. His whiskers tickled her fingers. *I don't want to love you,* she told herself, *but I already do.* She wrapped her arms around his neck, stood up on her toes and kissed Billy with all the emotion she had tried to hold back.

Just about the time he responded, the door to her uncle's office swung open.

"It's about damned time," Ben Holladay's voice boomed from his office, causing Claire to flinch and pull guiltily back from Billy.

Claire started toward her uncle. "Hello, Uncle Ben."

"What did they do?" Ben asked her with an odd look on his face. "Drag you behind the carriage?"

"It feels like it," Claire admitted as she hugged her uncle.

Ben frowned. "I thought that Billy would have taken better care of you." Then Ben glared at Billy. "Can't you see how fragile she is?"

Billy had to bite his tongue. He wanted to shout, she's only fragile because everyone treats her that way. Instead he said nothing.

"If it weren't for Billy, I wouldn't be here," Claire told her uncle. "He rescued me from the Dalton gang."

"So I heard," Ben said while he walked with Claire back into his office. "Your Aunt Ute was beside herself when she arrived. It took me two days to calm her down and assure her that Billy would find you."

"Well, thank you for your faith in me," Billy muttered as he stood in the doorway. "And it's good to see you, too."

Slowly, Ben smiled. "If I didn't have faith in you, I'd never have sent you back East. Now I'm going to take my niece home, and I believe there is a little guy who has been waiting for your return. Never figured you'd come back with a child."

Billy smiled. "How is Willie?" he asked as they started down the stairs.

"He's been a big help working around my stables," Ben said. "Willie told me he was now your brother."

"Looks just like me, too." Billy laughed.

Once they were downstairs, a commotion could be heard outside the office. It was just a minute before a man dressed in buckskins stormed through the door. He had riveting gray eyes, set off by a drooping mustache and blond hair that tumbled around his shoulders. He wore a Prince Albert frock coat that showed off broad shoulders. He seemed to look right through Claire.

"Holladay. Just the man I need."

"What's wrong, Wild Bill?" Ben asked.

So this was Wild Bill Hickok? Claire had heard stories about his daring deeds during the Civil War.

"Need another shotgun for the rest of my trip," Bill said. "Jake was killed early this morning."

Ben let go of Claire's elbow as he spoke. "Do you have passengers?"

"Yes, sir. And they ain't cottoned to this delay, neither," Wild Bill said.

Billy stepped forward. "I'll ride with you."

"But you just arrived," Claire spoke up. "You must be tired."

"I'll be fine," Billy said curtly, and then he walked off with Wild Bill.

Claire looked to her uncle for help.

"Don't fret. Billy will be all right." He looked at her appraisingly. "It appears that you and Billy have gotten to know each other very well," Ben finally said.

"I have spent a lot of time with him."

Ben held open the door for her. "And . . . ?"

Claire swept through the opening with as much dignity as she could muster. "I like him."

"Does he know?"

"No. And I don't want him to."

"Well, he's a fine man," Ben said, helping Claire up into the carriage. "You couldn't do much better," Ben admitted.

Claire gave a sigh. "I know. But my illness complicates things."

* * *

A week had somehow slipped by as Claire settled in with her uncle in his big sprawling house. It was only a little smaller than her home in New York.

Aunt Carla, who lived part of the time in New York and part of the time in Denver with Uncle Ben, had taken the children to England for the summer, so Aunt Ute had taken over running the household.

Claire thought that she'd be homesick, but she stayed busy enough exploring Denver and she tried not to think of home. She had regained her strength after her travels and had written two articles for *Harper's Weekly*. She shoved the last of the articles into the envelope. How she would love to see Ann's face as she read them.

Then Claire decided she had better let Ann know how she was progressing with Billy, and what had happened so far. The letter started out . . . *things haven't gone as well since we left Independence. Wish you were here to talk to. . . .*

Claire admitted to Ann that she loved Billy, but was unsure what she could do about that. She hadn't even seen Billy since she'd come to her uncle's house and wondered why he stayed away. She kept hoping that her uncle would say something, but he'd not mentioned Billy, and she wasn't going to ask him.

By the second week, Claire had become bored, and she knew she had to do something to keep her mind off Billy. She missed him more than she wanted to admit.

One morning, she was reading the *Rocky Mountain News* when she came up with a brilliant idea.

She'd go into town with her uncle and visit the *Rocky Mountain News* and do an interview with them.

Uncle Ben thought it was a splendid idea, so the next day, she dressed in a gray day dress trimmed with a plain white collar. She wanted to fit in with the local people. This morning when she looked in the mirror, she noticed she'd lost the pasty white look she'd had back East.

Once they were in town, Claire broke down and asked her uncle, "Have you seen Billy?"

He gave her a sly smile. "So you've missed him."

"I didn't say that. I was just wondering, that's all."

"Billy has been helping out until we could hire more people to ride shotgun. As a matter of fact, he should be pulling in sometime today, if you want to see him."

"If I happen to be at the office when Billy comes in, then I'll talk to him," Claire told him primly. "Look, there's the newspaper. You can let me off. When I'm finished, I'll walk over to your office."

Billy had never been so damned tired. The only sleep he'd gotten in the last two weeks had been on the stage, and he was looking forward to climbing into a soft bed for a good night's sleep.

The stage pulled to a stop. Billy retrieved the mail sack from under the seat as Rattlesnake jumped down to hold the door for the passengers.

"I'll see you, Rattlesnake," Billy said as he started for the office.

"You need to get some rest. You look sicker than a toad frog."

Billy nodded and hurried into the stage office.

He tossed the mailbag to the clerk, and then trudged upstairs to see Ben.

"You busy?" Billy called from the doorway, then entered anyway.

"It's good to see your sorry hide," Ben said. "You look like hell."

"Thank you," Billy drawled. "You're the second person who has told me I look like shit."

Ben chuckled. "I do appreciate you helping out until I could hire more men. These attacks are costing me a lot of money. If they keep up, I'm going to ask for Federal Troops as escorts. The mail must get through."

"I agree." Billy nodded. "How is Willie doing?"

"He's doing fine, but he keeps asking when you're coming to get him."

Billy smiled. "He probably thinks I'm going to get rid of him. I'll go get him tomorrow. Has anybody else asked?"

"As a matter of fact, Claire asked about you this morning. She's over at the newspaper, if you want to see her," Ben said. "Oh, before I forget—" Ben reached into his desk drawer and pulled out an envelope. "Your sister sent this to you."

Billy took the envelope and opened it up. He was frowning when he looked up again.

"Is there a problem?"

"I hope not. Brandy wants me to come home and talk to Mary about some crazy idea she has." Billy smiled as he got to his feet. "With Mary you never know what you'll be getting into. However it will be a good chance to take Willie out to the ranch and introduce him to his new family. There is going to be more than one surprised face when I arrive with a child in tow."

Ben leaned back in his chair. "You deserve some

time off. Take a few days. I know that Claire will be glad to see you, too."

As Billy left the office, all he could think of was Claire. He had hoped to get some rest before seeing her, but somehow his feet seemed to be taking him in the direction of the newspaper instead of the hotel. He'd tried hard not to think of Claire this past week, but that had proven an impossible task. The thought of holding her in his arms made his blood run hot and his footsteps quicken.

He was so glad he hadn't let Claire get under his skin, or he might do something foolish like ask her to marry him. Nope, he was just curious to see how she was doing.

Claire walked out of the newspaper and directly into Billy.

"Oh, my goodness," she gasped.

Billy steadied her. "You never know who you're going to run into," Billy said as he let her go.

She smiled brightly. "It's good to see you. Where are you going?"

"To find you," Billy said.

Claire's cheeks burned like a shy schoolgirl's. Billy looked so devilishly handsome; she'd forgotten what an effect he had on her. However, she noticed Billy had dark circles under his eyes and appeared very tired. "How have you been?"

"It's been a long couple of weeks," he admitted. "Come and walk with me. I'm going to get a bite to eat and could use the company."

They were about to cross the street when someone shouted, "Billy West!"

Billy turned to find Kincade and two hired guns on either side of the old man.

"Who is that?" Claire asked.

"Somebody who wants me dead." Billy heard Claire gasp, but he didn't dare take his eyes off the old man. "What do you want, Kincade?"

"I want you," the old man ground out slowly. Billy gave Claire a shove. "Get inside, Claire."

"Why?"

"Just do as I say. And do it now!"

The tone of his voice made Claire obey for a change without further argument. When she reached the door, she turned to see what was wrong and try to figure out why those men were shouting at Billy. Surely Billy was exaggerating.

Billy moved out toward the middle of the street and everybody else started clearing the street.

"You're a hard man to kill, Billy West," Kincade shouted. He stood with his feet wide apart, as did the men on either side of him.

"So you're the one that's been taking shots at me," Billy accused.

"You finally figured that out, boy."

"Look, Kincade. It was a fair fight. I didn't kill your son," Billy told him.

Kincade sneered. "You might as well have. It was 'cause of you, Jake was a cripple. It was cause of you that he took his own life."

The marshal walked out into the street, putting up both his hands. "All right, gentlemen. I don't cotton to gunfights in my town."

"It's been a long time coming, Marshal," Kincade said. "He killed my boy."

"I heard that was a fair fight."

"You didn't hear me, Marshal. My boy's dead. And it's his fault." Kincade motioned toward Billy.

"I can see you're pretty bullheaded, but three against one isn't fair, in my book," the marshal grunted. "Back your men off, and I'll let you both have at it."

Claire was petrified. She couldn't believe the marshal was going to let these two men shoot at each other. Couldn't the man see how tired Billy was?

She watched as the two gunslingers backed away. Billy and Kincade squared up in the street.

Wasn't the marshal going to do anything?

She had to do something to stop this. She couldn't let the man kill Billy. But what could she do?

Everything grew deathly quiet as the men stared at each other.

Claire couldn't stand still any longer. She had nothing to lose. She jumped off the boardwalk and ran toward Billy. Her scream of "No!" seemed to come from somebody else as shots rang out. She threw herself in front of Billy.

She couldn't let somebody shoot him.

She couldn't lose him yet.

She felt Billy's arms come around her just as another shot rang out. A searing pain in her right arm made her scream with pain.

Billy holstered his gun with one hand while he clasped Claire to him with the other. "You little fool." When he had a good hold of her he looked into her bright blue eyes. She stared up at him with tears trickling down her cheeks about the same time he felt the sticky blood on his hand.

Claire had taken the bullet for him.

And if it proved fatal . . . Billy looked at the old man who staggered to his feet because Billy had been merciful and had shot him in the leg instead of killing him—the wrath of hell would be released on Kincade. Billy would never show any mercy again.

The next time, he'd kill Kincade.

Billy scooped Claire up in his arms and headed for the stage office. Her head was cradled in his neck as he said over and over again, "Don't you die on me, Claire Holladay? We have unfinished business."

Chapter Nineteen

The Overland Stage office was full of passengers awaiting the next stagecoach when Billy burst through the door carrying Claire.

Everyone turned to gawk at him, but no one offered to help. They were too busy gasping and covering their mouths. One passenger said that Claire looked dead.

Ben was just coming down the stairs when he spotted them. "What the hell!" Ben bounded down the rest of the stairs and was in front of Billy before he could blink.

Billy felt like his senses had left him the minute the gun had been fired. Where he was normally sure of himself, he now found he couldn't think of what to do. So it took a few moments for Ben's words to register. "I—I need help. She's been shot."

"Take her upstairs," Ben instructed Billy. Then Ben turned to one of his men behind the counter. "Go fetch the doctor."

A middle-aged woman stepped forward. She

was dressed all in black, and a small satchel sat on the floor beside her. "I'm a doctor. Can I be of assistance?"

"If you're familiar with bullet wounds, follow us," Ben said and took off after Billy.

The woman nodded, then picked up her black bag and hurried after them.

Billy kicked open the door and carried Claire inside. When the doctor entered, she looked at Billy and said, "You'll have to place her on the sofa, if you please." When Billy didn't move, she said in a much firmer voice, "I cannot examine her while she's still in your arms."

Billy finally came out of his stupor and placed Claire on the green sofa that was behind Ben's desk.

Billy stood there, his gaze never leaving Claire's face. She was so lifeless. The bodice of her dress was soaked in blood down her right side. He had no idea how badly she was wounded. But she wouldn't have been in this situation if she hadn't been trying to protect him. And he couldn't very well relieve his frustrations by yelling at her as long as she was unconscious.

"How the hell did Claire get shot?" Ben shouted.

"You'll have to keep your voice down," the doctor instructed from behind them.

"Claire took a bullet meant for me," Billy explained. "She actually jumped in front of me. She did it before I could stop her. I told her to stay in the building, but of course she didn't listen."

"She's a brave woman," the doctor said, moving up beside them. "My name is Doc Susie," she said as she pushed Billy out of her way. She placed her black bag on the floor, then sat on the couch beside Claire.

Billy glanced at Ben. He looked like he wanted to kill somebody, and Billy couldn't blame him.

Ben spoke one word. "Who?"

"Kincade," Billy said. "I'll explain later after we get Claire taken care of."

"All right," Ben agreed and then added very quietly, "I knew I shouldn't have let her come out here. She's too delicate."

Susie picked up Claire's wrist. "What's her name?"

"Claire," they both said.

Doc Susie placed two fingers on the side of Claire's neck. "Her pulse is good," she said, "so I think you gentlemen can rest easy."

Billy took a deep breath. He wasn't sure he'd breathed at all since Claire had been shot. He'd reasoned that Claire wasn't dead, but he hadn't had the time to see how badly she was injured. "How is she?"

The doctor reached into her bag not bothering to answer the question. She passed a small bottle of smelling salts under Claire's nose, and Claire jerked and began to struggle. She started to cough as she blinked a couple of times before her eyes popped open.

"That's a girl," Doc Susie soothed. Then she looked over her shoulder at the gentlemen. "Are either of you her husband?"

"No," Billy said, and motioned to Ben. "This man is her uncle."

Claire was still coughing, so Doc Susie had to raise her voice to be heard. "It appears she has been shot in the shoulder, so it isn't life threatening. But I would appreciate both of you leaving me with my patient for a few minutes. And if you could find me some hot water and fresh bandages, it would be greatly appreciated."

Neither man moved.

"Look gentlemen, neither of you are helping me or Claire by standing there staring at her," Susie told them firmly. "I assure you she isn't going to die. Water if you please. . . . Now!"

Both men frowned at the bossy doctor before they left. Then Susie turned back to Claire. "First, young lady, let's tackle that cough of yours. It doesn't sound like a normal cough."

Claire was focusing now on the kind woman beside her. Where had she come from? The last thing Claire remembered was the gunfight in the street. She couldn't believe that the man actually shot her, but by the fire in her arm she knew he had. Remembering the panic on Billy's face, she thought he had been shot also, but she must have been wrong because she saw him before he left the room and he looked fine, thank goodness.

The doctor helped Claire to sit up, then held a bottle to her lips.

Claire felt the bitter liquid slide down her throat and start to ease her cough. Now she needed to concentrate on her other problem.

When Claire had finally ceased her hacking, she winced at the pain in her arm. "My arm," she managed to say between coughs. "It feels like it's on fire. Who are you?"

"I'm Doc Susie. I live in Fraser. It's high up in the mountains. I just happened to be in the stage office when they brought you in, and I could see right away that you needed a doctor. How did this happen?"

"Gunfight," Claire said, then added, "I was in the wrong place at the wrong time."

"Let me take a look at your shoulder." The doctor took a pair of shears and cut open the top of

Claire's dress. "I'm afraid you will not be wearing this dress again."

Claire smiled. The lady had such a gentle way about her that Claire began to relax. There was something about this woman that was comforting. She definitely had a mother's touch. "A gown is the least of my worries. How badly am I hurt?"

Doctor Susie gave her a smile. "It could be much worse. It appears that you're very lucky. The bullet went through the fleshy part of your arm instead of your shoulder, so I won't have to dig out a bullet and cause you more pain. However, it is going to hurt when I clean the wound, and I'm afraid you'll be sore for a while, but you'll be fine, other than having a nasty scar, which I hope in time will fade. As soon as the hot water gets here, we'll get you all fixed up. But I want to ask you about your cough before the men get back."

"How did you know what to give me for my cough?"

Susie laughed. "I am a trained physician even though I wear a dress. They told me your name is Claire. Are you Claire Holladay?"

"Yes I am." Claire nodded. "Do you know me?"

"In a way. I received a letter from Doctor Worden about you several months ago. Since I heard the men call you Claire and I'm in the Holladay office, I kind of put two and two together." She smiled. "Doctor Worden told me that you'd be coming this way, and he was going to tell you to look me up. Did he tell you?"

Claire frowned. "I was so busy right before I left, I never went back to Doc Worden's office. Did he tell you about my condition?"

Susie nodded. "You see, Claire, I have consumption, too. I came out here two years ago for my health, and I'm convinced that the disease can be cured with the proper care. It depends on how far your disease has progressed."

"You're cured?" Claire asked.

"Let's just say I'm better," Susie admitted. "I don't want to offer any false hope, but if you're willing to come and live with me for a while, I will try to help you."

Claire looked at the woman. She seemed so sincere. "They told me that there was no hope."

"Most physicians believe that there is no hope, but I'm not one of them. I won't lie to you. There are many who never survive this White Plague. Just think about it for now," Susie said. She squeezed Claire's hand. "When the time is right, you come to Fraser and find me."

"Thank you," Claire said with a nod, but she was doubtful. She wanted to believe, but she'd known disappointment in the past and that made her cautious.

The door swung open and Billy rushed in carrying a pot of hot water, and Uncle Ben followed with a tin pan and strips of white cloth in his hands.

Everyone was quiet while the doctor cleaned Claire's wound.

Claire glanced at Billy. He looked so tired and a little nervous. Normally, she couldn't tell how he felt, but maybe because he was so tired he'd let his guard down. Funny, he hadn't looked the least bit nervous when he'd faced the gunman. Could he really be worried about her? More likely he felt guilty, but he shouldn't. It had been her choice. The only thing she could remember was thinking that he was much too tired from lack of sleep and an easy target for the other man. She had much rather risk her life and spare Billy. He had so much to live for.

"This salve will help your wound close," Doc Susie said, gaining Claire's attention. She placed the white salve on both sides of Claire's arm and then put on the square pieces of cloth before taking the long strips and wrapping her arm.

The words the doctor had spoken kept rolling through Claire's mind. Doc Susie said *she* had consumption, and she was still alive. Did Claire dare to hope?

After Claire was neatly bandaged, Billy handed her a large shirt. "I thought you could use this to cover up until you can get home?

Claire accepted the shirt with a smile and then turned back to the doctor. "Thank you, Doc Susie."

"You're welcome. If your arm starts hurting, put it in this sling. Now I'd better get downstairs before I miss my stage. I'm taking a small trip, and will return in two weeks."

"We're thankful that you were downstairs, so Claire could get help quickly," Billy said.

Ben took the doctor's elbow and escorted her out the door. "Don't worry, ma'am. I held the stage for you. It doesn't move until I say it does. You know, for a woman doctor you aren't bad," Ben said.

Claire could hear Susie's laughter as they walked down the hallway.

Claire glanced at Billy and found he was staring at her again. "You haven't said a word to me," she said.

He pushed away from the wall and strolled over to her. After helping her stand, he enfolded her in his arms. It took him a moment before he spoke. "You scared the shit out of me!"

She noticed his voice shook a little.

"That was a damn foolish thing to do."

"I didn't want anything to happen to you," she murmured.

"Claire Holladay, I should shake some sense into you."

"I would rather that you kiss me," she said and twisted until she faced him.

He kissed her with such tenderness that she thought her heart would melt and the feelings running through her were much more than sexual desire. She'd known there was something special about Billy from the very beginning. He ended the kiss with a sigh and then gazed down at her.

"No one has ever risked his life for me," he said with a smile.

"I happen to think you're worth saving."

"Thank you, but in the future please remember I am fully capable of taking care of myself. I already had the drop on Kincade," Billy told her as he let her go. "Come on, we need to get you home."

Once downstairs, Ben told them the carriage was waiting out front. Billy escorted Claire to the carriage and helped her in, then he stepped back.

"You're not coming?" Claire asked as her uncle climbed onto the driver's seat beside her.

"I need to get some shut-eye," Billy said. She could see the dark circles under his eyes. He was only standing because of sheer determination.

Ben leaned around Claire and said, "Come on. You can sleep at the ranch. Since you've been gone for so long, I had Spot and your things taken to the ranch."

Billy stepped up into the carriage and took his seat beside Claire. Where most people in Denver rode on buckboards, Ben had had a special carriage made for him back East. The Holladays did everything first class.

Once they were on their way, Ben said, "You could use some sleep. Besides, you'll have to pick up Willie since you're going to your sister's tomorrow."

"You're going to your sister's?" Claire asked.

"Yeah. I got a note saying I needed to come home. Would you like to come with me and meet my family?" Billy asked.

"I've heard so much about them," Claire said. "I'd love to meet them."

"Good. Maybe I'll ride Firebrand. Thunder appreciates good horseflesh." Billy looked at Ben. "How did you like Firebrand?"

"Liked him fine right up to the time he kicked a hole in the stall." Ben chuckled. "He's a fine piece of horseflesh, but extremely temperamental. That's the reason I had Spot brought to the ranch. Willie suggested that Firebrand would calm down once Spot was stabled with him, and damn if the kid wasn't right."

Billy laughed. "I guess I never had the chance to tell you about Firebrand. He's the start of my ranch."

"Well, it's a good start," Ben admitted.

Later that night after dinner, when Willie had gone to bed and Ben had retired, Claire asked if Billy would like to go outside and sit on the porch swing.

The night was beautiful. There was a warm breeze and a full moon in the starlit sky.

"How is your arm?" Billy asked as he sat down beside her in the large white swing.

"It's throbbing a little," she admitted. "Will you help me put on this sling?"

Once she had her arm secured, Billy reached over and pulled her next to him so that her head was resting on his chest just below his chin. She sighed. She felt his head resting on top of hers. She hadn't been this comfortable in days. "Do you want to talk?"

"Nope," Billy said in a weary voice. "I just want to hold you."

Claire could hear his heart beating beneath her ear and it gave her comfort. She could sense that their relationship was changing and it scared her.

After a while she heard his deep breathing and knew he had fallen asleep. It was proof of how tired he was.

She wanted Billy in her life. She wanted to enjoy every minute she could with him, but she feared what they had couldn't last and one day she would have to walk away.

Could he handle her sickness? She wasn't sure, but for tonight she was just content with what she had, knowing that everything could change tomorrow.

Chapter Twenty

The next morning Claire took the extra time to put her hair up in a chignon, wanting to look nice for Billy's family. She chose an open pelisse over a petticoat of muslin in a rose-lavender that she thought complemented her complexion. She was probably the only woman in Denver who didn't have brown in her wardrobe.

Billy and Willie were waiting for her on the porch. The horses had been brought from the barn, so they walked down and mounted the horses with Willie riding in front of Billy, who was riding Fire-brand.

Fluffy white clouds were scattered across the clear bright blue skies. The sun was warm over-head when it slipped from behind the clouds.

Claire loved the weather in Denver. With its dry climate, she could breathe a little easier. She'd only had two coughing spells since she'd been here.

"How is your arm?" Billy asked as he rode beside her.

"As you can imagine, it hurts, but I'll live," she said with a smile as she rode beside him.

"I'd like to have seen a real gunfight," Willie said.

"No, you wouldn't," Billy told him. "Men actually get killed in gunfights, and a man dying isn't a pretty sight. They only make it seem glamorous in books and newspapers."

Willie twisted around looking at Billy. "Did you get the drop on him?"

"I did." Billy glanced at Claire. "Then Miss Claire kind of got in the way."

"I was trying to help. I thought you were too tired to defend yourself," Claire offered.

"I'm glad you didn't get killed, Miss Claire," Willie said and then completely changed the subject. "Do you think they will like me?"

"Yes. So don't worry about it," Billy assured him.

Claire liked the easy way that Billy had with children. He was a natural and would make a good father. She tried to picture what their child would look like. He'd definitely have dark hair. But—and with her there was always a "but"—they would never have children together, so why waste time dreaming about it?

They had ridden a few miles when Willie shouted, "Look!" He pointed ahead. "There it is."

Up ahead of them was The Wagon Wheel that Billy had spoken of. They rode through the gate, up a long driveway to the front of a lovely home. Claire was as nervous as Willie about meeting Billy's family. But the time was here, so she had to go through with it.

By the time they had dismounted and tied their horses, a woman came out on the porch to greet them.

Claire knew this had to be Brandy. Billy had talked about her so much, Claire felt like she knew her.

Brandy was beautiful. Her hair was long and a dark red . . . just the color of Brandy, which Billy had told her was where she got her name. Her hair swung freely around her shoulders, and Claire was glad to see that she wore a pale green gown instead of the popular brown.

"I see you've brought company," Brandy said.

The screen door flew open and a young boy came flying out of the house and down the steps, heading straight for Billy. Billy swung the child around before placing him back on his feet again and asked, "You been behaving?"

"Yep. Who's this?"

"I was just getting ready to tell you," Billy said. "Brandy and Scott, I'd like you to meet Claire Holladay, and this is Willie."

"It is nice to meet you," Brandy said. "I see Billy got you back home safely. Though I must admit it seemed like he was gone a long time."

Claire climbed the steps and extended her hand. "We had some trouble along the way, but we made it."

"Please, come inside. Dinner is about ready," Brandy said, then looked at Willie. "You have a handsome son."

"Oh, Willie isn't my son," Claire said as she swept past Brandy. "He's Billy's."

Brandy stopped before entering the house, and swung around. "I beg your pardon?" she said and looked directly at Billy. "Explain."

Billy started laughing. "You should see the look on your face." He felt Willie tugging on his breeches. "Yes, young man?"

"She don't like me," Willie said, almost hiding behind Billy.

Billy pulled the child out and then scooped him up in his arms. "She didn't like me much either when we first met. Trust me, she likes you. She's just hard to get along with."

Brandy gave Billy a frown before turning her attention to Willie. "Of course I like you, Willie. I just know that you can't be Billy's child."

"Nope," Willie said. "I'm his brother."

"Willie is our brand new brother," Billy told Brandy, sitting Willie back down. "You see, Willie is an orphan, too."

Brandy squatted so she could be on eye level with the child. "Welcome to our family. This is Scott, another brother."

"Hi," Willie said then rushed on, "I will work real hard."

Brandy nodded. "That's good, in this family, everybody works the same as the others, so you'll have chores of your own. Isn't that right, Scott?"

"Yep," He agreed. "Hey, this means I'm not the youngest anymore." Scott grinned. "How old are you?"

"I'm five," Willie said.

"You can stay in my room, Willie. I think I'm going to like being an older brother," Scott admitted. "Come on, I'll show you around," he said as he put an arm around Willie's shoulders.

Willie looked back at Billy for approval. "It's all right," Billy assured him.

Scott and Willie had started down the steps when Scott glanced down at Willie. "Have you ever milked a cow before?"

"Nope," Willie said.

Scott smiled slowly. "Really? I'll show you how.

It's easy." He glanced back at Billy. "I kind of like this brother thing."

Billy and Brandy starting laughing as they passed Claire.

"Did I miss something?" Claire asked, a little puzzled as to what was so funny.

Billy took her hand. "Scott has always hated milking that 'blame cow,' so we figure that he has finally found somebody to take over his job. It is the price paid for being the younger brother."

Claire laughed. With her three brothers, she'd always had to pay the price for being the youngest . . . until she got sick.

They moved into the kitchen where two young girls were setting food out on the table. "We need to set the table for two more," Brandy instructed. "Billy brought a guest and we also have a new brother, Willie."

Everybody started talking at once, asking questions about Willie and welcoming Claire.

When the back door opened everyone stopped talking, then Brandy said, "Good, we can eat now."

A large man entered the back door with Scott and Willie right behind him. Claire automatically took a step backward. She knew this was Thunder. He was bigger than life. She could see why everybody had turned to him for help on the wagon train.

After all the introductions were made, they took their places at the long table, Claire sitting next to Billy. It reminded Claire of her dining room back home and just for a moment she felt a pang of homesickness. How she'd loved those family meals with all the discussions of what had happened during the day and, of course, an argument or two always kept things lively.

The meal smelled wonderful. There was roasted wild turkey and mashed potatoes, with corn on the cob and butter beans. As the food was passed there was a lot of chattering as they brought Billy up to date on what had been going on since he'd left. While Claire listened she couldn't help thinking that people didn't have to be blood kin to be a family. It seemed families came in all sizes and Willie was fitting right in.

They had to get a stack of books for Willie to sit on, so he could reach the table, but he was grinning and enjoying himself. A lump formed in Claire's throat. It was probably the only time Willie had ever sat down for a family dinner, and that she'd never thought about it until now made her feel ashamed.

"Tell us, Claire. What made you want to travel to Denver?" Thunder asked.

Claire swallowed the lump in her throat. She didn't want to lie so she'd just tell him the part that she wanted them to know. "I'm a journalist for *Harper's Weekly*. I wanted to visit my uncle and see this part of the country. I thought I could combine my trip with writing a few articles. Let the people back East see what it's like out here. They think it is only a wilderness."

"I remember that, myself," Thunder said with a chuckle. "When I lived in Boston, they didn't think there was life beyond the Mississippi."

"You lived in Boston?" Claire asked.

Thunder nodded. "It's where I studied law."

They continued asking Claire questions about her family and the horse farm. She almost felt as if she were being interviewed as a suitable companion for Billy, which was ridiculous since Billy didn't want a wife. However, Mary remained quiet during the dinner and Claire wondered why. She could feel Mary watching her from time to time, but she didn't say anything.

Mary looked nothing like the rest of the family, who all had dark hair. Mary had thick blonde hair that hung in natural curls around her shoulders. And her eyes were the most unusual clear blue, as if you were looking in a pool of crystal clear water and you could never see the bottom. She was lovely.

"What is this I hear about a gold mine?" Billy asked.

She glanced at him, not sure what he was speaking of, but she soon found out because he was staring directly at Mary, whose cheeks had turned a vivid pink.

Scott broke the silence. "Yeah, Mary has a gold mine."

Mary took a sip of tea before she placed her glass on the table. "My mother somehow found out where I was living and sent me a deed to a gold mine. There was a note attached saying, 'This is to make up for all the things that I never gave you.' "

"After all this time," Billy said with a shake of his head. "I figured she'd forgotten all about you. Is the deed real?"

"It appears so," Thunder supplied.

Billy sat back in his chair, reaching for Claire's hand under the table. "So what are you going to do?" he asked Mary.

"I'm going to stake my claim and work it."

"Tell her how crazy that is," Brandy interjected.

Claire was enjoying this family discussion. It reminded her of when she told her family she was traveling West. It seemed this family argued just like her family. Maybe arguing was a part of all families. She could see by the set expression on Mary's face that she was determined and not about to back down.

"You don't know the first thing about mining," Billy told her.

"Are you fighting?" Willie asked.

"No, Willie. This is called a family discussion, so listen and learn," Thunder told the child. "It's normal around here."

Mary tossed her napkin on the table. "I didn't know anything about wagons, either, but I had to learn. And . . . if everyone will remember, I didn't want to travel West in the first place."

"We remember," everyone said at once, and then they all started laughing, breaking up the argument.

Billy turned to Claire to explain, "Mary wasn't always as agreeable as she is now, and she told us more than once she wasn't going West."

"Billy, can I talk to you alone?" Mary asked.

He slid his chair back. "Sure. Let's take a walk." He reached down and squeezed Claire's shoulder. "I'll be back in a few minutes."

Once they had left, Claire said to Brandy, "The meal was delicious. Can I help you clear the table?"

"Ellen and Mary cook so they are the ones to thank. They don't let me near a stove," Brandy laughed. "But you can help us clean up."

"If Brandy had cooked dinner, you'd be green by now," Scott joked as he got up and motioned for Willie to come on.

Thunder reached over and kissed Brandy on the mouth. "You take a lot of abuse over your cooking, sweetheart, but you do do other things well."

Claire thought that was sweet. She could see how much Thunder loved his wife. She hoped that someday someone would look at her like that.

"Willie, are you ready to help me with the cows?" Thunder asked.

"Sure. Scott has already showed me how to milk the cow."

"I bet he did," Thunder said with an arched brow at Scott.

Scott merely shrugged. "After we get through with our chores then we can play and have some fun."

"Oh boy," Willie said, following Scott out the back door.

After they left, Claire said, "I think Willie is already enjoying his new home. He is a very lucky little boy."

They began clearing the table. "I'm not surprised Billy brought him home," Brandy said. "He has always had a way with children. He'll make a good father."

Claire felt a small pain that she wouldn't be the mother of Billy's children. "I'm sure he will."

"What was Billy like when he came to the orphanage?" Claire asked.

"He had two black eyes and red streaks across his back where he'd been beaten," Brandy said. She tied an apron around her and began to tell Claire what she knew of Billy as a child.

As Billy and Mary walked along the path, they were quiet. Billy was giving Mary plenty of time to talk to him. He knew he'd always been closer to her than anyone.

When they finally reached the group of aspen

trees, she said, "Aren't you going to give me a lecture about wanting to mine for gold?"

"Would it do any good?"

"No," she admitted with a soft smile. "I know how crazy it sounds, but you should know better than anyone how I feel. We have always been so much alike. You must remember when you couldn't wait to get out on your own?"

"But I'm a man."

"Rubbish!" Mary snapped. "Women have desires, too, Mr. West. I love my family, but I want to find my own way. I can't live with Brandy and Thunder forever. I suppose one day I might find a husband or somebody special like you've found."

Billy stopped and looked at Mary. "And what makes you think that I've found somebody? I thought those rumors had stopped about me and Mandy."

Mary looked at him a long time before she said, "That's not what I was talking about. You don't realize it, do you? I can see the way you look at Claire. You love her."

"That's ridiculous," Billy shot back.

Mary's brow raised. "Is it?"

Billy started to say something and then stopped.

"Look, I should know better than anyone. I have loved you all my life," Mary admitted. "And I know when I've lost you." There were tears in Mary's eyes.

Billy reached out and hugged her. "Ah, Mary you have only thought you loved me because you haven't known anyone else. But I bet if you look at it real hard you'll realize that you love me like a brother, the same as I love you. We've been through a lot together."

Mary nodded her head and then pulled back.

"You're right. I don't know anyone else, and I never will, staying out here on the ranch. That is why I have to do this and make my own way."

"All right, I can see what you're saying. How about if I take you to this claim and make sure you have someplace to live?" He suggested. "That will make the whole family feel better."

A slow smile flitted across Mary's face, and then she reached up and kissed Billy briefly on the lips. "Claire is very lucky to have you."

Billy smiled down at Mary. "You're not losing me, Mary. We'll never stop being brother and sister, and if you get in trouble all you have to do is send word and I'll be there. As for Claire, she told me in no uncertain terms that she wasn't the marrying kind, so I don't know if she is lucky or not."

Mary looped her arm through Billy's when they started back to the house. "Have you asked her?"

"No."

"Then you don't know what the answer is. But if you don't ask her and you let her get away, you could be losing the most important thing in your life," Mary said.

Billy chuckled. "When did you get to be so wise?"

"Somewhere along the line, I must have grown up."

"It could have started with that dunking in the river," Billy teased.

"I'll admit that I didn't have the best attitude." Mary chuckled, too. "We've both done a lot of growing up, wouldn't you say?"

"Yep. Sometimes you wish things would never change, but life goes on and it has to change. I guess I'm trying to say that it's your turn to find out what is out there. And I don't want to lose you to someone else, either."

"You'll never lose me," Mary said. "I'll be your ornery sister forever."

"Ornery is right. I forgot about that part. You, finding a man will be impossible."

"Go to hell, Billy West," Mary said with a grin.

Billy chuckled. "When do you want to leave?"

"In two days."

The next day Billy and Claire had just finished supper and had walked out onto the porch to sit in the swing, while Uncle Ben retired. It was a lovely evening with a gentle breeze. Floppy had followed them, flopping down on his favorite spot in the corner.

"Does that dog ever run?" Billy asked as he and Claire sat on the swing.

"Sure he does," Claire said. "You just have never been around when he chooses to run."

Billy cut his eyes at Claire. "I'd have to see it before I believe it. Actually seeing him standing is rare."

"Don't pick on my dog," Claire teased. "He's just a sedentary animal."

"All right," Billy said, giving the swing a shove. "How are your stories coming along?"

"Good. I finally received a letter from Ann yesterday. She said my articles were well received at the office and the first should appear in the magazine next week. They especially liked the one about the Daltons."

"So your trip has been successful?" Billy asked as he slipped an arm around Claire. "Do you like it out here?"

"I think this trip was necessary for many reasons, and I love it out here. I don't think anyone can appreciate the beauty of this country unless they get to see it for themselves."

"I love it, too. I don't know, there is something about it that just says it's home."

At this moment, Claire couldn't remember when she'd felt so contented as she leaned her head on Billy's shoulder. The gentle breeze felt wonderful as they rocked slowly back and forth. She could feel the strength in Billy's arms and she felt safe. If only he could chase away all the demons in her life.

"You're quiet," he said in a low voice.

"I was enjoying the moment. It seem so perfect tonight," she admitted.

"I was thinking the same thing. I'm going to be leaving tomorrow."

"I thought you had a few days off from work," Claire said.

"It isn't work. I'm going to escort Mary to that gold mine of hers."

"Oh," Claire said in a small voice, already knowing that she'd miss him. "How long will you be gone?"

"I'm not sure. Will you miss me?" Billy asked.

Claire twisted and looked up at him. "Of course I'll miss you. But I can understand you wanting to take Mary and make sure she is safe. I really like your family."

Billy helped Claire to shift until she was stretched out on the swing, lying across his chest. He supported her back with his arm. "There, now I can see you when I talk. Are you comfortable?"

"Very."

"I'm glad you like my family. They like you, too."

"They remind me of my family."

Billy chuckled. "Yep, they are lively like your brothers." He stared at her with an odd smile that made Claire's heart jump.

"I'll miss you while you're gone," she whispered.

"Claire," Billy said and then paused again. He thought about what Mary had said. If he wanted something he should go after it and not worry that he wasn't a wealthy man. "I never thought I'd ask anyone this question, but I'm asking now. Will you marry me?"

"But you said you were not the marrying kind," Claire said trying to buy some time. She hadn't expected a proposal. If she'd been normal, she'd have been jumping for joy, but she wasn't a normal young woman, anything but.

"I didn't think I was the marrying kind," Billy admitted. "Then I met you." He smiled. "I realize that I've sprung this on you. Why don't you think about my proposal while I'm gone and give me an answer when I return? I cannot promise you the kind of life that you are used to, but I will tell you that I love you very much, Claire. Life hasn't been the same since I've met you."

Claire reached up and touched the side of his face. "I love you, too."

Billy's arms tightened around her, pulling her closer while his eyes held her spellbound. *Tell him, Claire,* she told herself, *tell him that you're not going to marry him, send him away and let him find someone he can make a life with.*

But Claire said nothing.

This one time she was selfish as she anticipated Billy's kiss. The first tender brush of his warm lips made her heart catch in her throat, and her eyelids fluttered closed. She loved this man so much she ached inside as she became lost in a dreamy world that only he could take her to.

What Billy intended to be a chaste kiss was rapidly changing as he tasted the sweetness Claire offered him. Her soft, beguiling mouth became the only invitation he needed as he gave in to his longings and deepened the kiss. She responded by wrapping her arms around his neck and pressing her body into his.

Clutching Claire to him, he gently parted her lips with his tongue and explored her velvety softness. The very taste of her was like no other before. He really wanted an answer before he left, but he could wait. She couldn't respond to him like this and say no. Yes, he was going to make this woman his wife, and build his dream with her.

Desire flared in his veins and something told him that he wanted to remember this night forever. He lifted his mouth and struggled to restrain himself, even as his blood pounded through his body. He knew, in her uncle's home, that he couldn't answer the desire that he saw in her eyes.

"You're so beautiful," he murmured. "I want to take this picture of you with me until I return." He brushed his fingertips across her warm cheeks, and found himself memorizing every facet of her delicate features and especially her determined jaw. He claimed her mouth again. By God, she was sweet.

His lips moved along her neck, and his self-control slipped a notch as he unbuttoned her blouse with dexterous fingers. Sliding his hand beneath her blouse, he captured a full, ripe breast, and rubbed his finger back and forth across her nipple until it hardened with desire.

When he heard her moan, he came to his senses

and looked down at her. "We had better stop. I don't think Ben would like it very well if I swept past him with you in my arms and took you up to my bed."

Claire smiled as she buttoned her blouse. "I don't think he would look kindly on either of us." When she finished buttoning her blouse, she leaned up and kissed Billy lightly on the lips. "I'll remember this night as long as I live," she murmured, then added, "Thank you."

Billy chuckled. "Well, at least remember it until I can return and provide you many more nights like this one."

The next morning thunder clouds had rolled in and threatened to let loose their rain drops as the thunder rumbled in the distance. Claire thought the day was perfect, as it matched the turmoil within her.

Tell him, Claire. The voice wouldn't leave her alone.

She stood on the steps and kissed Billy goodbye. Then she watched as he mounted his horse. He looked at her for a long moment before pulling his horse around.

Tell him, Claire.

She said nothing. She could only stand there and watch him ride off, watching until she couldn't see him any longer.

Her heart was breaking. Would she ever see him again?

And if she did, what would her answer be?

Chapter Twenty-One

As the weeks slipped by, Claire kept busy writing articles, and keeping her mind off Billy. He had been gone much longer than expected, and it gave her time to think that maybe she could marry him. A couple of weeks had gone by without any coughing spells.

Then one night Claire had a terrible coughing spell that left her gasping for breath. Her chest hurt worse than it ever had and when she looked down at her arm she saw phthisis for the first time.

Aunt Ute tried to give Claire her medicine but it wasn't working. Blood covered her handkerchief.

Claire managed to gasp. "It's getting worse."

Aunt Ute nodded in agreement.

Finally, when Claire had gotten her hacking under control, she gasped for air and asked, "What day is it?"

Aunt Ute thought for a moment before answering, "The first day of September."

Claire felt the blood drain from her face and suddenly she felt very cold and all alone. She was quiet for a few minutes. "This is the end, Aunt Ute."

"No, child. You mustn't think that way."

"I met a doctor a few months ago who said that I should contact her," Claire paused. "I kept hoping I'd get better, but now I can see that I'm not going to. I'm not sure this woman can help. I'm not sure anyone can help, but now I'm willing to try one last time and hope for a miracle.

"I've made up my mind, I'm going to see Doc Susie. She lives in Fraser, which I understand is high in the mountains. I know that you like it here so you don't have to come," Claire said.

"Nonsense!" Ute waved her hand brushing the suggestion away. "If you're going, I will be there with you, *liebchen.*"

"I can always count on you Aunt Ute. And I want you to know that has been a big comfort to me. Now let's start packing while I can still travel."

"What about Billy?"

Claire felt an icy dread seep through her. "I'll leave him a note, telling him goodbye."

"But you love him," Aunt Ute pointed out.

"That's why I'm leaving. I couldn't stand to have Billy watch me die. I couldn't handle the pity when all I want is his love. He deserves someone who can give him children and will always be with him. I'm not that person."

"I wish I could ease the hurt for you, child," Aunt Ute said and pulled Claire into her arms.

"I wish you could, too," Claire whispered, brokenhearted as she sobbed into her aunt's bosom.

* * *

The next morning everything was packed by the time Claire went downstairs to have breakfast with Uncle Ben and Aunt Ute.

Claire waited until breakfast was served before she made her announcement. "I'm going to Fraser," she finally blurted out.

She immediately got her uncle's attention as his head snapped up and he lowered his fork. Ben looked at his niece for a long moment. The deep, lavender circles under her eyes were more pronounced than they had been, and he could see the disease was robbing her of her youth. "Isn't this kind of sudden?" Ben asked as he leaned back in his chair.

"I know, but my condition is getting worse. I had a bad spell last night."

"I see," he said reaching for his cup of coffee. After he'd taken a sip he asked, "Why Fraser?"

"Do you remember the doctor who helped me when I was shot?"

"Yes, I do. Believe her name was Susie," Ben said. "Nice woman."

"Well, my doctor from back home sent my medical history to her. She thinks she can help me. I'm not sure if she can, but I'm willing to try."

"And what do you think of this, Ute?"

"I have not met the woman," Ute replied. "But I do know that Claire needs to do something to get better."

"I see." Ben rubbed his chin. "Then I don't blame you for going but don't you want to wait until Billy returns?"

Claire finally put her fork down, unable to eat. "I thought he'd be back before now, but my time is running out so I can't wait. You do realize this is the first of September?"

Ben nodded.

"Besides, I don't know if I could tell Billy in person that I don't want to marry him. I'm not sure I could stand to see the hurt in his eyes."

"So you're going to take the easy way out," Ben said with a frown, "and walk out on Billy just like everybody else."

"Don't be so hard on her," Aunt Ute told him.

"I'm not being hard. But it's very evident that Billy loves Claire, and he'll be coming home expecting to find her waiting for him."

"And that's the reason I must not be here," Claire insisted. "I must convince Billy that I don't love him anymore." She leaned forward on the table. "I have to see if there is a chance I can get well. If I can't, he will have lost me anyway. Don't you understand, I'm doing this because I love Billy? He doesn't deserve my problems."

"I think you are cutting Billy short," Ben said. "But I will abide by your wishes."

Claire breathed a sigh of relief. "Thank you." She felt so tired and her chest hurt, but she had to go. Reaching into her pocket, she pulled out a letter and laid it on the table. "I want you to give this to Billy."

"All right," her uncle agreed.

"Now that all that is settled, how do we get to Fraser?" Aunt Ute asked.

"By train. You'll be going into the high country. Thank God it's only September because when the winter months set in the only way you can get there is by train and sometimes that doesn't work because of the snow."

"Can we get the train from Denver?" Claire asked.

"Yes," Ben said with a smile. "Ute, you'll love

Fraser. It will remind you of home or at least the way I remember Germany. Fraser is eighty-five miles across the Continental Divide in the midst of 13,000-foot peaks. It's maybe fifty miles from Denver as the crow flies, longer any other way. I'll take you to the train whenever you're ready."

"We're already packed and ready to go," Aunt Ute said.

"We?" Ben asked.

"*Ja.* I wouldn't let her travel alone. Besides, the doctor could probably use a good nurse."

"And she'll be getting one," Ben said as he rose from his chair.

"We'll be leaving in a few minutes," said Claire.

When her uncle rounded the table, Claire hugged him. "Thank you for understanding. I'll miss you," she said. "I would like you to take care of Floppy for me. I'm afraid it will be too cold where I'm going, come winter. If something happens to me, make sure Willie gets him."

Ben nodded. "I'll do that. I think Floppy has adjusted well here. This morning when I went into my office, I found him on the sofa with his head on a pillow. He didn't move an inch when I came in."

Claire laughed, the first time in days. "Floppy does like his comforts."

Once they were under way, Claire felt like she was leaving her life behind her and a deep sadness settled in her. She knew that her heart was breaking because she was walking out on the one person she truly loved. After he read her note all that would change and Billy would hate her.

You're walking out just like everybody else has. Her

uncle's words rang in her ears, and the worst part was that it was true. She shut her eyes and took a deep breath, hoping the words would go away. As much as it hurt now . . . it would hurt so much more later. Sometimes life wasn't fair. She'd just have to put one foot in front of another and do what she needed to do and somehow she'd get by.

The steady rhythmic clack-clack of the train wheels began to soothe her as the train started its climb through the foothills. She stared out the window at the tall ponderosa pines. Her ears felt funny from the pressure, and she looked to Ute. "Do your ears feel strange?"

"*Ja.* Swallow," Ute said. "Better?"

"Yes."

"The higher we climb in the mountain, the more pressure you'll have on your ears. Just swallow and it will go away. You will get to use to it after awhile."

Claire smiled at her aunt. "You always know so much," she said. "I wish I were more like you."

Aunt Ute chuckled. "It's called age, my dear. The more years you live, the smarter you become. It is strange, but I have a good feeling about our trip. I feel that the higher altitude will be good for you and make it easier for you to breathe."

"Now that you mentioned it, my chest has stopped hurting. I hope you're right," Claire said and turned her attention back to looking out the window. "Look, there is a mountain up ahead." She had no more said it than they were plunged into darkness. Claire reached for her aunt.

"Do not worry. We are in a tunnel that runs through the mountain. We'll be out in a few minutes. Can you imagine making this tunnel?"

"No. It sounds impossible to me," Claire admitted.

In just a short time the train burst from the tunnel back into daylight.

A big Swedish lumberjack sat across from them. He wore a red plaid shirt and he held his black knit cap in his lap. "Dere's nothing for you little ladies to be worrin' about," he said with his heavy accent. "I've made this trip many times."

"*Danke* for your concern," Aunt Ute said. "Have you been in this country long?"

"About three years now," he said. "And you hail from Germany?"

"*Ja.*" Aunt Ute said. "It's nice to meet you."

They entered another tunnel and this time when they came out the car had started to grow hazy from the coal smoke, which accumulated with each tunnel they went through. It was also getting colder and Claire reached for her shawl.

"Tie your handkerchief over your mouth and nose, and it will help you breathe easier," the big Swede suggested.

Claire did as he instructed and it did help. She wanted to smile her thanks at the man. Instead she nodded.

"What is your name?" Ute asked.

"I am Joseph. I am a lumberjack with these other men," he said.

Claire leaned against the window as Ute and Joseph continued talking. It was the most Claire had heard her aunt talk in a long time and she was glad that Ute found something enjoyable about the trip.

If Billy were here, she'd be talking to him, too. She missed him already. God, how she missed him. It was funny how he'd come to mean so much to her in such a short time. But she wouldn't go back and trade one minute of their time together.

Love makes fools of us all was Claire's last thought as she drifted to sleep.

When she woke she heard Joseph saying, "This tunnel is called the Needle's Eye because the engineer can see a slit of daylight through it as he comes up the grade from Yankee Doodle."

"They have some strange names," Ute said.

As Claire straightened they were coming out of the tunnel. She turned and glanced out the window and her heart jumped into her throat; she was staring straight down 2,000 feet. She felt like the only thing holding the train up was thin air. Finally, she pulled her gaze away from the window, deciding it was too scary to watch any longer.

The train started to slow and the conductor came through announcing they were pulling into Arrow. All the lumberjacks told them goodbye and started off the train.

Joseph stopped beside Aunt Ute and said, "Tanks very much, missus, I enjoy our conversation. Maybe I will get to see you again sometime."

"Ja," Aunt Ute replied. "If you get to Fraser come by and see me."

Claire nudged Ute. "I think he likes you."

She smiled. "He's a fine man, *Ja.*"

"I agree. With that blond hair and blue eyes, he'd steal any woman's heart."

The train continued on chugging over the mountains. When Claire didn't think that they could go much higher the train pulled into the station where a big wooden sign that looked haggard from the weather proclaimed they had finally arrived in Fraser.

Claire stepped off the train and collapsed.

* * *

Billy and Mary were thirty miles away when they caught their first glimpse of Pikes Peak. The mountain rose to a majestic height of 12,000 feet and its apex was covered with perpetual snow.

As they wound their way around the mountain through lofty pines and cedars, the air grew much cooler so that they had to slip on their jackets. Billy wondered if there really was a mining town in this wilderness. They had ridden for miles without seeing anything other than antelope and a bear or two.

About the time he was ready to suggest turning back, they reached a small mining town. The rough wooden sign said they were in Gregory Gulch. In a field to the left was a herd of antelope grazing in a meadow. Everything appeared very peaceful, or was the word dead?

"This isn't much of a town," Billy said as they sat on their horses looking down a dirt street that had log cabins scattered on both sides. Each brown cabin looked alike—some didn't even have windows.

"I'm not sure what I was expecting, but it wasn't this," Mary admitted.

"Do you want to go back?"

"No. I'm determined to make this work. If a little hard work will bring me gold and independence then I can handle this. However, I am glad we stopped and picked up supplies and heavy clothes. It is the middle of August, but it's cool up here."

"Yes, it is," Billy said. "I guess we should go to the claims office first and find out where your claim is located, and then we can see about finding you someplace to stay."

"I really do appreciate your help," Mary said.

Billy smiled at her. "That's what brothers are for."

It was easy to find the recorder's office because it was in the middle of the buildings and had a big sign hung on the side. When they dismounted they found a line waiting to see the clerk so they had to wait.

Finally Mary made it to the desk. She took out her deed and handed it to the man. It took him a few minutes to read it over. He reached under his desk and pulled out a very large book that looked like it contained a variety of maps.

After flipping several pages, he frowned and reached for a brown book on the edge of his desk. He turned back and forth between several pages until he found what he wanted. He scanned the page with his index finger. "Ah, yaw," he said and tapped the spot with his finger before looking up at Mary. "You have a problem."

"What is the problem?" Mary asked.

"Somebody has already filed a claim on this here land."

"But this is a legal document. I've had a lawyer look it over," Mary insisted, and then added, "What can I do?"

"I'd go see Marshal Stanley. Maybe he can straighten this out for you."

Billy stepped forward. "Where do we find the marshal?"

The clerk pointed. "Two doors down on the right."

"Do you know the name of the other owner?" Billy asked.

"Let's see," the clerk looked down. "Oh dear, it's Big Jim McCoy. He's an Irishman with a mean temper."

"Great!" Mary rolled her eyes. "Just what I need."

They took their horses and pack mules with them and tied them outside the marshal's office.

Upon explaining to Marshal Stanley the problem and showing him the deed, he sent a deputy to get Big Jim.

Fifteen minutes later Big Jim McCoy strode into the office shouting, "Who the hell is trying to steal my claim!"

The man made two of Billy. McCoy was broad shouldered and wore faded overalls with a blue flannel shirt, and had a gun and a bowie knife tucked into his work belt. He wasn't a young man, but a weathered veteran.

As soon as he saw Mary, he removed his wide-brimmed hat displaying his black hair streaked with gray. "Ma'am," he said with a nod.

Turning his attention back to the marshal he said. "Now who is this cussed sidewinder?"

"I am," Mary said and stepped in front of him. "My mother sent me the deed." She handed him the papers. "As you can see, it's legal. It says nothing about me having a partner."

Big Jim snatched the deed from her.

Billy was proud of his sister not backing down from Big Jim. As a matter of fact, she looked more like an angry cat with its fur standing straight up. Big Jim would scare most men with his thick black beard and long black hair that was streaked with gray.

After Jim read the deed, he threw it on the marshal's desk. Then he pulled his deed out from a pocket and tossed it beside hers.

"That deed used to belong to Toothless Tom. When he left he told me I could have his part 'cause he was through with mining," Big Jim told the marshal.

"Do you have any paperwork to prove that, Big Jim?"

Big Jim frowned. "A man's word ought to be good enough."

"Not when it comes to property. As you well know, many have been killed over property disputes," Marshal Stanley told him. "The way I see it, you have a new partner."

"But she's a female," Big Jim pointed out the obvious.

"What's wrong with that?" Mary snapped.

"Plenty," Big Jim said and looked directly at her. "Mining is damn hard work and you're puny. 'Sides every man would be after you once he saw you, and I don't have time for such."

"I've already thought about that," Mary informed him. "I'm going to dress as a man and keep my hair under a cap so everyone will think I'm a boy. As for work, I intend to work just as hard as you. What I lack in muscle, I'll make up with brains."

"I doubt that," Jim shot back.

Mary stepped closer to the man. "Well, Big Jim, you don't have a choice."

He glared at her. "You're a mouthy little thing."

"So I've been told," Mary said.

With that comment, Big Jim started laughing and all the tension in the room eased. "All right. I give you two months before you're running back home." He looked at Billy. "Who's he?"

Billy pushed away from the wall where he had thoroughly enjoyed the exchange between these two. It seemed Big Jim had a wild cat by the tail and didn't know quite how to handle her.

"I'm her brother, Billy West."

"Good. You can help her."

"I'm not staying," Billy told him.

The Irishman appeared as if his patience was all but gone. "Is she plumb loco? Life ain't easy up here."

"So I've tried to tell her," Billy said. "But as you can see, she has a mind of her own."

"I can also speak for myself," Mary informed both of them.

"See," Billy said with a shrug.

The marshal cleared his throat. "Then it's settled. You both have equal ownership in the mine. If one of you dies, then the other inherits full ownership. Is that agreeable?"

They both nodded.

"Good," Marshal Stanley said. Then he scribbled the agreement on both deeds. "Sign here that you agree. Myself and Mr. West will witness the signatures." When the signatures were obtained, the marshal said, "Good. Now get out of my office. I have work to do."

Once they were outside, Big Jim asked. "Where are you staying?"

"I don't have a place yet," Mary said.

"Well, there ain't no empty cabins around here."

"Oh," Mary said as she stopped by the three pack mules loaded with supplies."

"These yours?" Big Jim asked.

Mary nodded.

"How about if I make you a deal?" Jim said with a smile. "Seeing as I can't get rid of you, why don't you throw your supplies in with mine, and you can stay with me."

"I'm not so sure about that," Billy said.

"Don't go getting your dander up. I have the

biggest cabin up here with two bedrooms. It's a little ways up the hill. She'd have her own sleeping quarters. 'Sides which, I'm old enough to be your Da. I have a daughter your age back home."

So an agreement was made.

Billy stayed another month to make sure Mary was settled in and could handle everything. Then he decided he needed to worry more about Big Jim than Mary. She already had the man eating out of her hand.

When it was time to go, Billy did have a talk with Jim and told him if he ever made the mistake of hurting his sister that Billy would return with a vengeance.

Big Jim nodded.

Billy gave Mary a hug. "You take care of yourself."

"I will," she said in a soft voice. "You take care of yourself and my future sister-in-law."

Billy smiled. "I will."

He rode off with a peaceful mind about Mary. She was going to make it on her own. As he started down the mountain heading for home, he realized that he'd been gone much longer than he'd expected. He wasn't sure of the day but it must be two months since he'd left. He did know that he was more than ready to see Claire. God, he'd missed her.

During the days he'd stayed pretty busy, but at night when all was quiet, his thoughts were always of Claire. She made him happy. She gave him a sense of purpose.

He felt that most of his life he'd had no direction. He'd been wandering, never sure exactly what he wanted to do.

Now he knew.

He wanted Claire. Together they would start

their own horse farm. With her knowledge, he knew that they would raise the best horseflesh around these parts.

Looking back, Billy realized that he'd been looking for Claire all his life and he was going to make her his wife as soon as he returned. No more waiting.

Suddenly, as he rode toward Denver, life seemed perfect.

Chapter Twenty-Two

The minute Doc Susie saw Claire, she ordered her to bed, and that was fine by Claire. She hadn't realized how exhausted she was from the physical strain of traveling.

Claire slept for two days.

Upon waking the morning of the third day, she found a big difference in the way she felt when she got up. The mornings were cold and the air dry, making it easier for her to breathe.

She wrapped a comforter around her and wandered into the big kitchen where Susie was preparing breakfast and Aunt Ute was stacking wood in the potbelly stove.

"Good morning," Claire said from the doorway.

Aunt Ute swung around. "She up."

"Good. Now we can talk about your new routine while you're here," Susie said. "How do you feel?"

"Much better," Claire said with a yawn as she took her seat at the table. "I didn't realize I was so tired."

"When you're tired, the disease takes over your

body. Now here is what we're going to do," Susie
said, setting a steaming bowl of hot oatmeal on the
table with fresh fruit and cream. As she poured
everyone coffee, she said, "We are going to give
you a regimen of rest, healthy food, and fresh air,
and when you're stronger we are going to add
plenty of exercise."

"Do you think this will work?" Claire asked.

"It has for me. Some doctors like to prescribe a
whiskey-cure. They think it stimulates the appetite
and is a relaxant. But I disagree. I think it con-
tributes to listlessness and depression. So what we
are going to do is walk once a day over to my
neighbors and go to Bossy, his milking cow."

"Why?" Claire asked as she ate her warm oatmeal.

"We are going to squirt milk from the cow's teat
directly into a bottle and then we are going to
drink the milk right away."

"And that helps?"

"Yes, it does," Doc Susie assured her.

"I would like to help you in your practice," Aunt
Ute said.

"Good. There are times I can use all the help I
can get," Susie said.

And so the autumn days went by as Claire sat
outside in the warm sunshine, sipping her coffee
and staring up at the aspen leaves shining like
pure gold. It was so much easier to breathe up
here. The sweet air seemed to rush bubbles of oxy-
gen into her scarred lungs. And slowly she began
regaining the strength she'd lost long ago.

Every morning she'd go to the calendar to mark
off the days until it was the last day in September.

As she held the pencil in her hand, she realized that she'd been living on the edge, waiting to die. She'd been to so many doctors who'd never been able to help her that she'd really doubted Doc Susie could do anything. It was the last day of September and she was still alive. Now she dared to hope that she would live.

And of course, Billy was foremost in Claire's mind. Did he hate her for leaving him? Would he understand when she saw him again and explained? All these questions were running through her mind when she told Doc Susie one night at dinner, "I feel so much better. When will I be able to return to Denver?"

Susie stopped eating and looked directly at Claire. "I do not advise you going to Denver." Seeing the surprised look on Claire's face, Susie reached out and placed her hand over Claire's. "The climate here in Fraser is beneficial to your recovery. I've seen tuberculosis patients leave only to suffer a relapse, and sometimes it was fatal. My advice is to continue with your routine of vigorous exercise, rest, and plenty of fresh warm milk."

"But he'll forget me," Claire slipped and said. She hadn't meant her thoughts to come out, but she wanted to see Billy so bad that it hurt.

"Who?" Susie asked.

Aunt Ute could see how choked up Claire was and answered for her. "Billy West, a young man from Denver, asked Claire to marry him. Claire thought she was dying so she left town before he came back, not wanting to burden him with her problems."

Susie looked at Claire sympathetically. "No wonder you've looked so sad. You could send him a note and let him know where you are."

Claire shook her head. "No. I need to do it in person. I left him a note telling him that I didn't love him, so I'm sure he hates me by now."

"That is the sign of true love. You sacrificed yourself for him," Susie said in a soft voice. "But I can assure you of this, there is a fine line between love and hate. If he loves you, he'll find you one way or the other."

"He must hate me," Claire said, realizing that there was more than one way to die inside.

Billy West did hate Claire with every fiber of his being.

He had returned home, going to the ranch immediately, only to be told that Claire and her aunt had left. So Billy had ridden to Ben's office, opened the door and demanded an explanation.

"You were gone a lot longer than expected," Ben said when Billy slammed into his office.

"And she couldn't wait?"

"Sit down," Ben instructed.

"I don't want to sit down. Where is Claire?"

"She's gone."

"Why do I feel like you're playing a game with me?" Billy growled. "Where did she go and when is she returning?"

Ben didn't answer as he stared at Billy for a moment. Finally he said, "Claire won't be coming back."

Billy felt like he'd been slugged in the stomach as he sank down on the chair in front of Ben's desk. "Why?" Then Billy remembered what he'd said all along. "It was because I don't have the money the Holladays do, isn't it?"

"No, that isn't it at all," Ben said.

"It sure seems like it to me."

Ben opened his desk drawer and pulled out the letter. "Here, she left this for you. Maybe it will explain."

Billy took the envelope and tore it open. The script was delicate, just like Claire.

Dear Billy,
I so much don't want to hurt you, but sometimes we have to do things we don't want to do.
For reasons that I can't disclose to you, I'm leaving Denver and will not be returning. Believe me this is for the best.
Have a good life, Billy West. You deserve the best. Find somebody who loves you and can give you children.

Claire

The second time he read the letter, he felt his hopes and dreams crumble around his feet. She hadn't even said she loved him. Maybe she never had. She left him like everyone else in his life had.

Something within Billy died as he crumpled the letter and glanced at Ben across the desk. "When do I return to work?"

"As soon as you want to," Ben said. "Listen, Billy, I'm sorry that I can't tell you more, but I promised that I wouldn't. There are things that you don't know."

"I don't really care, Ben," Billy said, his voice void of emotion as he got to his feet. "Tell Rattlesnake I'll be ready to ride in the morning."

Ben watched as Billy left his office. It was on the tip of his tongue to tell Billy that Claire loved him very much. But Billy wouldn't listen to anything now. If only Ben hadn't made that promise . . . but he'd only promised not to tell Billy. What if he told someone else?

With that idea rumbling in his head, he quickly penned a letter to the one person who could get Billy to listen to reason.

As he sealed the letter, Ben thought, now with a little luck and a few prayers maybe a miracle could happen. He didn't even know how Claire was doing. He only knew that if she'd died, someone would have let him know.

The next two months became a blur to Billy. He worked all the time and took foolish chances, because he didn't care if he lived or died.

Rattlesnake had become a nag, fussing at him like an old mother hen. But Billy didn't care. He'd ceased caring from the moment he'd read that letter. The one time he'd dared to open his heart to a woman, she'd ripped it to shreds.

"Do you realize that it's almost Christmas?" Rattlesnake said as they rolled into Denver.

"So?" Billy replied.

"Thought you might be going out to spend some time with your family at The Wagon Wheel. It's been a while since you've seen them."

"Nope. Let them enjoy the holidays. I'm not in the mood to celebrate," Billy said in a voice that Rattlesnake thought sounded pretty much like the boy was dead.

"Iffen you ask me, you ain't in the mood for nothing," Rattlesnake complained.

"That about sums it up," Billy said as the stage pulled to a stop.

"This ain't any of my business," Rattlesnake said,

"but you need to start living again. Ain't no woman worth it."

Billy glanced up at Rattlesnake. "You're right. It isn't any of your business." Billy went into the stage office and deposited the mailbag and then left.

He had a room over at the hotel, but he wasn't quite in the mood to sleep yet. Glancing at the saloon, he thought maybe some good whiskey could numb him a little . . . make him forget.

He'd just stepped off the sidewalk when someone called out, "Billy West."

Billy turned at the familiar voice to see Heath Holladay strolling up toward him. What was he doing here?

"What the hell have you done to my sister?" Heath shouted, and gave Billy a good right across the jaw.

"Done to your sister?" Billy said as he rubbed his jaw. Then he squared up his body with Heath's. "I've been dying to beat the shit out of somebody and you're as good as any."

Billy landed a left into Heath's middle. Heath grabbed Billy around the middle and down they went swinging and landing punches until they both were too tired to swing again.

"I'll give up if you give up," Heath finally said.

Billy took a deep breath. "It's either that or we kill each other."

"So how the hell have you been?" Heath asked.

Billy slowly got to his feet then reached down to help Heath up. "You got a funny way of greeting people."

Heath gave Billy a lopsided grin because his lip was so swollen. "Got your attention, didn't I? Let's go somewhere where we can talk."

"I was just headed for the bar," Billy said. "You throw a mean right, Holladay. I can feel my eye swelling already."

They got a table in the corner and ordered a cool wet rag, coffee, and Scotch. After they got their faces cleaned up, Billy spoke before Heath could say anything. "I don't want to talk about your sister."

"Well I do."

Billy started to get up, but Heath caught his arm. "Don't make me have to lay you out again. I'm going to tell you something that you don't know. After I tell you, if you want to leave then you can."

Reluctantly, Billy sat down. "She left me," he said.

"I know." Heath nodded. "And I can imagine how you're feeling, but she had a good reason to leave."

"Yeah, sure," Billy said. "If that's the only reason you came here, then you're wasting your time."

"You are mule-headed," Heath complained, and then he took a sip of his Scotch. He frowned and wrinkled his nose. "I've had better."

"You're out West." Billy pointed out the obvious—that things were not as good out here as back East. "Why are you here?"

"After receiving a letter from Uncle Ben and Aunt Ute, I figured I needed to come out here and straighten some things out."

"You heard from Ute?"

"Yes. It was a very informative letter," Heath told him and then he leaned on the table and met Billy's eyes square on. "Claire is dying."

Billy gripped the table. He was so choked up, he reached for the remainder of Heath's Scotch and gulped it. After he got through coughing, he looked at Heath through watery eyes. "Why?"

Heath sat back and smiled. "Well, at least I know you love her. Let me start at the beginning. Claire came to Colorado to die. The doctors back East told her she only had until September to live—"

"But it's December," Billy interrupted.

"Let me finish."

"Tell me she's alive," Billy insisted.

"She's alive. Now drink your coffee and be quiet. It's apparent you can't handle Scotch," Heath teased him.

Billy reached for his coffee cup. "Go to hell."

"Anyway, Claire wanted to experience things she'd never been able to because of her health. She has had consumption the last few years. We thought it was just a cough and she'd get better, but that wasn't the case, so we had no choice but to approve her decision to travel out here.

"Then somehow you managed to worm your way into her affections." Heath grinned. "Uncle Ben said she was devastated when she left Denver, but her condition had grown worse and she wouldn't make any kind of commitment to you knowing that she was going to die." Heath stopped to order another drink.

Billy felt like a complete jerk. Her coughing had been so much worse than she'd let on. And the whole time he'd been blaming her for leaving him because he wasn't good enough. Then he remembered something she'd said. *Some of us don't have tomorrows.* Billy's jaw tightened. She had done everything because of him. But how was she feeling now?

"I would have stood by her," Billy said.

"Yes but there were others who didn't," Heath

told him. "When she told her fiancé, he broke the engagement, wanting nothing more to do with her."

"He was a jerk anyway," Billy said, now wishing he'd punched out the bastard.

"Well, the other reason Claire left was that she'd heard of a doctor that might be able to help her. So she went to the doctor who Aunt Ute said has practically cured Claire."

"Where is she? And why didn't Ben tell me?"

"Claire, still thinking that she was going to die the end of September, wouldn't let him," Heath paused to finish his drink. "The last letter we had from Aunt Ute said that Claire had built her own house and was starting to buy horses. She said that the doctor warned her that she couldn't leave Fraser and come to Denver for fear that she'd have a setback. But Aunt Ute said she still speaks of you with longing, and Ute kind of thought that you'd make a good Christmas present for Claire . . . that is if you still care."

Billy had to take a couple of sips of hot coffee before he could speak. "When do we leave?"

"How about in the morning?"

"I'll be there," Billy said. "Now tell me why you were the one who came out here?"

"Because I was the only one who could beat some sense in you just in case you proved to be stubborn, which of course you were." Heath tried to smile but his lip was too swollen.

"Thanks, Heath," Billy said, then decided the mood needed to be lightened. "You and I both make a sorry sight. Your lip is swollen and my eye is almost shut tight."

Heath stood and threw some coins on the table. "Guess nobody will mess with us on the train."

* * *

Claire got up and walked to the window. She took the end of her gown and wiped the frost from the windowpane. They had had fresh snow. What a beautiful Christmas they would have.

She moved over to the fireplace and tossed two more logs on the fire then poked at it until the red-hot coals came to life.

Today was Christmas Eve. Henry, the neighboring farmer, had helped get her tree into a bucket and placed it in front of her big window that overlooked the mountains. Now all she had to do was decorate it. Aunt Ute and Doc Susie were going to come over and help her string popcorn and cranberries. Aunt Ute said she'd make some gingerbread men for the tree.

So Claire's afternoon would be full, but today she just couldn't shake this empty feeling she had inside. She'd managed not to think about Billy during the last month, but she wondered how he was doing. Did he ever think of her?

How she'd love to take the train to see him, but this time of year sometimes the trains couldn't get through. Well, she might as well get her mind on other things. If she thought of Billy much more, she'd start crying.

As she dressed and went to get a bottle for her warm milk, she did promise to write her family and Ann and tell them she was alive and well. Then maybe they could come and visit during the summer. She also wanted to ask Ann if she still had a job because there were several stories up here just waiting to be told. Especially about the famous doctor who'd made a difference in everyone's life. A lot of the children in Fraser would be dead if it wasn't for Doc Susie.

No matter what happened, Claire vowed that she wouldn't be sad today. She was alive—something she didn't think was possible a few months ago. And she would be thankful to Doc Susie forever.

A blizzard howled outside as the train crept over the trestles. Billy and Heath both thought they were in purgatory . . . only it was cold instead of hot.

The potbelly stove in the railcar had been stoked full of wood, yet it barely kept the chill out of the car.

Finally, the train pulled to a stop. Crosby, the conductor, marched through the railcar shouting, "Corona! Passengers may leave the train until further notice."

Billy stopped the conductor. "We don't want to get off. We want to keep going."

"We can't," Crosby said. "We have to wait for the rotary snowplow to clear a path for us, and there is no water in the Corona tank."

"What does that mean?" Heath asked.

"Well, we're all right. We have water for the boiler, but if the snowplow breaks down . . . we don't have spit to fill it up. If we don't make it, we'll have to back her up clear to Yankee Doodle."

"Let's pray that it doesn't," Billy said. "Is there any more wood for the stove?"

"I'll bring you a few more pieces, but up here it's cold. You can boil an icicle at this altitude without ever melting it, so warmth is not a commodity."

"That's comforting," Heath mumbled to Billy

after the conductor left. "I feel like an icicle as it is."

The train started moving at a very slow pace as the snowplow tossed the snow off the tracks. It took them an hour to go three miles.

Everybody huddled under their coats and wrapped scarves around their necks. The potbelly stove was no match for the fierce wind blowing against an uninsulated train car.

"Are you sure Claire is up here?" Billy asked.

"That's what the letter said, but how she picked the Godforsaken icebox is beyond me. I hope we live to tell her," Heath grumbled and snuggled further down in his coat.

Their Christmas Eve supper was wonderful. Claire, Aunt Ute, and Susie all worked to fix the roasted turkey and stuffing.

After supper, Aunt Ute and Susie retired to the living room to finish decorating the Christmas tree. The blue spruce filled the room with a wonderful fragrance. It was almost like being outside, only warmer. The one thing that Claire had done to her house was to have a fireplace put in every room and double walls to keep the heat inside. In Fraser you could never be too warm.

Claire prepared cocoa and brought the steaming mugs into the living room and set them on the table in front of the sofa. "I thought you might like something warm," she said.

The fire was crackling and popping in the background as Susie and Ute strung the popcorn garland around the tree.

"It's beautiful," Claire said. "I think the popcorn

is just the right touch. Now if I could figure out how to hang the icicles that are clinging to the eaves of the house, we'd have a sparkling tree."

Ute glanced over her shoulder. "We could always douse the fire."

Claire laughed and then sat down and picked up a bowl of cranberries. "No thanks, I like my fireplace."

"*Ja,*" Ute agreed. "This one reminds me of our fireplaces back home. See how the flames have a blue tinge?"

Claire nodded.

"It means we are going to have good luck."

"I like that," Claire said as she handed Ute a mug of cocoa.

Susie joined them and they started stringing cranberries as the fire crackled in the background. Claire kept glancing at the blue flames. So far she'd had good luck with her health. She never felt dizzy anymore and she rarely coughed. But luck still hadn't brought her the one thing she wanted most of all. . . .

"This blizzard will bring us at least a foot of new snow," Susie said.

Claire glanced at the frosty windows. "I would hate to be out there tonight. It's so cold."

"*Ja,*" Ute said. "You know, this is one of the best Christmases I've ever spent."

Claire pricked her finger with the needle. She shook off the pain, then said, "I think it is for me, too. Of course, I'd love to see the rest of my family, but this peace and quiet is very relaxing."

Just then someone pounded on the door, and Claire jumped. Then she got up. "I wonder who that can be? It's too cold for anyone to be outside."

She pulled open the door. Henry McPhail stood

there, bundled up so that all she could see were his eyes. "Henry," Claire said.

"Is Doc Susie here?"

"Come in," Claire said. "Get out of the snow."

"What's wrong, Henry?" Susie asked.

"The train got stuck about a quarter mile outside of town. A small avalanche caught it. We've got three sleighs outside, but just in case someone might need medical attention, we came by to get you. Can you come?"

"Of course. I'll get my coat," Susie said.

Claire stood up. "We'll all go."

"Better bundle up then," Henry told them and turned toward the door. "I'll send the other two sleighs ahead. They've already started digging people out, and I'll wait outside for you ladies."

As Doc Susie got her coat, she said, "I'll get my bag. Claire, you get the brandy, and Ute, get some of the warm stones and blankets. These men are going to be very cold. I just hope it isn't too late."

Chapter Twenty-Three

The horse-drawn sleigh sped through the night, gliding over the snow and ice. A full moon overhead bathed the night with enough light to make everything look like crystal, shimmering in the wind.

Claire pulled her scarf up over her mouth and nose to keep the frigid air at bay. Then she said a prayer that all the train passengers would be all right. She felt sad when she thought of the men heading home for Christmas Eve now stranded in the snow, perhaps their lives threatened.

Tonight they would need a Christmas miracle.

As they neared the locomotive, she could see steam rising into the black night. Everyone was shouting as they ran back and forth to the train.

The sleigh slid to a stop beside the other sleighs. The town folks had already started carrying out the passengers. A few were walking, but most of the passengers had to be carried out.

Claire, Susie, and Ute wasted little time bounding out of the sleigh. Mr. Loan, the local banker, pointed to the next to last railcar. "There's still a couple of men in there. See what you can do for the ones we've brought out."

The women visited each man, wrapping them in blankets and giving them a sip of brandy. For some reason Claire kept looking toward the railcar. The next thing she knew she was wading through the snow toward the car as if something were pulling her. Ute followed.

Claire climbed up into the railcar where two men sat, their heads slumped over.

"They have hypothermia," Ute said from behind her.

"Let's see if we can get some brandy in them, and get them on their feet," Claire said.

She shook the first man. His eyes barely fluttered open. "You're going to have to help us get you out of here," she spoke in a loud voice, "Drink this." She unwrapped the scarf from around his neck so he could drink. The first thing she saw was a stubborn jaw.

"Heath!" Claire screamed. "Hurry, drink this."

Ute supported Heath's head while Claire held the bottle to his lips. He took several sips. Finally he looked at her and mumbled, "We found you."

"What are you doing here? Never mind, I can ask you later," Claire said, wanting to hug him but knowing time was of the essence. She and Ute pulled Heath to his feet, then Ute helped him off the train while Claire looked at the other man.

She rubbed the man's cheeks. "You need to wake up, sir. I must get you out of here." She took off his scarf, too, revealing long brown hair.

"Billy?"

Billy was babbling incoherently as Claire forced him to drink the brandy. Finally, as the liquor warmed him, he began to focus.

"Here, drink some more," she insisted.

After Billy had taken another swig, he said, "I'm dead, aren't I?"

"No but you will be if I don't get you out of here," she said, feeling her tears freezing. With a strength she didn't know she possessed, she pulled Billy to his feet and threw his arm around her shoulder.

"You left me," Billy murmured.

Claire ignored him. "Come on, you're going to have to help me. Take a step."

"You left me," Billy said as they slowly moved out of the train and into the snow.

"Yes, I did. But I'm not leaving you now," Claire said. "We'll talk about this as soon as you get warm."

They managed to get the men into the sleigh, then wrapped them in quilts and warm bricks. Billy and Heath were the last two men off the train. The rest had already been taken someplace warm.

Soon they were racing toward home.

Two hours later, after hot baths and a couple of hot toddies, Billy and Heath sat by the fire wrapped in blankets. Finally their teeth had stopped chattering so they were able to carry on a conversation. The color had returned to their faces.

Heath held a warm cup of cocoa between his hands as he looked up and asked, "So, Claire, how are you?"

"For once in my life I can say better than you,"
she said with a smile as she settled on the couch.
"I'm so glad to see you both. It's an unexpected
surprise. But how did you find me? Uncle Ben,
right?"

"No." Heath shook his head. "It was Aunt Ute."

Claire swung around to her aunt. "You wrote
him."

"*Ja.* It is my Christmas present to you," Ute said
with a smile.

"Thank you," Claire said and then she asked
Heath, "How is everyone back home?"

As her brother began talking Claire noticed that
Billy had yet to say anything. He just stared at her.
She wondered what he was thinking. Had he made
the trip because he missed her? Or just to find out
why she left? They really needed to talk, but not
until they could be alone.

Doc Susie came out of the kitchen and placed
her black bag by the door. "Let's take your temper-
ature one more time, and then I'm going home,"
she said.

"You're welcome to stay here," Claire offered.

"I don't take up much room," Heath offered
with a smile.

"Heath," Claire exclaimed with a shocked look.

"Here." Susie placed the thermometer into
Heath's mouth. "You're in no condition to be making passes, young man."

Claire could not believe how forward her brother
was.

Finally, Claire turned her attention to Billy.
"How are you?" she asked, feeling as if they were
absolute strangers. This wasn't how she'd pictured
their reunion. And then it dawned on her that

maybe Billy was acting so strange because Heath had told him of her condition. She sighed. It was happening again.

"I'm fine, Claire," Billy said.

Heath took the thermometer out of his mouth, and said. "He isn't fine. He's miserable."

"Shut up, Heath," Billy warned.

"See this fat lip he gave me?" Heath pointed to his lip. "Just proves how miserable he is."

"You didn't bother to tell her that you gave me the black eye first," Billy pointed out.

"Why were you two fighting?" Claire asked.

"Over you," Heath said.

"Oh," Claire murmured, not knowing what to say.

Finally Doc Susie had managed to take both men's temperatures. "They are both normal," she said as she shook down the thermometer. "I think I'll call it a night. Unless you need me to referee these two?"

"If they don't straighten up," Ute said, "I'll take them both on." She looked at each man. "And I won't be kind."

Heath smiled. "It's Billy, Aunt Ute. He's hard to get along with."

After Susie left, Aunt Ute stood up. "Heath, I think it's time that you retired for the night."

"I'm not tired," Heath grumbled. "I can stay up a couple more hours at least."

Billy glared at Heath.

"All right. All right." Heath stood, wrapping his blanket around him like a robe. "I know when I'm not wanted. See you in the morning, puss," Heath said, then nodded toward Billy. "See if you can't straighten out this ornery cuss. Uncle Ben says he's been impossible to live with and he's going to get himself killed."

"Go to bed, Heath," Billy ordered. "You talk too much."

Finally, they were alone.

Claire put a couple of logs on the fire before she sat back down again and looked at Billy. "I'm glad you are here," she said softly.

"You left me," Billy said.

"I had to leave."

"I know," Billy paused, and she glimpsed his sadness. "Heath told me all about your condition," Billy said as he shifted in his chair. "What hurts is that you didn't trust me enough to tell me yourself."

"I did it for you," Claire said. "Don't you see, we could have gotten married and then a couple months later I would be dead? Accepting the dying was hard enough, but leaving you would even be harder."

"But I'd rather have a few months with you than no months at all," he said, shoving out of his chair.

Claire stood too, worried that he would fall. "Should you be getting up? You've had a rough night."

"Sweetheart, I've been through a rough couple of months. But I've not been through near as much as you have," Billy said as he stood in front of the fireplace. He opened his arms, "Come here, Claire."

She flew to him.

Billy wrapped his arms around her, holding her so tight she could hardly breathe. But the comfort she received from him now was worth dying for. This was what she'd longed for. "God, how I have missed you," she murmured into his shirt.

He rested his head on top of hers. "When I returned home and found you were gone, I felt like my heart had been ripped out."

"I'm sorry I hurt you. You must know it wasn't easy for me to walk away," Claire said and then pulled back so she could see his face. "I want you to know that I'm much better. This climate has done wonders for my health, but I cannot tell you that I'm completely well. I could take a turn for the worse and die in a couple of months."

Billy looked at her with those soft brown eyes of his, and she could see love in them as he said, "None of us know when we'll die. I could be dead in a month. I just know if that were to happen that I'd want to spend my last month with you."

"Oh, Billy," Claire whispered as she slid her arms around his neck. She didn't bother to hide the love in her eyes. He captured her lips with a blistering kiss that was much hotter than the fire that was behind them. Lost in the stormy kiss, she barely felt him swing her up into his arms and carry her over to the couch. Gently he placed her down, and then bracing his arm on the back of the couch he said, "You still haven't answered my question?"

"What question?" Claire asked.

"Will you marry me?"

She smiled. "Do you still want me?"

Billy touched the side of her face. "Yes."

"Do you realize that I need to live here?"

"I can raise horses here as well as anywhere." He paused. "Any more questions?"

She looked at him shyly and asked, "Do you love me?"

Billy leaned down and just before he kissed her he answered, "With all my heart."

"Yes, I will marry you," Claire said and then pulled him down for a kiss as she told him over and over again how much she loved him. "You know, I once thought that if I could see you one more time and hold you that I would die happy." She smiled. "But now I know that once would never have been enough. I want forever."

Billy rolled to the back of the couch and then positioned Claire in front of him until they both could see the Christmas tree and the big window.

The wind had stopped blowing and now big snowflakes were falling softly outside as they lay there looking at the Christmas tree.

The room was bathed in candlelight and warmth. Billy glanced around feeling completely at home. Of course a lot of that had to do with Claire. As long as he had her, he'd be happy. He stared at the beautiful Christmas tree. He couldn't remember the last time he'd had a tree.

"You know, I didn't get you a Christmas present," Billy murmured.

"Yes, you did," Claire said as she snuggled next to him. "You gave me you. That's the best present of all."

Billy smiled. "Merry Christmas, darling."

Author's Note

I can't begin to tell you how many letters and e-mails I had on DANCE ON THE WIND. They all said the same thing—we want more—we want to know what happened to all the characters. It seems these people took on life and you really cared about them. That means I did my job.

Here is book two—Billy's story. I've tried to bring back most of the characters so you'll get to see all your old friends again. The next book will be Mary's story.

I must tell you how much your comments about the book helped. You even gave me ideas that I never had, so if we're lucky maybe one day all the characters will have their own book. Please write me, and let me know what you think of UNTIL SEPTEMBER. You'll get to meet some new characters. Let's see what you think of all the new people.

I think that Heath definitely needs his own story. And then we have all the characters from CHRISTMAS IN CAMELOT that you've asked for. Just maybe there will be many stories down the road.

Please check my web page for contest information. The Christmas basket was so successful—over 1000 entries—I will probably do another basket. But as always, the first fan who writes a letter about this book will receive a special gift from me, and the first five will receive an autographed cover.

Keep those cards and letters coming. I do answer all fan letters. A SASE is appreciated.

May all your dreams come true.

Brenda K. Jernigan
80 Pine St. W.
Lillington, N.C. 27546
Bkj1608@juno.com
http://www.bkjbooks.com